Pretty Maids

by

Pat Patterson

ALSO BY PAT PATTERSON

The Morning Glory Gang
A Long Time Comin'
Rocket Man
Freaknic!

This book is dedicated to my granddaughters. Love and kisses to my lovely ladies, Lil' Angie, Shelita, Courtney, Shandrika, and Tayla.

Published by ProMagic Digital Media

http://www.lulu.com/patpatterson

PRETTY MAIDS

ISBN: 978-0-578-01818-8

Cover design by Jose Angel Pardo

Editing: Jeannette Patterson, Marian Bickenbach, Anji Rainey, Mike Patterson, and newcomer, Shandrika Morris.

Published and printed in the United States of America.

Prologue

August 25, 1990.

It had rained off-and-on for the past ten days. That morning, the TV weatherman called it the worst rainy spell in a decade. A large cold air mass, rolling down from the North, met head-on with a cluster of storm cells sweeping up out of the Gulf of Mexico. For days, the two weather fronts were locked in mortal combat, but neither could move the other as they hovered over the Georgia-Florida line, leaving large sections of both states completely drenched.

Madison County was perhaps the hardest hit by the bad weather. Towering oak, maple, and magnolia trees – some more than one hundred years old – fell victim to the deluge when the water-soaked earth reached its saturation point and could no longer contain their sprawling roots.

Several cars and homes were damaged or destroyed by the branches of the fallen trees. Some of the county's historic antebellum mansions, which were spared by General William Tecumseh Sherman during his march through Georgia, suffered immeasurable damage.

In Wrightsburg, Georgia, the county seat, tonight's weather was the worst yet. A huge lightning bolt struck the ground, then traveled a ziz-zag pathway back to the sky before finally exploding to create a patchwork of light against darkness and the brief illusion of daylight. A loud clap of thunder shook the ground as torrents of rain spilled from the heavens and the winds blew violently.

A pale young woman, of about twenty, wearing a brown-fringed leather jacket with a matching band strung tightly around her head, appeared in the dim light of a street lamp. Rain plastered her blonde hair to her head and made her bell bottomed jeans stick to her slender hips as she stepped into the street.

The lights of an oncoming car outlined her silhouette in the darkness as it turned the corner. The car slowed, and then stopped in front of her. The passenger side door swung open, and a man's booming voice rang out, "Get in! You'll catch your death out there!"

Without hesitation, the girl got into the car, and then it pulled off.

The burly driver craned his neck toward her. "What in the world are you doing out here so late? And don't you have a raincoat or an umbrella?"

The girl stared blankly ahead, but did not speak. Chagrinned, the man regrouped and tried again. "Well, where are you going?"

Still gazing ahead, the girl spoke ever so softly. "I was trying to get home ... but I got lost."

"Where do you live?" he asked.

"One thousand ... Amsterdam Avenue," she said, speaking so softly the man could barely hear.

The man pondered as he drove. "I think I know where that is. It's not far from here."

The rain came harder now, heavy drops drumming against the roof of the car like streams of pellets shot from an army of air guns. The windshield wipers flailed back and forth wildly, fighting a losing battle to maintain just a small field of vision for the driver. By now, all of the other windows were fogged-up beyond sight.

They rode on in silence as he carefully navigated the tiny streets, being extra careful in the blinding rain. Finally, the man pulled the car to the curb in front of a large brick building. He turned and stared at the girl, who sat motionless. "Hey! There's no house here!"

The rain splattered into his face when he lowered the window and gazed out. "Are you sure this is the right address?" he asked. "This is the new high school."

There was no answer.

He slowly turned to face an empty seat. The girl was gone.

"Hey! What the hell?" the startled man exclaimed.

Befuddled, he sprang from the car and bolted around to the other side. Then – just as suddenly as it had started – the rain stopped as the man just stood there, staring out into the nothingness of the night.

Chapter 1

Cameras rolled as Ginny Westbrook posed, dramatically reciting her lines to Marcus, a young actor. "I'm leaving you, Marcus," she said.

"But, Darling, I can't live without you," Marcus said, despair creasing the brow of his handsome brown face.

"It'll be hard," she said reassuringly, "but you must go on."

Ginny turned and exited stage right.

"And, cut. It's a wrap," the director yelled excitedly, and then turned to Ginny. "*Magnifico,* Ginny! I'd say you have another hit on your hands!"

A young woman, wearing spectacles and carrying a leather-bound appointment book, pushed between the two of them before they could embrace. "Miss Westbrook, we really must hurry," she said, looking down at her notes. "Your talk show taping begins in one hour."

"Al-right," Ginny said demurely. Then a flash of excitement came over her face. "Did they deliver my new sports car?"

"Yes, ma'am, and *it* is beautiful."

Ginny grinned as she fell into step with the young woman and walked across the soundstage. "Anything else?" she asked.

"Yes," the girl replied. "Your publisher called. He's furious that you haven't approved the galleys for your new book, and--"

Ginny stopped suddenly. "Look, he'll just have to wait ... like everyone else!"

"Alright, I'll tell him. Oh, and Miss Westbrook, I almost forgot."

"What?" Ginny said.

"Your lunch date is here."

Ginny covered her mouth with her hand. "Oh, my God, so did I."

She sighed in exasperation, paused, and then spoke again. "Which one is it, Denzel or Wesley?"

Suddenly the door sprang open and a teenage boy, wearing a football jacket, baggy pants, and a cap turned backwards on his head, rushed up to them. "Hey, Redbone! Whatz-happenin'?"

Ginny looked up in dismay, and then screamed at the top of her lungs. "Sonny James, what are you doing in my dream? You get out of here!"

"But, Ginny--" the boy pleaded, reaching out to take her arm.

"No," Ginny cried as she turned and bolted through the doorway.

"Ginny, Ginny ...," he shouted, running behind her.

Miriam Westbrook stood in the bedroom doorway calling out to her daughter. "Ginny, Ginny, get up."

A startled Ginny awoke. She twisted and turned in bed before finally sticking her head from under the covers. "What?" she said.

"Get up. Have you forgotten? You don't want to be late on the first day of school."

Ginny groggily sat up in bed, knuckling the sleep from her eyes. "Aw, Mom."

"Come on now," her mother said before going back downstairs to finish making breakfast.

It took all the strength she could muster, but Ginny pulled on her robe, stuck her tiny feet into her bedroom slippers, and then padded down the narrow hallway to the bathroom. Before getting into the shower, she looked longingly into the mirror on the medicine cabinet door. Ever since she could remember, Ginny seemed to have been constantly searching for something. For what? Only God knew. She, had no earthly idea.

But even at this early hour and without a hint of makeup, Ginny Westbrook was strikingly beautiful. Her perfectly formed oval face, with too-perfect nose and teeth, had an incredible radiance. Her full mane of sandy brown hair curled naturally as it cascaded across her shoulders, stopping midway her back.

With both hands, Ginny parted her hair and pulled it away from her face as she looked deeply into the green-flecked gray eyes that stared back at her. The reflection from the tiny light bulb above the mirror made her eyes seem to sparkle. On occasions such as this, she could sometimes glimpse a trace of her father's face in her own.

She and the tall sturdy-built man had the same high cheekbones, but their complexions were entirely different. While his was rough and black as a tar bucket, Ginny's creamy alabaster skin was baby-smooth.

But Ginny could see little or no resemblance to her mother. Miriam Westbrook was a tall willowy woman with an extraordinarily plain dark-brown face. She had smooth skin, but her hair, which she religiously submitted to the curling iron each week, was short and unruly.

This morning was no different from any other, and Ginny found not a hint of that for which she was searching. Most seventeen-year-old girls would've killed for her looks, but there were some times – such as now – when Ginny Westbrook felt they were a curse. *Who am I?* Ginny asked herself.

Turning away from the mirror, she twisted the shower knob, and then stood watching as the water began to flow. Pulling a black barrette around her hair, looping it through again so that it piled her hair high atop her head, Ginny slowly disrobed and stepped into the shower. Soon the small room filled with steam, which clouded the mirror along with her mind.

By the time Ginny entered the kitchen, Charlie Westbrook had already polished off a helping of pancakes and sausages and was working on another stack. He was not shy about piling on the calories, and it pleased Miriam to no end when he heartily ate her food and praised her cooking.

Plus, he would burn those calories and more by the time he finished his truck route.

Before the day was over, Charlie would help load and unloaded more than a hundred large cases of produce, which he delivered from the Chandler farms to the restaurants up in Atlanta, Savannah, and sometimes as far away as Chattanooga, Tennessee.

"Morning, Dad," Ginny said and kissed him on the cheek.

Ginny poured herself a glass of orange juice from a pitcher, sitting on a nearby counter, and took a seat at the table. When she pulled her chair closer to his, Charlie knew that his little princess wanted something. He also knew exactly what it was. And as usual, it was going to be terribly difficult for him to say no to her.

"Try these," Miriam said, placing a small stack of pancakes in front of Ginny.

"No breakfast for me, Mom," she said, pushing the plate aside. "I'm getting fat."

Nothing could have been further from the truth. Ginny stood five-foot-six in stocking feet, and had a lean athletic body, which was kept trim by years of exercise and dance. Since kindergarten, she had studied ballet, modern dance, and tap, and had excelled in basketball, fast-pitch softball, and track before her junior year in high school. Then suddenly, Ginny's tastes ran toward more intellectual pursuits, drama and journalism, both of which were now her passions.

"You're not getting fat," Miriam said firmly. "And even if you were, you're not leaving this house without something in your stomach."

"Aw, Mom," Ginny said in mock disdain. "Okay, I'll have wheat toast, but no butter."

Miriam shook her head in exasperation as she dropped two pieces of wheat bread into the toaster.

"How's my baby?" Charlie asked.

"I'm okay, Dad," she said, and then took a tiny sip of juice.

"You don't seem too excited," Charlie noted. "You know, going to a brand new school and all."

"I'm not. It'll be the same old tired students and teachers, just in a new building."

Miriam, carrying a plate of pancakes and sausage for herself and toast for Ginny, joined her family at the table. "This is your senior year, Ginny," she said. "This should be your most enjoyable time."

"It will, Mom. Don't worry."

Ginny leaned over and clutched Charlie's arm just as he attempted to lift a forkful of pancakes to his mouth.

"Dad, did you think about it?" she whispered.

"Think about what?" Miriam chimed in after overhearing. "Charlie, what are you two cooking up? You are not buying this girl anything else. We have college to think of next year."

Ginny turned to her mother. "Mom, I need a car. Everybody has one but me. And I'll get that scholarship, for sure."

"Listen, young lady, don't you ever take anything or anyone for granted. Because when you do--"

"I know, you'll be letting yourself in for a big disappointment," Ginny said cutting her off. "Mom, you've said that a million times."

"What do you mean by that, Miriam?" Charlie cut in. "You're not happy with what I've given you?"

"No, Charlie, it's nothing like that. I just want Ginny to do more than I did. It's only natural."

"Mom, there's nothing wrong with being a nurse."

"You kidding me? The hours are crazy and the pay stinks."

"But, Honey, look at all the good you do for so many people," Charlie added. "By the way, what shift are you on this week?"

"That darned night shift, three 'til eleven," Miriam said contemptuously. "I hate it!"

"Oh, well, we do what we have to do," Charlie said.

They finished eating in silence.

Charlie pushed his plate aside and turned to Ginny. "Now, little lady, explain to me why all of a sudden you need a car. It's not like you have to walk, the bus stops right out front. Now back when I was in school--"

"But, Dad, some days I have to stay after school to work on the newspaper," she said, now cutting him off in mid-sentence. "Don't forget ... the journalism scholarship?"

"Ginny, I still don't see why you need a car," Miriam said. "You can use mine when I'm not working."

Ginny wiped the crumbs from her mouth with a napkin and turned to Miriam. "Mom, I don't want to ride that bus to school anymore. The children tease me!"

"What?" Miriam said. The look on her face was one of absolute shock. Her mind quickly returned to her own childhood when comments about her lanky body and plain face abounded. The one thing Miriam felt confident about was that her wonderful beautiful daughter would never have to suffer those indignities.

In an attempt to hide the teardrops rolling down her face, Ginny turned away and rose from the table, but Charlie grabbed her arm as she passed and gently pulled her back to him. "Tease you?" he said in a voice of genuine concern. "Wait a minute. What in the world would anyone have to tease *you* about?"

"About my color," Ginny shot back as she moved toward the counter where her notebook lay. "They call me hideous names. I hate it! I hate them! I hate me!"

Miriam rose from the table and hugged her daughter, lovingly stroking her hair. "Honey, you've seen the picture of your great granddaddy. He looked so much like a white man that they used to call him 'White-man Joe.' "

"I know, Mom. We studied about how family traits skip generations," Ginny said. "But why does it matter so much to everyone?"

"It shouldn't," Miriam said. "But you just ignore them, and they'll stop."

"I don't think so, Mom," she said. "And why do I have to look like him? He's your granddaddy, but you don't look a thing like him."

"It's genetics, Baby," Miriam laughed, attempting to lighten the mood. "Who can explain it?"

Miriam pulled back from Ginny, holding her at arms length. "But look at you. Look how pretty you are. And don't forget your cousins on the Florida side of the family, they're fair skinned, too."

For the moment, this appeased Ginny. She remembered that at the age of ten, Charlie had piled them all into his station wagon and driven the three hundred miles to Pahokee, Florida, to attend Miriam's great aunt's funeral. She had enjoyed playing with her cousins, Louise and Baby Jane. They were almost as light skinned as she was and never taunted her about the slight difference in their skin colors.

Charlie rose from the table, took Ginny's hand, and pulled her to him. "My baby ... my sweet baby," he said, shaking his head disconsolately as he spoke. "Ginny, you're intelligent, talented, and very beautiful. Those kids at school are just jealous of you."

Although she knew her father was biased and always prone to stretch the truth – especially where she was concerned – Ginny hoped that at least some of this were true. Anyway, she loved to hear him say flattering things about her. And for the moment, it was the salve needed to soothe her wounded being.

Then Charlie stood back and looked deeply into Ginny's eyes. "We can't stop people from saying cruel things about us," he said. "But don't you ever let anything that anybody says get you down. Is that clear?"

"Yes, Daddy," she said, wiping the last tear away from her eye with the table napkin.

"And ... well, I guess it's about time that we upgraded your mother's car."

Ginny's eyes widened with excitement.

"And they don't give you a thing for trade-ins these days," Charlie continued.

"Oh, Daddy, I love you," she said hugging him tightly.

Then Charlie pulled away. "That's if," he said.

"If, what, Daddy? I promise. I'll do anything."

"If you come straight home from school and finish dinner for your mother while she's working late."

"That sure would be a help," Miriam said, smiling at her daughter. "I'll get things started, but you know how your daddy loves his cornbread hot."

"I'll cook it for you, Daddy. I'll have your dinner *ready* by the time you get home, *everyday*. You just wait and see."

Charlie gave her a stern look. "Ginny, one more thing."

"Yes?"

"On the days you have to stay after school, make sure you don't take the shortcut through Simpson's Woods," he said. "Some pretty weird things go on back in there."

Miriam, who was now packing Charlie's lunch box, looked at him sarcastically. "Yes, when we were in school, I heard about some of those *things.*"

"Yeah, but things are different now," he said, turning back to Ginny. "You stay away from those woods, young lady. Is that clear?"

"Yes, sir."

"How is Sonny?" Charlie asked, changing the subject. "I hear he's gonna be first string again this year. Hey, why don't you ride with him until I can get a line on a good car for your mother?"

"No way," Ginny blurted angrily.

"What? Did something happen when he took you to the prom?" Charlie asked, his eyes widened now with the concern that comes along with the territory of every man who has a teenage daughter.

"No, Daddy, Sonny just needs to grow up. He's too childish."

Miriam began to laugh hysterically as she placed Charlie's lunch box on the table.

"What's wrong with you?" he said quizzically.

"You're just remembering how you were," Miriam reminded him.

"Aw, go on, woman," Charlie said, waving his hand in dismissal. He picked up his lunchbox and kissed them both on the cheek before walking toward the door.

"Where're you headed today, Honey?" Miriam asked.

"Got a quick trip up to Atlanta and back," he said. "I should be home in time for dinner."

"Good," Ginny said, beaming. "I'll make you something special."

Ginny picked up her notebook from the counter and walked out behind Charlie. "Wait, Dad, I'll walk you to your truck."

When the two of them reached the front door, Ginny stuck her head back into the doorway and laughed. "Mom, did anything happen when Dad took you to the prom?"

"None of your beeswax," Miriam said, playfully tossing a dishrag at Ginny, who neatly sidestepped the wet cloth and grinned.

Then she and her father walked arm-in-arm to the big white truck, bearing the same blue and white *Chandler Enterprises* logo that Charlie wore on the breast pocket of his gray khaki shirt.

As did a goodly number of the town's thirty thousand or so residents, Charlie had known no employer other than Chandler Enterprises, which was a major provider of produce to the Southeastern United States. While still in school, from the eighth grade until graduation, he picked peaches and pears during the summer break. After graduating high school, Charlie went to work full-time on the loading docks. Now he drove the two-ton delivery truck or an eighteen-wheeler, depending on the season.

They were in the middle of harvesting season and produce came straight from the fields of Madison and surrounding counties, so all he had to do was make deliveries. During the off-season, however, Charlie and his road partner, Jay Dee, would lead a team of eighteen wheel tractor-trailers all the way down to the docks of Miami, Florida, to pick up produce that came in from South America.

Miriam was also no stranger to the Chandler payroll. Until she finished her practical nurse's training, she had worked either part-time or full-time in the processing plant, where she and the other women canned peas, butterbeans, and okra, which were sold under the Chandler label in supermarkets across the South. It was said that if you ate canned peaches, pears, or fruit cocktail in Georgia, Florida, or Alabama, it probably came from the Chandler plant.

Charlie had always been a formidable athlete – he played tackle on the old segregated Carver High's football team – but had not been much of a student, so he had no illusions about attending college. The family's hopes of getting their first college graduate rested firmly on the broad and able shoulders of his brother, Billy, who was not only a stellar athlete but an able student as well.

Billy Westbrook was the star halfback on the then newly integrated Madison High's state championship football team. He was also on the starting-five of the basketball team and his Class B record for the 100-meter sprint stands to this day.

When Billy turned down a football scholarship to the University of Georgia, instead volunteering for the United States Army, both family and friends were shocked and saddened. After boot camp, he shipped out to Vietnam. Unfortunately, Billy Westbrook … never made it back.

It was within this context that they were all depending on Ginny to carry the Westbrook banner into some college or university – which one did not matter.

Chapter 2

As she moved toward the bus stop, Ginny had a sense of dread and foreboding unlike any she had ever felt before. At seven thirty in the morning, the sun was already shining brightly. *It'll be another hot muggy day,* she thought. Then a smile came to her face as she had a more pleasant reflection. *There'll be big doings up at the new school today, and Ginny Westbrook, star reporter for the Chandler High Chronicle, will be on the scene to document the momentous occasion for the annals of history.*

Ginny had not yet decided whether she would become a famous actress or a successful news-anchor for one of the major networks. She was sure that either would be well within her grasp. *No big thing,* she had decided long ago. Ginny Westbrook would be prepared for either or maybe both.

She would win her scholarship to the University of Georgia, where she would major in journalism, as did Charlene Hunter – the first black to graduate from the prestigious department – and take a minor in theater. Then upon graduation, she would simply flip a coin. If it came up heads, she would take the first flight out of Atlanta to New York, and if tails, it would be the bright lights of Hollywood for Ginny Westbrook.

Or should I change my name, she pondered before deciding, *definitely not,* just as the bus made a screeching sound and came to a stop in front of her. Now Ginny recalled herself from an inner world of pleasant thought and put on her "game face."

The students laughed and talked among themselves until the door opened, then they grew silent. Two black boys, sitting near the front, confronted her as soon as she walked up the steps.

"Redbone," one of them shouted.

"Hey, Red, the other said, "what's happenin', baby? You wanna go out tonight?"

Ginny's first impulse was to ignore them and move to the back of the bus, but she had taken just about enough abuse from those two. This year, things would be different.

"Let's get this straight," she scowled, grabbing the second boy by his collar and squeezing it tightly. "I am not your baby! And if you and I were the only two people left in the world, I'd cut my throat."

The bus roared with laughter and some of the students began to taunt the boy, who pulled back just as she released him, banging his head on the steel rod above the seat. "Aw," he cried.

"Alright, you two," Minnie Wilkes, the bus driver, said, "I ain't havin' none of that mess this year. And, Johnny, why can't you leave that girl alone?"

"Hey, I was just tryin' to be friendly," the boy said, rubbing the back of his head.

Ginny struggled through the tight aisle space, brushing the leg of a black girl as she passed.

The girl pushed her. "Get off me, you old yellow dog!"

"Well ex-cuse me," Ginny said, with a mixture of anger and sarcasm.

Margo Johnson, a pudgy dark-skinned girl with a pretty face, pointed to a seat beside her as she called out, "Ginny, over here."

Ginny finally slipped into the empty seat beside her friend. "Thanks, Margo."

"Child, don't let them fools get you started," Margo said. "They jus' be trippin'. Ain't none of 'em got no sense."

"You've got that right," Ginny replied, and then smiled at Margo, changing the subject. "How was your summer?"

"Girl, don't ask. I've been runnin' a day care center."

"A day care center?"

"That's what I call my house," Margo said, and then rolled in laughter. "I spent the whole summer lookin' after my bad brothers and sisters. I told my mama, 'You keep on goin' out gettin' these babies, you'd better stay home and keep 'em.'"

"And what did she say?"

"Nothin', she just slapped me."

They both laughed raucously.

"I wish I had some brothers and sisters," Ginny said, sounding serious.

"Child, no you don't," Margo warned her.

Sensing someone staring at her, Ginny turned to see a girl sitting in the corner of the bus. She was wearing hippie-styled clothing, white blouse, brown fringed-leather jacket, and matching headband. Their eyes met before Ginny sheepishly turned back to Margo.

"Who is that new girl back there?"

"New girl? Where?" Margo asked, craning her neck to look around the bus.

"That white girl in the corner," Ginny said. "She's got some weird looking clothes. And it's certainly too hot for that leather jacket."

Margo turned to look back, but Ginny pulled her arm. "Don't look, now. She'll know we're talking about her. But she's sitting right behind us, over in the right-hand corner."

Margo slowly turned and looked toward the empty corner seat, then turned back to Ginny. "What girl?"

Ginny was stunned as she, too, turned and stared at the empty seat. "She was …" Her voice trailed off.

"Girl, them fools got you trippin'," Margo said.

"I know that's right," Ginny said, turning to look again. Still seeing no one, she shrugged and shook her head.

The school band played *The Stars and Stripes Forever* as teachers, a few parents, and the entire student body stood facing the front of the building. Joe Oliver, the town's mayor, Francis Murray, the school's principal, and Tyson Chandler, Jr., sat behind a podium facing the audience.

Mayor Oliver was a short squat man with a full mane of gray hair. In his early sixties, he was the oldest of the onstage trio. He looked to be the consummate politician and walked with the swagger of a man in power. The mayor, like most politicians, also had the gift of gab and used it unsparingly.

Ty Jr., as he liked to be called, was the son of an empire builder. He was a tall well-built man, in his forties, with dark hair piled high on his head, although his temples were graying. He, too, walked with an air of importance, steeped in both breeding and money.

In his late thirties, Principal Murray, a man of average size except for the small spare tire developing around his midsection, was relatively young for a school principal. Like many his age, he was a victim of premature balding and had but a few strands of long black hair, which he brushed across the top of his head in a laughable attempt at disguising his balding pate.

Mr. Murray was homegrown, coming up through the ranks. He graduated from the old Madison High School, returning to his alma mater after college to teach Social Studies. He has never left.

Behind the dais, a gigantic blue ribbon sealed the entrance to the building. The band stopped playing, and then Mr. Murray walked to the podium.

"Students, teachers, parents, and friends ... I welcome you all here today on this most auspicious occasion."

As Mr. Murray continued, a huge white boy pushed through the crowd with Sonny James and three other boys following closely in his wake. They were all wearing royal blue T-shirts with white lettering that read, "Big Blue Wave, First String." The letters encircled a depiction of a white football with blue stripes circling each of its pointed ends. "Hey, look out," the big boy yelled, "comin' through."

As the entourage made its way from the back of the crowd toward the front steps, a small black boy pushed back. "Hey, watch where you're going," he said.

The big white boy shoved his chest into the smaller boy's face. "What? What?" he asked menacingly.

"You don't have to be so pushy," the small boy replied.

"Listen you little pipsqueak--"

"Hey, Pike, let's go," Sonny said. "We'll see that lil' punk later on."

The boys pushed on until they had sidled up to Ginny and Margo. Ginny recoiled when Sonny touched her arm.

"Hey, Red, what's been goin' on?" he said in a low sexy voice.

Ginny stomped her foot in exasperation. "If anyone else calls me that today, I swear--"

"Hey, baby, don't go off on me," he said. "I meant it as a compliment. Ain't nothin' like a fine red woman. Anybody will tell you that."

Ginny snarled at him. "Oh, you make me so sick."

Sonny grabbed her arm. "What? You think you're too good for me?"

Ginny struggled to free herself from his grip. "Stop it, Sonny, you're hurting me!"

Suddenly Margo hit Sonny with her notebook. "Sonny James, you turn her loose!"

Noticing the altercation, Jerry Robinson, Ginny's English teacher and sponsor of the school newspaper, called out to them. "Hey, you people up there, quiet down."

Sonny gave the hefty teacher an angry glance, but released Ginny. As he and his boys reluctantly walked away, Sonny turned to Ginny. "You're still mine, and if I catch you hangin' out with that white boy again--" He frowned and shook his fist at Ginny. Sonny James was clearly angry, and all who knew him understood that this was *not* good.

As the saying goes, some people are born with silver spoons in their mouths, but Randolph (Sonny) James was born with a football in one hand and a basketball in the other. This was to be expected since his mother, Sylvia, was one of the best basketball players in the county, male or female, and Bob, his father, was the quarterback of the 1975 State Championship football team. Instead of the traditional blue for baby boys, Bob lined Sonny's crib with a green blanket with white stripes, so that it resembled a football field.

Robert and Sylvia James, proprietors of the Rib Shack, a popular soul food café, used the lion's share of their profits to plot out the athletic future of their baby boy. From the age of ten, Sonny James had attended every major sports camp in the South. Summers were spent on the campuses of the Georgia Institute of Technology, the University of Georgia, Auburn University, and Florida State University, where he was coached and tutored in the art of becoming a point guard in basketball and a football quarterback.

Sonny's one-on-one training had paid off in spades. Last year, he led the basketball team to the state finals, where they lost at the last second – on what some said was the worst call by a referee in basketball history. But football was Sonny James' true calling.

The *Atlanta Journal's* sportswriter, Jimmy Cavan, predicted that this would be the year that history would repeat itself. Sonny James would emulate his father and lead Madison County to its second state title.

To his family and the town's football fans, this tall, tan, and handsome boy could do no wrong. Sonny was the favorite son and was treated as such by his parents and many of the townspeople. When Sonny James was crossed, there was a penalty to be paid. As he stood in the midst of his ardent followers, they remained perfectly still and silent as Sonny huffed and puffed. *Ginny Westbrook would get hers,* he thought.

At the podium, the principal drew his monologue to a close and began his introductions. "So it gives me great pleasure to introduce our Mayor, the honorable Joe Oliver."

The crowd applauded as the Mayor walked to the microphone. "Thank you, Francis. I am truly honored to be here, today..."

Mr. Murray grimaced as he took his seat. He hated to be called by his first name. Francis was a girl-sounding name.

Back in the crowd, Ellie Benson, one of the new teachers, turned to Jerry Robinson. "I thought he would go on forever," she said.

Mr. Robinson laughed. "You haven't seen anything, yet. The Mayor is the *real* windbag."

"Oh, yes, politicians," she said, and then crossed her arms as she shuffled from one foot to the other.

It was getting hotter now and the crowd was growing restless. The audience had already been standing for thirty minutes, and there was still another speaker to go.

"Those flowers on the podium are so beautiful," Ellie said, pointing to the large urns of multicolored roses, hydrangeas, chrysanthemums, and lilies.

"Courtesy of the principal," Jerry said. "The man has the greenest thumb in Madison County."

"Our principal?"

"Yep, you should see the flower garden in his back yard. It is exquisite. They say he has a secret formula for making fertilizer."

"Well, I've heard a lot of stuff about him, but not that."

"What'd you hear?"

"That, at times, he can be an ass-hole."

They both sniggled.

"Well, that can be," he said, "but basically he's a good guy. But if you have a question where you really need 'yes' for an answer, ask it after lunch."

"After lunch, why?"

"He's diabetic, and when his insulin runs low, he can be a grouch. He goes home for lunch every day to take his shot and fix his special food, for himself and his mama. She's got it, too, and now she's an invalid."

"Oh, how horrible," she said with a grimace. "He's not married?"

"Divorced. His wife and his mother couldn't see eye to eye."

"Oh, one of those."

Back at the podium, the Mayor finally sat, and Ty Jr. took the microphone. "It was my Daddy's wish that after his death, our old home be torn down and the land given to the city. It was indeed gracious of the mayor and the town council to pass it along to the school board, whose members saw fit to build this magnificent edifice."

There was only scattered applause. It had been a long morning and the heat and oratory were taking its toll on the audience.

"It is truly an honor to have this school named for the Chandler family," Ty continued. He nodded to two custodians, and they pulled ropes on either side of a tarp covering a sign above the doorway. The tarp fell away from the sign that read, "Tyson Chandler High School."

The audience applauded wildly.

The custodians removed the podium and handed a giant pair of scissors to Ty Jr. The principal and the mayor joined Ty as he placed the large ribbon into the blades of the scissors. Mitch Bradley, the editor of the *Wrightsburg Herald* – the town's only newspaper – sprang from the crowd, wielding a camera. "Hold it, smile," the white-haired man directed.

The three men turned and smiled as his camera, along with several others, flashed. Jerry Robinson pulled a 35mm camera from its bag and joined the other photographers. Mr. Robinson was recording the event for the school's newspaper.

"I would like to dedicate this building in memory of my father, Tyson Chandler."

Ty Jr. ceremoniously cut the ribbon. The bell sounded just as it fell to the floor. The custodians open the doors, and then the students flooded into the brand new building.

A swirl of students filled the hallways. They all laughed and talked, greeting their friends and welcoming each other back from the summer break. Ginny, who had been taking copious notes for the school newspaper, turned to Margo as they stood under the massive arch of the intersecting hallways. "Who do you have for homeroom?"

"Benson, the new teacher," Margo said.

A week earlier, parents and students had attended "Open House," where they were given a tour of the new building, received their schedules, and met their homeroom teachers. Ginny was assigned to her favorite teacher. "I've got Robinson," she said with a smile.

"See you after school," Margo said as she turned to leave.

"Not today. I have to work on the school paper."

Margo laughed and shook her head. "Oh, I forgot, you're one of them brainiacs."

"You go on, girl," Ginny said, smiling at her only true friend. "If I don't see you at lunch, I'll see you in the morning."

Margo walked down the hall to the west wing, where she was immediately swallowed up by the throng of students. Ginny walked in the opposite direction, and then quickly ducked into the restroom. She placed her notebook on the counter beside the sink before slowly studying her reflection in the mirror.

Pulling her hair back with both hands, Ginny stared at the mirror image of her face. Nothing had changed. The face – too white for black and too black for white – stared back, as usual. Frustrated now, Ginny shook her head in resignation. *Oh, whatever,* she said silently.

After relieving herself, Ginny ran water into the basin, rinsed her hands, and then looked up. As she reached for a paper towel, out of the corner of her eye, she caught just a glimpse of a reflection in the mirror. Caught by surprise, she felt a tingling sensation over her entire body and the hairs on the back of her neck stood straight up.

It was *the girl* from the bus. Ginny turned to greet her. "Oh, hello, my name is…"

The girl was gone.

Ginny stood transfixed. All at once, she felt a cold chill run up and down her spine and smelled a musky scent that seemed to be a mixture of mildew and Lilac water. Ginny quickly wiped her hands, picked up her notebook, and ran – as fast as two feet could carry her – from the restroom.

Like all high schools, Chandler High had its share of cliques and factions. Although the school had been integrated since 1970, most were still delineated according to race. Others were determined by social status and financial standing in the community.

Descendants of the county's most prominent families, the Steeles, the Chandlers, the Hamptons, and the Meriwethers, banded together almost naturally. The group had no particular name, but they knew who they were, and so did everybody else. This collection of rich snobs hung together, that is, until it fit their fancy to do otherwise.

"Going slumming," they called it when a Meriwether or a Hampton girl dated a star football player or an unusually handsome boy of lesser means, or if one of the rich boys slipped around with a pretty "peasant" girl, which they did with some regularity. In such cases, it was made abundantly clear from the outset that this kind of relationship could never be taken seriously. There was never a case where one of them married beneath their station, neither boy nor girl.

Then there were the sons and daughters of Madison County's black elite, the Wannabees –they were called behind their backs – insinuating that they wanted to be white. Their parents were doctors, lawyers, morticians, and even one was a Superior Court judge. The Wannabees dressed and acted like their white counterparts and played by the same rules regarding friendships with their poorer classmates.

The most extreme of these assorted collections of students, however, were the all-black hip-hoppers and the all-white flaggers. The hip-hoppers were called such for their love of hip-hop and rap music. The boys wore baggy jeans and pants, slung low on their hips, and extra large T-shirts, worn outside their pants. Some of them wore baseball caps turned backwards or to the side, and colorful basketball shoes, the kind endorsed by Magic Johnson and Kareem Abdul Jabber, star pro players of the day.

The girls that hung with the hip-hopers were called "hootchie-mamas" and dressed provocatively in tight jeans or too short miniskirts. The blouses or skimpy tops they wore had plunging necklines or exposed midriffs, sometimes both. The boys drove low-slung throwback cars, from the '60s and '70s, with oversized speakers that blasted the newly emerging rap music – by artists such as Luther Campbell aka Luke Skywalker and his 2-Live Crew – to excruciatingly high decibels as they cruised through the campus.

The flaggers were named for their blind dedication to the Confederate flag. The boys dressed in jeans and cowboy boots, drove pickup trucks, and listened to blue grass music. Their trucks had once been adorned with waving Confederate flags until the school's principal outlawed all flags, other than the "Stars and Stripes." Now the flaggers had to settle for small flag decals stuck on their truck tags and in the corners of their windshields. Attempting to show fairness, Principal Murray also banned Malcolm X T-shirts, which were worn by another all-black group of students.

The flagger girls wore skimpy tops and extremely short cutoff jeans or Daisy Dukes' as they were called. The scant outfits were named for a girl who appeared in an old TV show, called *The Dukes of Hazzard*, which was sometimes filmed in Dooly County – about fifty miles down the road.

Chandler High also had its share of odd birds, the ones who wore spiked hairstyles, dyed green and pink, and preferred heavy metal music. They, too, had no particular name other than "weird," and no one noticed when a few black students infiltrated their ranks. There were also other groups that crossed ethnic lines: the computer geeks, the science nerds, and the history nuts.

The most integrated of all groups, however, were the athletic teams, both male and female. When they were cut, they didn't bleed red, but royal blue. Members of the Big Blue Wave – as each team in season was called – were blood brothers and sisters, as were the townspeople whenever they played. Last year, when the Big Blue Wave boys' basketball team made it all the way to the semifinals up in Macon, robbers could have backed up moving vans to the town and made off with everything.

Only the sick and infirmed were left behind with a skeleton crew to look after them. If the church hour, eleven o'clock Sunday morning, was the most segregated time in Madison County, then kick-off time, seven o'clock, Friday night, was the most integrated. When the county's twenty-five hundred screaming fans converged upon Griffith Park to meet the enemy on the gridiron, there was no black or white, only blue and white, the school's colors.

The first day back at school had gone about as well as could be expected for Ginny. Not bothered that she didn't fit into any of the cliques, she had gotten used to being an outsider. At lunch, she shared a table with her friend, Margo, and a grossly overweight new girl called Cha-Cha, who had just moved to town from Atlanta. Cha-Cha, a nonstop talker, filled them in on how she came to live with her grandmother. The main reason being that her stepfather had tried to rape her.

Cha-Cha knew about, and had an opinion on just about everything, including the goings-on in the city and the latest fad diet, which she was sure would help her to lose the extra fifty pounds she had been trying to get rid of since grade school. Their conversation had been pleasant, but not up to Ginny's intellectual level. But it didn't matter. Cha-Cha was Margo's friend, and any friend of hers, Ginny concluded, was to be welcomed. Anyway, Ginny Westbrook was running way short on friends, male or female.

Later in the spring, when tryouts and rehearsals would begin for the school play, Ginny would be in her element. Last year she'd played the leading role in *Romeo and Juliet*. A tall stringy boy named Dewey Colton played Romeo. The couple had caused a stir in the community with their interracial onstage kiss. This year, they were all looking forward to doing *A Star is Born*. Miss Mixon, the drama coach, was a bit player in one of the original road productions, years ago.

But until then, there were only two times a day when Ginny felt really alive, when she was in Mr. Robinson's Advanced Placement Language Arts class, and the time spent working with him on the school newspaper. Mr. Robinson was one of the few teachers at Chandler High who didn't just stand up and talk down to you, but engaged the class in meaningful, thought-provoking dialogue.

Not only was he open to student's ideas, but also expected, no, he demanded that they have them. Ginny truly loved this type of give-and-take and responded well to the challenges he issued. As far as she was concerned, Jerry Robinson was the most knowledgeable man Ginny Westbrook had ever met.

Chapter 3

When Ginny entered the newspaper office after school, Mr. Robinson was sitting at one of three desks, each holding a computer workstation. The screen of the computer he worked with showed a crude black and white photograph of the morning's dedication ceremony.

Ginny was pleasantly surprised by the modern office that came with the new school. For the past two years, they had worked out of a converted book closet. "Mr. Robinson, is all this really ours?" she asked excitedly.

Mr. Robinson laughed as he turned to Ginny. "It truly is. Come take a look at this program."

Ginny rushed over to the Apple Macintosh, marveling as he moved the curser around the screen with the mouse, then deftly dropped a picture into a mock-up of the newspaper.

"Photoshop," she exclaimed. "I've heard of it!"

"And that's not all. We have the latest version of *Microsoft Word,* and this is *Aldus PageMaker,*" he said, pointing to the screen. "It's a new program made especially for newspapers and the like."

Then Mr. Robinson nodded toward the digital scanner. "And this is what I used for this morning's pictures."

"I know, I know," she squealed in delight. "With all this new stuff, we can print the paper up right here."

Just then, Sarah Steele breezed into the room and looked cynically at Ginny. "What in the world is all the fuss about? Haven't you people been exposed to modern technology?"

"And I suppose you have," Ginny said, turning to return Sarah's cynicism but was too excited to do so.

"The computers in Daddy's office are much better than these," Sarah said snidely, running her long thin, finely manicured, fingers across the keyboard of a nearby machine. "I used the Mac all summer, and I'll be using them next year at Tech."

"Hello, Sarah," Mr. Robinson said. "How was your summer?"

"Oh, hi, everybody, I forgot my manners," she said. "And my summer was … so-so."

Sarah Steele was one of the true bluebloods of Madison County. Her family history could be traced back to General James Oglethorpe's landing at Savannah. Both of her great-granddaddies fought in the Civil War – the Great War, they called it – and were among the founders of the city of Wrightsburg.

Next to Chandler Enterprises, Steele Construction was Madison County's most lucrative business, and employed most of the other part of its population that didn't call Ty Chandler, Jr., *Boss.* The new school had been the company's latest project.

Sarah was born with the proverbial silver spoon in her mouth, and she had not taken it out except for the times when she needed the extra space for her foot, which was quite often. Her admission to Georgia Tech would be by something called "legacy." Translated, that meant that her daddy went to school there and that he was also a major contributor to the institution. Although, to hear her go on about this and that, you would surely think otherwise.

"Aw, Sarah, don't be such a grouch," Mr. Robinson said, getting up from the computer."

"I'll be right back," he said. "We'll get started as soon as Dewey gets here."

Ginny was filled with excitement and her eyes sparkled as she moved from workstation to workstation, in awe of one technological wonder after another. Sarah slung her leather tote bag on the editing table and took a nearby seat. The charms on her sterling silver bracelet, which matched her long earrings, jangled as she dug deep into the large bag and pulled out a bottle of water.

Ginny felt the faintest twinge of jealousy as she looked at the statuesque beauty, with a head of luxuriant black hair, now reclining on one chair with her feet propped up on another. She looked at the trendy color-coordinated outfit Sarah wore, and then down at her own clothes, which until that very moment, Ginny had thought to be stylish.

Sarah wore a soft white chiffon blouse with a narrow tightly-stitched dark-blue border around its ruffled front and collar. Light blue opaque stockings accentuated her matching blue miniskirt. Sarah's blue soft - leather shoes probably cost as much as Ginny's entire outfit.

Although she considered herself a conservative dresser – she wouldn't have been caught dead in one of those "hootchie-mama" outfits – more than a few of the designer names such as Pierre Cardin, Ralph Lauren, and Liz Claiborne could be found in Ginny Westbrook's closet. But today she wore a simple white cotton blouse and tan summer skirt. The matching flat shoes she wore were stylish, but comfortable for the long walk home.

Sarah's fashionable clothes came straight from the finest department stores and boutiques of Atlanta, but Miriam Westbrook found most of Ginny's outfits at Marshall's, T. J. Max's, and other discount houses.

Money does matter, Ginny thought, *and one of these days I'm going to get me some.*

Between sips of bottled water, Sarah prattled on endlessly about everything and really nothing in particular. She criticized the Chandler's for waiting so long to bequeath the land to the city, the city for taking so long to deed it over to the school board, the principal, the mayor, and Ty Chandler, Jr., for making them stand in the sun for over an hour – she hadn't worn her sun screen – and finally, how dull the town and its boys had been that summer. "Ginny; are you listening to me?" she asked, sensing that she had lost her singular audience.

"Yes, I'm listening," Ginny replied, and then recapitulated Sarah's entire soliloquy.

Suddenly Sarah moved her feet from the chair and sat up straight. "You know, I really don't have time for the newspaper this year."

"Sarah, if you don't have time, then why are you here?"

Sarah gasped in disbelief. "You really don't have a clue, do you?"

"Clue, about what?"

"Your portfolio, silly," Sarah said. "You simply must have lots of extra curricular stuff in it to get into a really good school, and I just have to get into Tech so I can take over Daddy's business one day."

"Is that right?" Ginny said more than asked.

"Oh, I forgot," Sarah said sharply, sensing the patronizing tone of Ginny's voice, "you all have affirmative action. You don't have to worry about gettin' in school."

Ginny felt as if a stake had just been driven straight through her heart. She felt like placing her hands around the sterling silver necklace that Sarah wore and squeezing it until the impressions of its geometric designs were firmly imprinted upon her throat. Determined to take the high road, however, Ginny just laughed, shook her head, and then said facetiously, "Well, good luck to *you*, good old *Georgia Tech*, and to your *dear old dad*."

"What's so funny?" Mr. Robinson asked, walking through the door. "And where is that Dewey?"

Just then, Dewey popped his head into the doorway. "Somebody looking for me?" he asked with a wide grin on his face.

They all looked on in awe as he entered the room. Dewey Colton had left school for the summer a pale and bespectacled hundred-fifty-pound weakling with crooked teeth, but now he was tan and muscular. Ginny's heart skipped a beat as she stared at Dewey. He was strikingly handsome.

"Dewey, is that really you?" Sarah said, blushing. "Where are your Clark Kent glasses and scrawny body?"

"Hi, everybody," he said, now smiling even more to show off the new caps on his teeth. "Yes it's me. I'm wearing contacts and I'm working out now, weights, running, karate, the whole nine yards."

Mr. Robinson held up his hand, and Dewey gave him a high-five. "Boy, you're really buffed," he said, looking down at the small spare tire developing around his waist. "I might have to join you."

Then Dewey looked lovingly at Ginny as she sat at the computer, and she bashfully returned his smile. "Hello, Ginny," he said softly. "How was your summer?"

"Fine, Dewey. How was yours?"

"Good," he said.

When he was sure that the others were not looking, Dewey looked at Ginny. "But I missed you," he mouthed, smiling when she dropped her gaze and blushed.

"Well, this is it," Mr. Robinson said, moving from the computer and sitting behind his desk. Dewey and Ginny took seats beside Sarah.

"If no one else signs on, it'll be just us four," he began. "But, with the new technology, we should do just fine. Dewey, you'll have sports as usual."

"Okay. Anything special?" Dewey asked.

"Yes," Mr. Robinson said, looking contemplatively. "Let's take a new angle, and try to put a name and face on some of the jocks. You know, show their human side."

"Got it," Dewey said.

"Sarah, you take the new teachers," he continued. "Do the usual. You know, name, rank, and serial number."

"Whatever," Sarah replied placidly.

"And, Ginny, why don't you focus on the new school?" he said.

"I'm already on it," she said. "I took notes this morning."

"Good, I've got some great shots for you. You can take your pick later," he said. "Oh, and try to get an interview with Ty Jr. See if you can dig up some history on the old man. Find out why he was so willing to give up prime property for a school building."

"Oh, alright," Ginny said, blandly.

"What?" Mr. Robinson said, noticing that Ginny's exuberance had severely diminished. "What's wrong?"

Ginny sighed, hesitated, and then shrugged. "I just thought, with all of the new stuff ... that we could do something different this year."

"Like what, Ginny?" Dewey asked.

"I don't know, something ... like real news."

"Ginny, we do real news," Mr. Robinson said pleadingly. "But we can't *make* the news, we can only report it."

"I know. That's what's wrong with living in a small town. Nothing ever happens," she said, almost sadly.

"Well, that's it. Let's get cracking," Mr. Robinson said.

Dewey headed over to inspect the new laser printer and scanner, and Mr. Robinson and Ginny went back to the computer terminal – the one with the picture.

Sarah stood, gathering her things together to leave. "Well, little Miss Pulitzer, I hope we can find enough excitement to keep you in town until graduation," she said sarcastically to Ginny. "Well people, if that's all, I have better things to do."

As she walked to the door, Sarah pressed a slip of paper into Dewey's hand and whispered to him. "You look good. Call me tonight."

Dewey opened his hand and smiled as he looked at the number scrawled on the paper. A tiny heart was drawn at the top corner of the note.

Although it was called the fall semester, school actually began in summer, late August. The football team and cheerleaders had even started practice two weeks earlier. At four o'clock in the afternoon, the sweltering sun still blazed unmercifully on the wilted brown grass of the school's football practice field as each group began to assemble for their practice sessions. A few cheerleaders had already gathered at the sideline, and small groups of boys, carrying large gym bags, ambled toward the field house to change into practice uniforms

A tall muscular boy, with a mane of curly black hair, pulled his Chevy Malibu into the parking lot and got out of the car. While he went around to the trunk to get his gym bag, his passenger put the final touches to her makeup. She applied lipstick to full sensual lips, just a touch of blush to her well-defined cheeks, and then used a powder sponge to remove the shine from her pert upturned nose. She then gave her long platinum-blond hair a few final strokes of the brush, and then fluffed it back up with both hands.

Heads turned as Joe Meriwether opened the door, and Beth Campbell exited the car. Although of only average height, she had a more than amble bosom, shapely broad hips, and a razor thin waistline. The white letters stenciled across the front of her tight fitting royal blue T-shirt identified Beth as a cheerleader. But the letters across her back clarified that she was, indeed, cheerleader captain. The almost blinding white shorts she wore revealed her long tanned and shapely legs.

Joe was handsome by any standard. His piercing blue eyes were set deeply into a well-chiseled face, under thick eyebrows that matched his jet-black hair. Standing six-foot-two and weighing in at an even one hundred ninety pounds, Joe's athletically trim body was well tanned by his regular summer stint as a lifeguard at the city's swimming pool.

Joe and Beth were Chandler High's ideal couple, and today, they looked every bit the part as the two of them strolled, arm-in-arm, across the parking lot and onto the field. When they reached the center of the field, Beth kissed Joe on the cheek before skipping off to practice. Joe returned her peck, and then turned toward the field house.

Sonny James whispered to his cohorts – the big white boy and three other black players – as they walked past Joe, and then they all laughed loudly.

Joe rushed to catch up with Sonny and his friends. "What did you say?" he asked angrily.

The boys continued laughing as Sonny turned to face Joe. "Nothing," Sonny said with a smirk.

"You lie! I heard you!" Joe shot back.

Sonny turned to walk off. Then thinking better of it, he turned back to Joe. "Alright, I said it looked like Beth titted up over the summer. Now what?"

Now Sonny's boys laughed even more raucously. Joe rushed toward Sonny, but the big white boy stepped between them. "Hey, man," he said, "we can't have any dissension on the team. We've got a chance to go all the way this year!"

Cooler heads prevailed and the two boys parted and walked away in opposite directions. Suddenly Sonny stopped and turned toward Joe. "If you think you have an exclusive on that," he shouted, "you've got another thought coming."

That did it! Joe could take no more. Angrily, he turned and ran toward Sonny, who had already turned to meet him. The two of them clashed with such ferocity that even the big white boy was afraid to intervene. By now a crowd had gathered. Some of the boys egged them on, but the cheerleaders – especially Beth – screamed their pretty little heads off.

Coach Dixon, a powerfully built black man, rushed to separate them. "Hey, you guys, break it up!"

But even the coach – who stood six-foot-five and was a former pro football player – was not equal to the task. It was only after several assistant coaches had joined the fray that the two boys were pulled apart. Coach Dixon was livid, as well as scratched and tired from the struggle.

"What's wrong with you guys?" he shouted maniacally, while desperately trying to catch his breath. "Are you crazy? You two are supposed to be the leaders of this team, and just look at you!"

The two boys, also a bit worn, huffed and puffed as they glared at each other.

"Get to the field house, all of you!" the coach said. "And when you get dressed, give me ten laps!"

This had been neither the first tiff between these two boys, nor would it be the last. Until the second game of last season, Joe Meriwether had been the team captain and starting quarterback. Trailing badly in the fourth quarter, things got worse when Joe went down with a twisted knee.

Sonny came in and led the team to an unexpected victory and, although his injury was ever so slight, Joe was never able to regain his first string position. Sonny went on to become the team's leader and star. This year, he was named starting quarterback and team co-captain, relegating Joe Meriwether to a role he had never played before, second string.

Dewey was wearing a backpack for his own books, but he carried Ginny's under his arms as they walked down the street. He playfully pirouetted in front of her. "Well, how do you like the new me?"

"You look great, Dewey, but you were always handsome to me," she said, reaching for her books. "But this is far enough. You'd better turn back now."

"No," Dewey said, pulling the books out of Ginny's reach. "Why can't I walk you home?"

"You just can't, Dewey. You just can't."

"Look, Ginny, you can't deny what happened between us."

Ginny facetiously cupped her hands to her mouth as if making an announcement. "Bulletin, bulletin, it was a stage kiss. We were just a-c-t-i-n-g."

"No," Dewey cried. "It was real."

Ginny couldn't remember what had shocked her most on that fateful night, when Dewey slipped his tongue into her mouth or when she, not only did nothing to stop him, but also let it stay there for a moment before returning the favor.

Later, she had passed it off as being caught up in the moment, with the applause of the crowd for an outstanding performance. However, the week after *the kiss*, the two of them *had* gone out, but not on a real date.

One night when they stayed late at the city library, researching a story for the newspaper, the two of them shared hamburgers and sodas at Barney's Burger Barn. Afterwards, she let Dewey walk her home. The kiss they shared that night on her front porch *was* real.

So was Charlie's anger when he caught them in the middle of the act. He flipped on the porch light and was totally indignant when she tried to introduce Dewey. To this day, Ginny *could not* understand the irritation her father showed regarding the matter.

The next day, word of the night at Barney's had spread to Sonny James, who was also fit to be tied. Ginny and Sonny had dated off-and-on since the tenth grade, but she just didn't think of herself as being his girlfriend.

Although she couldn't deny that she was physically attracted to him. After all, he was a hunk, and all of the girls at school, black and white, were throwing themselves at him. Ginny knew for a fact that more than a few of them had found the target, but she didn't care.

Ginny and Sonny simply didn't like the same things. They were on two different levels and had absolutely nothing in common. She liked all kinds of music and movies. And of course, there were her three passions, writing, theater, and dance.

The only thing she could be sure that Sonny liked, other than sports, was slobbering all over her face – in what he called a kiss – while he used his hands and arms like octopus tentacles.

Fending off Sonny James was like playing goalkeeper for a ice hockey team. As soon as one shot was deflected, you had to prepare for the next while wondering from which direction it would come. Though sometimes she didn't mind as much as others.

It really bothered Ginny, however, when Sonny continued to pressure her about "going all the way," something she had no plans for, and certainly not with Sonny James.

Sonny's conversation was mostly monosyllabic with a few contractions thrown in for variety. But she and Dewey could talk until the wee hours of the morning about any and everything, and sometimes did via telephone. That was until Miriam overheard them at three o'clock one morning, last spring.

That called for another long talk with Charlie, whom she loved immensely and didn't want to hurt. He gave her a long list of reasons not to date a boy of another race, so Ginny promised never to see Dewey Colton again.

Mostly, though, Ginny dated Sonny because of Charlie, who like many others, dearly loved the man-child athlete. On the few occasions when he had cajoled her into inviting Sonny for dinner, Ginny didn't have to worry. Charlie would hardly let her get a word in edgewise, even if she had one and wanted to. She didn't on both counts.

Additionally, Ginny had not been altogether truthful with her father about what really did happen last spring after the Junior-Senior Prom. They had an awful fight when Sonny wanted her to go to a room he had rented at the Starlight Motel. She scratched his face, and then he took her straight home. Ginny heard that he picked up Mary Brewster, a red-haired trollop who waited tables at Pappas' Drive-in, and the party went on as scheduled.

Ginny still had not reconciled why it upset her so much when Margo filled her in on all the gory details. She had not gone out with Sonny since. After then and up until school let out for the summer, she would sometimes let Dewey walk her part of the way home after working on the newspaper.

"I love you, Ginny," Dewey said, reluctantly placing her books into her arms. Then he gently placed his hands on her shoulders, turning her so that she faced him. "I want *you* to know it, and I want the *world* to know it."

"Oh, Dewey, you're so sweet," she said, "but I don't know. Things are just too complicated right now. And I--"

Dewey moved close and placed a finger to his lips, and then silenced Ginny by touching the finger to hers. "Don't fret, my love," he said softly. "Until tomorrow."

For the second time that day, Ginny Westbrook's little heart skipped a beat or two as she watched Dewey Colton turn and walk down the sidewalk. His steps quickened and soon turned into a trot. He was running late for his karate class, which was taught by Master Moto, a no-nonsense master of Karate, Tai chi and Tae Kwan Do.

Shortly, Dewey hastily entered the converted storefront studio. The small, but compelling, Japanese man looked up at the clock on the wall. Dewey stopped and bowed. Master Moto bowed in return.

"Mr. Colton, you are one of my better students," he said. "You could be my best, if only you would work on your--"

Dewey finished the sentence for him. "Discipline. I know, Master Mo, I won't be late again."

Walking in the opposite direction, Ginny looked at her watch and remembered her promise of making dinner for her father. She hesitated at the entrance to Simpson's Woods and grimaced, remembering her other promise – not to take the shortcut.

At first Ginny slowly walked past the arching wrought-iron sign gaping over the never-closed gates. Then she stopped and looked at her watch again. Noticing the lateness of the hour, Ginny turned and sprinted back through the entrance, following a trail that led deep into the forest.

On paper, Simpson's Woods was a city park, named for Colonel Jedadiah James Simpson, one of Madison County's native sons who served under Robert E. Lee in the Great War. In reality, however, it was just five square miles of landlocked property, which the city purchased when competing land developers couldn't agree on which portions were usable.

Determined to waste nothing, the city cleared portions of the land for the park. A statue of the colonel still stands at its entrance, bearing testament to the city's good intentions.

After the Depression, dwindling resources took their toll on not only Wrightsburg, Georgia, but also the entire nation. Since that time, the woods had been used for various purposes. The lane that the city cleared for access to the never-fully-developed park served as the ideal shortcut from the south side to the central part of town.

Other parts of the forest, once used for family outings, still served as a clandestine playground where children could come – unbeknownst to their parents. The boys could become pirates in search of buried treasure, cowboys chasing a band of renegade Indians, or a famous general leading his troops into battle. A girl could be magically transformed into a fairy princess who reigned over an entire phantom kingdom. Ginny had done this since the age of ten, so she knew the woods like the back of her hand.

In later years, during the spring when the wildflowers bloomed, she loved to take the shortcut through the lane, which halved the distance from downtown to her house on Cherry Lane. Sometimes she would find a spot under her favorite oak tree and curl up with a good book.

While engrossed in her novels, she was no longer Ginny Westbrook, the girl from Madison County, but Ginny, the world traveler, actress extraordinaire, or sometimes, airline pilot. Only the sky was the limit. She loved those times spent in her world of make-believe, a world where good always triumphed over evil, and nothing was impossible.

There were two parts of Simpson's Woods, however, that were definitely off limits to Ginny. The first was a section on the backside of the woods that served as a lovers' lane and a place for other surreptitious meetings. With the influx of drugs in the early '70s, this area had become an open-air market for drugs and sex, and still was to this day.

Then there was Witches' Hollow, where only the most courageous souls dared venture. It was located at the center of the park, far away from any street or access road. Many tales and fables were told of malevolent goings-on in the hollow. It was rumored that back in the 1800s, a witches' coven used it for human sacrifices. On certain nights when the moon was full, some still claimed to hear the mournful wails and cries of their victims.

Chapter 4

The husky middle-aged man, wearing only an undershirt and boxer shorts, sat slumped on a threadbare sofa. A can of beer was propped on his sagging belly as he dozed between watching snippets of the *Late Late Show*. In the foyer of the house, a humongous black Rottwieler stirred from his sleep and emitted a low growl. The dog then ran to the front door, barking ferociously as he jumped up and down, scratching at it with his paws.

"Duke, pipe down out there," the surly man yelled from the living room.

Although it was still during the Dog Days of summer, there was a distinct chill about the night. The wind blew briskly, leaving a swirl of early fall leaves in *the girl's* wake as she quickly walked past the house and continued down the street.

At another house across the street, a little brown Chihuahua howled fervently as it, too, scratched at the front door. A diminutive old woman reached down and picked up the still barking dog.

"Something frighten Mama's little baby?" she asked softly, stroking the Chihuahua's head. "Come on let Mama get you some milk."

Moonlight cast a shimmering glow around *the girl's* straight blonde hair as she turned into the driveway of a modest two-story house.

For some reason, Ginny had slept fitfully all that night. She tossed and turned, and then awoke with a start. She shuddered and sat straight up in bed, sensing a presence in the room. "Who's there?" she asked, her voice filled with fright.

And then Ginny saw her. She was standing at the foot of the bed. It was *the girl* from the bus, surrounded by an eerie shimmering glow of light.

The girl reached both hands out to Ginny. "Help me," she said in a low raspy voice.

Terrified, Ginny opened her mouth to scream, but no sound escaped her lips. Suddenly *the girl* turned and spirited out the window. Inexplicably, Ginny rose from the bed and followed her through the window, although it was closed. She felt a sense of weightlessness as *the girl* took her by the hand and lifted her high into the heavens.

They were flying over the city. At first, Ginny was terrified, but then, her terror slowly subsided and turned to perverse pleasure. She liked it. No, she loved it.

Things were beautiful from way up high. Ginny's sandy brown hair and *the girl's* blonde tresses blew wildly in the wind as they passed over the lights of the downtown area. Then they were over the new school, which looked like a toy building below. Off in the distance, Ginny could see Chandler Enterprises. The fleet of trucks was parked in front of the loading dock in preparation for the next morning's runs.

Now they were directly over Simpson's Woods. Ginny looked down at the statue of Colonel Simpson, and then she could see the familiar trail that led to the old oak tree, where she had whiled away so many summer days.

Suddenly they were no longer in the air but on the ground, running through the forest. But now, *the girl* was leading Ginny deep into areas of the woods where she dared not go. *The girl* was leading her into the dreaded Witches' Hollow. "No," Ginny cried out voicelessly. She tried to stop, but couldn't.

Then a fog settled over the woods. Ginny found it not only difficult to keep up with her, but now she could barely see *the girl*. But then she disappeared into the fog, altogether.

"Stop. Wait. Who are you?" Ginny called out. This time her voice worked, and she could once again see *the girl* in front of her. But out of nowhere a long arm reached out and snatched *the girl* by the collar, violently pulling her into a gaping hole in the ground.

"Help me," *the girl* shrieked.

Ginny paused, and then cautiously approached the hole. Reaching the precipice, she peered down into the darkness. But *the girl* was gone. Now there was only a skeleton, a fleshless carcass with a horrific looking green glow emanating from its eye sockets as they stared up in ghastly horror. All of a sudden Ginny was in the hole with the skeleton, and someone was shoveling dirt into it.

"Aiiigh," Ginny screamed as shovelful after shovelful of dirt covered her. "Help! Get me out of here! Help!"

Miriam grabbed Ginny's arms as she thrashed wildly in bed.

"Ginny, Ginny, wake up!"

Finally, Miriam was able to shake her awake. Ginny sweated profusely, and upon awakening, the moisture caused her body to chill. She shook in heaving sobs as tears ran down her face. Miriam Westbrook wrapped her arms around her weeping child and rocked her back and forth – as she had done so many times before.

"Oh, Mom, it was so real," Ginny said, her voice trembling from fear. She kept shaking her head as she looked up into Miriam's eyes.

"Honey, it was just a bad dream," Miriam said in an attempt to be reassuring, but she was stung by the fright that she saw in her daughter's eyes.

Later, when Ginny had mercifully slipped into a peaceful sleep, Miriam sniffed the air. She turned the lamp off, then thought better of it and turned it back on.

When Miriam reached their bedroom, Charlie, whom she had persuaded to let her handle the situation after Ginny's terrifying screams had awakened them, was already back in bed, but not asleep. He turned just as she slipped in beside him. "Is she okay?" he asked.

"Yes," she replied hesitantly, "but there was something strange."

"Strange, what?" Charlie said, now sitting up in bed with a look of great concern on his face.

"A familiar smell," she said, "like lilac toilet water, I think. I don't know."

"A smell?" he said, sounding a bit bewildered."

"And I can't swear it," she continued hesitantly, "but that room was as cold as ice."

"It was just the air conditioner. You know she keeps her vent wide open."

"I'm sure you're right. It's probably nothing. Go back to sleep," she said. *But the air conditioner wasn't on*, Miriam said to herself. She flipped the switch on the lamp, and then all of Cherry Lane turned dark ... except for Ginny's bedroom.

If anyone had been there to watch, in the light of the small lamp beside her bed, they would have seen *the girl*, sitting – on silent guard – in Ginny's rocking chair at the foot of her bed. *The girl* rocked to her heart's content until near the break of dawn.

Then she was gone.

The next morning when Ginny got on the bus, the boys taunted her as usual, but on this day, she was no match for them. The boys were not really her enemies. They all held secret – and some not so secret – crushes on the pretty girl whom they deemed to be out of their league.

Actually, Johnny Riggins, the short dark-skinned boy who led the mockery, had been Ginny's escort to their seventh grade spring dance. Although the two of them had not dated since, they had maintained a cordial relationship until the tenth grade, which was when Sonny James entered the picture. At first, Johnny was just disappointed and turned sour, but now it seemed that he was her mortal enemy.

Walking through the gauntlet of black faces that sneered at her and whispered curses, Ginny did not react. The girls taunted her out of jealousy and the boys out of spite, although both groups knew there would be a price to be paid if Sonny James ever found out about their shenanigans. But they all knew that Ginny would never tell. She was too independent for that. The few white students who rode the Cherry Lane bus were always cordial to Ginny. This only served to further inflame her darker enemies, especially the females.

For fear of seeing *the girl*, she dared not look to the back of the bus, so Ginny moved straight toward the seat, which like clockwork, Margo regularly saved for her. She spoke softly as she slid in beside Margo. "Hi, Margo."

"Hi, Ginny."

Ginny said nothing else, but sat rigidly and looked straight ahead.

Margo stared at her for a long time, and then finally said, "What's wrong with you?"

"Nothing," Ginny said, and continued to stare straight ahead. Neither of the two girls spoke another word.

Finally, the bus pulled into the driveway of the school, and they disembarked. When they reached the intersection in the school's hallway, Margo broke the ice, "Lunch?" she asked.

"Maybe," Ginny said, and then they parted ways.

Margo was visibly concerned. Something was wrong with her friend and she meant to find out what it was.

Ginny cast a cautious glance at the restroom as she quickly walked past and skittered into her homeroom class.

Ginny spent most of the day walking around in a daze. She didn't remember whether or not she had eaten any of the food Miriam placed before her that morning. Maybe she did. It was her favorite, raisin bran muffins and freshly cut fruit that Charlie brought daily from the loading dock. She did remember that there was very little conversation with her father.

Today, he and Jay Dee would be driving down to Cordele, Georgia, where they would pick up a load of watermelons and cantaloupes. He always brought cantaloupes home when they were in season, knowing how much Ginny loved them. And, oh, yes, soon they would all be driving up to Beaudry Ford in Atlanta, where Charlie had gotten a really good deal on the Ford Taurus that he and Miriam shared, but was referred to as hers.

At lunch, Ginny had been a total zombie, which did *not* seem to bother Cha-Cha one iota since it gave her more talking time. But Ginny's trance-like state left Margo even more distressed. The whole time, Ginny gave one-syllable answers to the questions the other two girls put to her.

"Did you go out with anyone this summer?" Margo asked.

"No."

"Are you going to the back-to-school dance with Sonny?"

"No."

"If you ain't going with Sonny, could you fix me up with him?" Cha-Cha said.

"No."

What's wrong with you?" Margo said.

"Nothing."

In Mr. Robinson's language arts class, it had been more of the same.

What's wrong with you, today?" he said.

"Nothing,"

"Is there anything I can do?"

"No."

Finally, it was nearing the end of the sixth period. If the rest of the day had gone badly for Ginny, sixth period was going even worse. Mr. Chester was one of the most boring teachers in the school. The history teacher was also the president of Madison County's Heritage Society, which was said to be a cover for the Neo-Klan movement.

Yesterday, the two of them had crossed swords about the role of African Americans in early America. He had not forgotten the run-in – neither had Ginny.

"Present," spoken during roll call, was the only word she had uttered since entering the classroom. Mr. Chester stood in front of the class, poking verbal holes in the picture of General George Washington crossing the Delaware, which was taped to the blackboard.

"Whoever heard of anyone standing up in a boat, especially in the middle of an icy river," he said, and then everybody laughed, except Ginny. She had felt a stir of excitement upon seeing that one of the men in the boat was black, but let it pass. This was a bad day for Ginny Westbrook, and she wanted to keep it that way. Instead of commenting on the soldier's race, she let it ride, sinking deeper into her blue funk.

As she had done with Sarah Steele, Ginny was able to keep up with the old professor's simplistic dialogue without interrupting her train of thought – which was as it had been all day – about *the girl.*

Who was she? Where did she come from? Was she real or was it all a dream? Which was it?

"Which was it, Miss Westbrook?" Mr. Chester, who was now standing directly over Ginny, asked again. "Was it, by plan or accident that the Revolutionary War began?"

Both, came the answer, rising up from Ginny's subconscious. But before the thought could be vocalized, a voice came over the intercom. It was the principal with the afternoon announcements. Ginny uttered a sigh of relief as she looked down at her watch. No, it was only two forty-five, much too early for the end-of-day announcements. *This must be something special,* she thought.

In the principal's office, Mr. Murray swiveled around from his desk to face the intercommunication machine. A distraught woman, with her clothes and hair in disarray, sat beside him as he picked up the microphone from the table and spoke. "Students, before we leave for the day, there is an urgent appeal from a parent that I would like for you to hear."

He placed the microphone down in front of the woman who looked to be in her early fifties, but was actually in her late thirties. And if you could look past the years of hard living reflected in her face, you would have known that she had once been quite beautiful.

As if she could be seen over the intercom, the woman made a valiant effort to pull her bleached blonde hair back into place and straighten her dress before she spoke. "For those of you who don't know me, I'm Lizzy Campbell, Beth's mother," she said in a trembling voice. "I hate to disturb you, but … last night…"

Lizzie's voice failed her.

45

Elizabeth (Beth) Campbell was named after her mother. When she was a child, family members took to calling her Beth and her mother Lizzy so as to distinguish between the two of them. Lizzy fought back tears as she continued. Mr. Murray took a tissue from a box on his desk and held it out to her.

"Beth didn't come home last night. It is so unlike her to do this. It's totally out of character," she said, taking the tissue and dabbing at her eyes. "If anyone has seen her, I'm asking that you please come forward with any information you might have."

"As Mrs. Campbell has stated, Beth is missing," the principal added after taking the microphone from Lizzy, who was once again in tears as she had been when she entered his office.

"Beth was last seen at Barney's Burger Barn," he went on. "We are sure that this is all some kind of terrible misunderstanding, so if you have any information as to the whereabouts of Beth Campbell, please stop by my office before leaving campus."

Shortly after the last bell sounded, the office door opened, and Faye Drummond entered with her head held down. She shyly looked up at Mr. Murray and Lizzy Campbell.

"Mr. Murray, I'm Faye Drummond."

"Yes, Faye, I know you," he said. "You're good friends with Beth."

"Yes, sir," she said. "I have some information."

Chapter 5

The two women laughed and talked amiably as they walked across the parking lot toward their respective cars.

"See you later, Myrtle," Lola Morgan said, inserting the key into the car door and flipping the lock.

"Okay, girl, take it easy," Myrtle replied before walking on toward her car, which was parked further down.

Before getting into the 1980 Camry, Lola checked the back seat. There had been some strange occurrences lately, and she was not about to take chances with her safety. As she pulled the car out of the parking lot and into the flow of traffic, a blue sedan, parked across the street, pulled away from the curb and fell in behind her. Whenever the gap between the two cars widened, the sedan would speed up, but when the distance seemed too close, it slowed again.

At first, Lola paid little attention to the car's headlights that glared in her rearview mirror. She tapped her fingers lightly on the steering wheel in time to Aretha Franklin's "Respect," blaring from her car radio, then began rocking from side to side and humming along with the old song she had first heard as a child. Once again, the sedan came too close, and then slowed to a crawl. This time, the amateurish maneuvers of the driver caught Lola's attention. She quickly snapped the radio off and adjusted her rearview mirror to better see the headlights, which now grew smaller and smaller as the two cars distanced themselves from each other.

"Well, here we go again," she said aloud.

For the past two nights, Lola had the feeling that somebody was following her home from work. *Is it that doggoned Ralph?* she thought. *No way. I'd know his Cadillac anywhere. Maybe the bastard's got somebody following me.*

She was now more angry than frightened. As the green light turned yellow, Lola pushed the accelerator to the floor. The Camry lunged into the intersection, and then made a wide swerving left turn in front of the oncoming traffic. Horns blared from the two cars she had almost hit as Lola quickly pulled to the curb of a side street and turned to look back.

There was nothing. The car that had been following her was gone, having either run the red light or been no more than a figment of her imagination.

Janie Morgan looked so much like Lola did when she was the same age that it sometimes scared Grandma Hattie silly. After dinner, the young girl sat at the dining room table with a math book propped open, but with only a few problems worked on the sheet in front of her.

Math was definitely *not* Janie's subject. Hattie and Lola sat in the living area across from the open-air dining space. Hattie was hand stitching the hem of an expansive wedding dress that lay sprawled across the sofa and another chair while Lola anxiously pretended to watch TV.

"How're you comin' over there?" Hattie asked Janie.

"Fine," Janie lied.

"Are you sure?" Lola added.

"I'm doing alright," she said. "The new teacher just gives too many problems."

Just then, there was a melodious chime as Lola's pager went off. She picked it up and walked toward the kitchen, looking at the number displayed on the small screen. Reaching the kitchen, she punched the numbers into the wall unit and waited as the phone rang on the other end of the line.

"Hello," said a deep male voice.

With the music and loud talking in the background, it was obvious to Lola that the call was coming from a bar.

"That you?" he asked.

"Yeah, it's me," she said.

"I'm coming over."

"About what time?"

"Late."

"Good, the later the better," Lola said, and then hung up the kitchen phone and walked back into the living room.

"Was that Ralph?" her mother asked.

"No."

"Who was it?"

"Nobody you know, Mama. Just somebody from work."

"Lola, are you and Daddy Ralph gonna get back together?" Janie asked.

Lola hated that her daughter chose to call her by her first name, but it seemed that by the time the two of them really got to be friends, all of the motherly names were all used up. Janie couldn't use "mama," because it confused her when Lola, Ralph, and her Uncle James, who lived in Macon, called Hattie that.

"Where in the world would you get an idea like that?" Lola said.

"I heard Grandma Hattie and Daddy Ralph talking about it."

"Mama," Lola said in a voice of vexation, "would you *please* stay out of my business?"

That did it. Hattie Morgan blew her top. "Your business … your business … it's my business, too. When you left your child here for me to raise … that made it my business!"

"Grand-ma," Janie said, her young brow creasing with lines of frustration.

Janie felt frightened when the two women in her life fought, which lately was quite often. She had lost her mother once and was horrified at the thought of it happening again.

"Mama, not in front of the child," Lola said, and then left the room.

Lola walked down the narrow hall and entered the small bathroom. Its pink and white décor clearly staked it out as being for women only. It had been years since a man had lived in this house. Pink lace valances adorned the tiny window and white shower curtains, festooned with large pink flowers, hung above the old-fashioned claw-foot bathtub.

Lola quickly stripped off the white blouse she wore and stepped out of her blue slacks, dropping them both to the floor. Shedding her bra and panties, she added them to the pile, pushing it aside with one bare foot.

Reaching for one of the large pink towels up on the rack, Lola caught just a glimpse of her reflection in the full-length mirror on the back of the door. Fingering a bit of flab around her belly, she decided to take a closer look, slowly examining her body, from the top of her head, with its glossy-black permed hair, to the bottom of her feet, where finely pedicured toes matched her immaculately done fingernails. *Not bad*, she thought, smiling, *to be pushing forty*.

Suddenly Lola froze with fright. There was a noise outside the window. To her, it had the distinct sound of a foot stepping on a twig. She quickly flipped the light switch, and the tiny room went dark. She then slowly tiptoed to the window and peered outside. In the moonlight, she could see all the way to the fence that separated their property line from the storm drain, which ran the length of Jasper Road.

Girl, you trippin', Lola said to herself. *It's probably one of the neighborhood boys trying to sneak a peep*. She turned the light back on and walked over to the bathtub.

"Well, I hope you enjoyed the show ... whoever you are," she said aloud with a smile.

It was around two in the morning when the chime of the pager on the nightstand awakened Lola Morgan from her half-sleep. Ignoring the irritating sound, she pulled her flannel nightshirt over her head and stuffed it into the laundry hamper before walking over to her dresser.

She sprayed just a touch of body mist along the curve of her neck and behind each ear, and then as an afterthought, between her breasts.

Then Lola ceremoniously slipped into a red almost-transparent teddy, which she had agonized over for almost an hour before purchasing from Victoria's Secrets, and then padded barefoot to the kitchen. She quietly unlocked the door and stood waiting until she heard a faint tapping on it. She opened the door and a tall hulking figure of a man quietly slipped inside.

Towering over her, the man immediately encircled her waist with his arms, drawing her close, his lips in search of hers. But without a word, Lola avoided the kiss and gently pushed him aside. Taking him by the hand, they tiptoed lightly down the hall to her bedroom. She could hear Hattie snoring as they eased past the bedroom that her mother and daughter shared.

The next morning, Lola pointed the Camry towards Highway 29 for the drive into Wrightsburg. On the way to work, her mind drifted back in time as she thought about her current predicament.

Lola Morgan knew that she didn't have an earth-shattering face – her nose was a little too wide and her lips a bit too thick – and that it was her voluptuous body that caused heads to turn when she walked down the street. This much she had learned when she was about the same age as her daughter, Janie, who would soon be fourteen. Back then, it was routine that she would walk the three miles from their house – on the outskirts of town – to Perryman's Fabric Shop to pick up supplies for her mother, the town's seamstress.

At first, young Lola went unnoticed as she slipped into town to buy the needles, threads, and zippers that Hattie Morgan used to turn out the sumptuous wedding gowns and prom dresses, which were her staples. Any girl or woman, black or white, who was anybody in Madison County, could be counted among those who wore Morgan originals.

After Lola's body began to bloom and take on the characteristics of the woman she was destined to become, the men and boys would always turn to stare as she passed, sometimes to the chagrin of their female companions. In the afternoon, hustlers and con men who made their living in the dead of night – in pool halls, gambling houses, and houses that offered up other services of the female type – came out for their daily dose of sunlight.

The men would sit along the railing in front of the Blue Moon Cafe or loiter in front of Dick's Pool Room before going back to the cover of darkness. Whenever they were out and Lola walked past, they would whistle and give catcalls.

Initially the fancy looking men – who were always dressed to the nines in silk suits, alligator shoes, and stingy brim hats – frightened her. But she soon grew to love it, especially when it was smooth talking Johnny Adams doing the whistling. Johnny was a tall, lean, ladies'-man who was the spitting image of Billy D. Williams. When she was fifteen, Johnny Adams introduced Lola Morgan to the ways of the world in the back seat of his Buick Riviera.

Lola stopped when the traffic light turned red. "It'll be another hot one," she said aloud. The light turned green, and then she pressed down on the accelerator. The Camry darted into the flow of traffic as her mind again drifted back through the maze of time.

Her short fling with Johnny had come to the attention of her family, thanks to Irene Watson, one of their nosey neighbors. When she spotted them, parked in Johnny's Buick behind Lowman's Cotton Gin, Irene didn't let her feet leave the street until half of Madison County knew of the scandalous affair.

Lola's father, Howard, had been bowled over when his barber, between snips of his scissors, whispered the gory details into his ear. Thus began the rift between Lola and her parents, which to this day has not entirely healed.

Anyway, that was the first time her body got her into trouble, but it would *not* be the last. Her shapely figure had also served her well. When Lola Morgan hit the Big Apple, she did it with a bang. Black was just becoming beautiful when she walked into the Ford Modeling Agency.

In order to cash in on the shift in marketing products toward minorities, there was a dire need for models of a darker hue who would – as they put it – photograph "Black," much to the dismay of lighter-skinned hopefuls.

One look at the curvaceous girl with the dark chocolate skin, and the management team gave her a contract on the spot. This was not to say that Lola was a creature of beauty but no substance. She was an honor student during her high school days and even into two years of college.

Lola had a saying, "Accentuate the positive and eliminate the negative." It was not really her saying, but came from the lyrics of a song that was popular during World War II. Nevertheless, she followed its edicts religiously. Lola Morgan knew that her body was her positive, and she did everything within her power to keep it perfectly honed – aerobics three times a week and eating right.

She had not gained over ten pounds since being crowned Miss Madison High School, back in 1970, still maintaining that golden ratio of breasts-to-waist-to-hips that proved to be so attractive to men. Lola's waist had grown a few inches, but so had her bosom and her most viable asset of all, her behind. When he first met her, Johnny Adams had called it a truckload. It still was.

The town had been in an uproar when Lola left Ralph Whitaker, son of the local mortician, at the altar. She didn't really leave him at the alter. They never made it that far. As the big day neared, Lola got cold feet, gave the ring back, and called off the wedding. Little did he know it, but Lola Morgan had done Ralph the biggest favor of his dull and boring life.

The baby that she carried in her belly – that to this day, Ralph thinks is his – was really fathered by her sociology professor up at Clark College in Atlanta, where she was going into her junior year. Lola wanted desperately to tell her family the truth, but it would've killed her father. Refusing to marry the baby's daddy was shock enough to the lovable old man's heart, but to divulge that the true father was a married man, living somewhere up in Atlanta, would have been too much.

Lola didn't love Ralph, but liked him well enough not to make his life miserable. She just couldn't see herself living in Wrightsburg for the rest of her life, but Ralph had already paid down on a plot of land across the street from his father's home and mortuary. Wrightsburg for life, in-laws across the street, Lola Morgan *did not* think so.

Anyway, it didn't seem to matter. After the birth of Janie Lynn Morgan, all involved fell madly in love with the little angel. It tore at Lola's heart when she left for New York to stay with her Aunt Maude, where the plan was for her to find a good job, and then send for her daughter.

The others back in Madison County never cared that Lola never sent for Janie. Although she lived with Howard and Hattie Morgan, the toddler was gleefully passed from one set of grandparents to the other.

Later, when Ralph married Edna, a young woman who came from Eufaula, Alabama, to teach kindergarten, they too joined the grandparents, making it a tri-fecta affair. Janie had enough clothes at each of the three houses, which she rotated among like the revolving door of a department store, to outfit a classroom full of children.

All hell broke loose, one Christmas, when Lola came home and tried to take Janie back with her. She had never seen such outrage from all parties concerned, so Lola tucked tail and went back empty-handed and brokenhearted.

Although, upon her arrival, Lola Morgan had taken New York by storm, things quickly tapered off. She was fairly successful as a runway model for a few years, but at that time, big breaks were few and far between for black models. And after all, she did *not* have a "cover girl" face.

Then things took a dramatic turn for the worse. In a strange twist of fate, it was she who was left standing at the alter. Well, not really at the alter, but left waiting for a divorce that would never happened – between her married lover and his wife.

Disgusted and low in spirit, on a whim, Lola took the entrance exam for the New York City Police Department and passed it with flying colors. She decided to take the job until she could figure out exactly what she really wanted out of life, but soon discovered that not only did she like patrolling the streets of Manhattan, but also was also quite good at it. Within ten years, Lola had risen to the rank of junior grade detective.

Then one day, she got the distressing call to come home. The man whose strength she had borrowed from during her trying times, now needed her. Howard Morgan had fallen victim to a debilitating stroke. At first, she used her vacation and sick time to travel back and forth to help Hattie attend to him as he grew progressively worse.

Then one day, her father mercifully slipped into a coma and never awakened. It was only after the funeral that Lola discovered what she really wanted out of life. It was her daughter. During the months of trips to and from New York, the two of them had drawn closer to each other. Janie had cried all day before she was to leave, and secretly, Lola did, too.

She had driven the rental car all the way back to Hartsfield Airport in Atlanta and was waiting at the gate for her plane when it finally hit her. Lola Morgan was going to get her life back, and there was no time like the present.

When she got back to New York, Lola moved like a whirlwind. Within a week, she had turned in her badge, gun, and resignation to the NYPD, stripped her apartment of anything of sentimental value, and left instructions with her aunt Maude to dispose of whatever was left. They had no problem subleasing her apartment on the lower Eastside. Lola received a substantial check from a retirement fund she wouldn't be around to use, part of which she left with her aunt in case the sub-lessee defaulted on the rent.

On the way home, she stopped in Atlanta as usual, but this time instead of renting a car, she paid cash for the green 4-door Camry sedan and drove the eighty miles home to Madison County. Hattie and Janie were shocked to see Lola standing at the front door with suitcases in both hands, like a scene from a really bad movie. Nonetheless, Janie was overcome with joy.

But poor Ralph Whitaker.

Ralph, whose wife had been killed in a tragic accident a few years earlier, thought somehow that he might've had something to do with the return of the prodigal daughter. He now had high hopes of rekindling the love affair. Lola had added fuel to the fire when – in a moment of grief over the death of her father – she had gone to bed with him.

And, occasionally, she still did when the two of them might have dinner together to talk about their daughter's future. Sometimes one thing led to another, but how Ralph could ever think that dinner and a piece of tail would translate into reconciliation was totally beyond Lola's comprehension.

And to totally complicate matters, Lola Morgan had done it again. She had sunk back into her old bad habit. Once again, she had picked the wrong man. *But this time, I'm going to do something about it,* she thought. *I'll nip it in the bud.* Lola sighed and shook her head as she pulled the Camry into the parking lot of the police department.

The Madison County Police Department, under the able leadership of Chief Russell Callahan, had grown from himself and two officers, in

1978, to a staff of twenty. Two sergeants supervised fourteen uniformed officers who routinely patrolled the city streets and county roads, served warrants and eviction notices for overdue rent, and provided security for the county courthouse.

The newly formed investigative arm consisted of two detectives, Louis Brazell and Lola Morgan, plus a crime scene investigator, Brian Pollard. Lou, a transplanted Floridian, from Miami, was on his third strike as a law enforcement officer. After being called up on charges of excessive violence in two different departments in two different states, he had gotten this last-chance assignment through one of his former supervisors, a good friend of Chief Callahan.

For a long time, Lou had handled the investigations alone since he was the only officer on the force who had studied investigative techniques at the police academy, a prerequisite for the job.

Then Callahan, a graduate of the University of Georgia's criminal justice program, wrote a proposal and got a federal grant to fight the drug trade that had begun to spread its ugly tentacles out from Atlanta into the outlying rural areas. Under the grant, he was able to hire five additional patrol officers, one detective, and a crime-scene investigator, bringing the staff to its current level.

Lola Morgan relocated back home just in time to get the new detective job. At first, she and Lou were constantly at odds with each other, and it seemed that the noble experiment in crime fighting was *not* going to work, but that was a long time ago.

Mayor Joe Oliver thought that both detectives were a waste of taxpayers' money. After all, there hadn't been a murder in Madison County in thirty years, although there was a missing person a while back. Lou and Lola investigated burglaries, robberies, and other assorted misdemeanors, including marijuana use by teenagers.

The two of them spent most of their time rooting out the drug dealers that drifted in and out of the county, peddling everything from pot to the newest scourge, crack cocaine. The team's biggest bust, to date, had been two unemployed chemistry majors who made crystal methylene – a new designer drug made from cold medicine and farm fertilizer– in a farmhouse and sold it out of their apartment. Some called the deadly drug, crank, out of deference to its poisonous cousin, crack.

At the morning's roll call, Chief Callahan met with the day shift, assigning a list of specific duties for the two sergeants to split between their commands. Then he called Lou and Lola into his office.

"Alright, you two," he said, taking a seat behind his long oak-paneled desk, "have a seat."

Lola took the chair in front of the desk, and Lou pulled up another from the conference table on the other side of the room.

"Well, it looks like you two can finally start earning your keep," the chief said sadly. "We've got a missing person."

"No, kidding," Lou said, attempting to control the adrenalin rush, having noticed the chief's tone of voice.

The two detectives never really had a case they could sink their teeth into.

"Aw, how, horrible," Lola said. "Who is it, do I know them?"

"I don't know, maybe so," the chief said. "But I sure do. She's from my old neighborhood."

The chief picked up a copy of last year's Madison County High School yearbook from his desk and opened it to a pre-marked page, turning it so the two detectives could see the encircled picture of a girl.

"This is Beth Campbell. She went to the library two nights ago, but never made it back home."

"Is that right," Lou said, more than asked.

"Now, I know the usual forty-eight hours haven't passed, but I know her and her mother, and she's already having prissy fits about finding her daughter."

"Okay," Lola said. "We'll get right on it."

"Great," the chief said. "Her mama will appreciate that."

Then the chief handed Lou a card with Lizzy Campbell's name and address scribbled on it.

"We'll get cracking," Lou said as he and Lola rose from their seats.

"Oh, two things," the chief added.

"What?" Lola asked.

"The girl *has* done this before."

"Done, what?" Lou asked.

"Stayed out all night. She and her mother can sometimes be at odds with each other."

"I can understand that," Lola said, slowly nodding her head.

"So, if that turns out to be the case, kinda keep it quiet. Alright?"

"Sure," Lou assured him. "That's one. What's the other?"

The chief turned to another pre-marked page in the yearbook. "This was the last person to see her."

Lou and Lola said their goodbyes and started down the long hallway toward the cubicle that served as their office.

"Lou, we've got to stop this," Lola said without breaking stride. "I can't do it anymore."

"Do what?" Lou asked, grabbing Lola's arm and pulling her around to face him. "What's wrong?"

"What we're *doing* is wrong! It's your wife. It drives me crazy when I see her at aerobics," Lola said before turning and stalking off down the hall.

Catching up with her, Lou walked alongside Lola. "I've told you a million times, the woman is my wife in name *only*. Our marriage was over long before you came back to Wrightsburg."

Lola stopped short, detouring into the women's restroom. Inside, she took a moment in front of the mirror to calm herself. Things were definitely not going as she had planned. The new case, if it turned out to be one, was too important for the two of them to be at odds.

After the case, she told herself. *After this case, I am definitely going to make some changes in my life.* She sighed and blew off one last bit of steam before leaving the restroom. Lou was waiting patiently outside the door.

Lola and Myrtle Davis, a patrol officer and a good friend, were the only females on the force. A departmental policy did not allow intra-force relationships, although it was never enforced, at least not to his knowledge, Lou had said. Both she and Myrtle had broken the rule.

Myrtle had been dating Kyle Richardson, a sergeant, for over a year. They were even thinking about getting married. But Lola knew in advance that *their* relationship would probably be acceptable to both the members of the force as well as the Wrightsburg community. They were both white.

There had always been sexual tension between the interracial partners, but Lola and Lou finally crossed the line while on an all-night drug stakeout, three weeks earlier.

Later that day, Lou and Lola rolled onto the campus of Chandler High School. Lou pulled the unmarked sedan into the parking lot next to the football practice field.

"Do it?" Lou asked, smiling as he turned to Lola in the seat beside him.

"Do it," she said, grinning from ear to ear.

Lou's foot floored the accelerator, and the car hurdled the curb and climbed onto the field. The tires dug up divots of sod as he drove underneath the goal posts toward the sideline. Running toward the car, Coach Dixon furiously waved his clipboard in the air yelling, "Hey. You can't do that."

The car stopped, and as Coach Dixon approached him, Lou flipped out his badge and shoved it into his face. "Can't do what?" he said.

"Look, I don't care if you are the police," the coach said angrily. "You can't drive *that* car on *this* field."

Lola emerged from the other side of the car. "Cool your heels, Willie," she said with a note of familiarity. "You'll have a heart attack."

Coach Dixon acknowledged her comments with his own note of acquaintance. "Oh, it's you. What do you want?"

"Looking for Joe Meriwether," Lou said, now in a huff, not liking the familiarity between Lola and the coach. "Is he here?"

"Maybe, maybe not," he replied. "What do you want with him? You got a warrant?"

"Nah, this is just a friendly visit," Lou said. "It's about the Campbell girl's disappearance. Wasn't he her boyfriend?"

"I *am* her boyfriend," Joe said, suddenly appearing out of the pack of players that had now gathered around their coach. "You talk like she's dead."

"That's why we're here," Lola said. "Maybe you can tell us if she is or isn't."

"Be careful, Joe," the coach said. "You don't have to answer their questions if you don't want to."

"He's right," Lou said. "But we can do it now, or we can do it later. Here, or at the station, it doesn't matter to me."

The players now gathered around the car.

"No! I'll talk to 'em," Joe said. "I've got nothing to hide."

"Well … alright. The rest of you, back on the field," Coach Dixon said, turning to the players.

Lou came around the car, then the four of them just stood there, facing each other.

"That's a good boy, Joe," Lou said. "Now we have an eyewitness who says that you may have been the last person to see Beth Campbell."

"Not only that," Lola added, "but Faye Drummond says that the two of you had a violent argument."

"Naw, naw, it was nothing like that," Joe protested. "We quarreled, but it wasn't violent."

"What was it about?" Lola asked.

"Nothing, really. Just something somebody said."

"What did they say and who said it?" Lou asked.

Shyly, Joe turned away. "Nothing. It was really nothing."

Lou – sensing that the moment was right to move in for the kill – stood toe to toe with Joe, now looking him squarely in the eye. "Now look, boy!"

Coach Dixon could take no more of the harassment of his player, so he stepped between them. "Enough of this! I must ask you to leave, Detective. Come back when you have a warrant!"

"No, no," Joe protested. "I don't want anything like that."

Joe breathed deeply. "If there's anything I can do to help find her, I want to do it. She's *not* dead. Beth *is not* dead!"

"Why don't we all have a seat over there," Lola said, pointing toward the bleachers.

"I met her at Barney's after she came from the library," Joe began. "And...

That night at the Burger Barn, Joe, Faye Drummond, and another boy were sitting in a booth. Faye and the boy joked with each other as they ate burgers and fries. Joe nursed a soda, anxiously looking at his watch. "What time did she say she was coming?" he asked Faye.

"She didn't say, just whenever she finished at the library," Faye answered.

Much later, Beth Campbell, with books in hand, walked through the door and casually strolled over to the booth. Joe stared angrily, standing aside so she could slide into the booth beside him.

"Hey, everybody," Beth said cheerily.

Joe remained silent as the other two exchanged greetings with Beth. When Faye and the boy had gone back to their chatter, Joe finally spoke.

"What took you so long?"

"I told you I had a paper to finish," she said firmly.

Irately, Joe sprang from the booth, pulling Beth up by the arm. "Let's go! We've got to talk!"

Beth snatched her arm back. "Look, Joe, don't you start with me tonight! I'm just not up to it!"

Joe pulled at her again. "Let's go, I said!"

"Joe, you leave her alone," Faye screamed.

Then Beth composed herself and rose to her feet. "It's alright, Faye. I'll see you tomorrow."

After a hasty retreat from the Burger Barn, Beth angrily turned to Joe as he pulled his car into the street. "For the last time, Joe, I don't care what your friends say about me. It's not true!"

"They're not my friends! But why do they keep saying it, if it's not true?"

"I've had enough," she said sharply. "Stop, I'm getting out!"

"Well, get out! I don't care!"

Joe stopped the car, and Beth got out. Rubber burned and tires screeched as the Malibu pulled off, and Beth walked slowly down the street into the darkness.

Lola looked at Joe suspiciously and spoke more sharply than she had intended. "Wait a minute. You mean to tell me that you left your girlfriend *alone* on a dark street!"

"No, I didn't leave her," Joe said with a look of anguish on his face. "I just drove around the block, but when I came back, she still wouldn't get in the car. Beth was stubborn like that. And, anyway, it's not like we live in Atlanta or something."

"That'll do for now," Lou said, bringing the questioning to a close. As they turned to leave, Lou glowered over at Coach Dixon. "And I'll be seeing you later, cowboy."

On the way back to the station, Lou wanted desperately to confront Lola about her prior relationship with the football coach, but remembering her earlier tirade, thought better of it. They rode silently until Lola turned to him and spoke.

"Something just doesn't gel, Lou."

"Yeah, I know," he said. "The chief said the librarian told him that Beth was *not* there that night."

"Yes, I remember."

Chapter 6

The Campbell's doublewide trailer sat on a corner lot of the Orchard Park Trailer Camp, setting it apart as being among the best on the lot – the pick of the litter over the singlewide variety. Some units on the back lots were little more than campers, but all were old and weathered.

Lou and Lola climbed the cinderblock steps and knocked on the front door. Shortly, an eye appeared in the peephole, the bolt slid back, and Lizzy Campbell opened the door. "Oh, thank God you're here," she said. "Y'all come on in."

The Orchard Park community was named such because of its proximity to the Chandler fruit orchards. Over the years, there came to be an Orchard Park Dry Cleaners, an Orchard Park Package Store, and once there was even an Orchard Park Drive-in Theater, all of which were owned and operated by the Chandler family. And certainly not the least among the family's holdings was the Orchard Park General Store, which usually saw to it that the migrant workers left town just as dirt poor as when they had arrived.

The itinerant workers who came to pick fruit during the harvesting season didn't like to mix with the townspeople and kept to themselves down in Orchard Park, much to the delight of the citizens of Wrightsburg. Actually, they felt more at home with the blacks, with whom they worked alongside in the orchards.

The plot of ground where the trailer park sat was once a tent city. The itinerants would drive their jalopies and pickups to town and pitch a tent until the peach and pear seasons were over, and then they would pull up stakes and head on down to Florida in time for the orange, tangerine, and grapefruit picking.

But when old man Johnny Campbell, Ty Jr.'s granddaddy, built the first food processing plant, he needed workers year-round, so he bought ten house-trailers from the Bluebird Manufacturing Company down in Fort Valley, and had them mounted on concrete blocks in tent city.

On that very day, the community of Orchard Park was born, and to this very day, it still serves to separate the poor whites from the rest of Wrightsburg, Georgia.

As they entered the living room, Lou extended his hand, and Lizzy eagerly shook it.

"I'm Detective Brazell and this is Detective Morgan," Lou said, pointing toward Lola, who also extended her hand to the frazzled looking woman.

"I'm sorry it took us so long to come," Lola said apologetically. "We couldn't officially declare her missing for two days, but that didn't mean we weren't doing anything."

"That's right," Lou added. "We've already talked to her boyfriend and the girl across the street."

"You mean Faye?" Lizzy asked, ignoring the reference to Joe Meriwether.

"Yes, Faye Drummond," Lou replied, looking down at his tiny note pad for confirmation.

"Come on back to the kitchen," Lizzy said, ushering Lou and Lola in and guiding them through a small, but neat and tidy, living room into the kitchen area. "I've got a fresh pot of coffee, if you want some."

"That would be nice," Lola said.

"Y'all have a seat," Lizzy said, pointing to a bright red and chrome dinette set. "I'll get the coffee."

Lou and Lola pulled chairs from under the table and took seats as Lizzy took a small pot of coffee from the burner of the apartment-sized gas stove.

"Mm'm," Lola mused, taking in the pleasing aroma of the freshly brewed early morning drink, "real coffee."

"That's right," Lizzy said, "brewed the old-fashioned way."

"Yeah, that does smell good," Lou added. "What's the secret?"

"Heat," Lizzy said, placing three large white mugs down on the red plastic tabletop, a throwback from the '60s, and filling each one to the brim with the steaming dark brown liquid. "You have to start with cold water. Some of the big restaurants even use ice water. Just bring it to a slow boil, but you also have to keep it hot."

"I'll have to try that," Lola said, adding cream and sugar from the small containers on the table before taking a long sip.

"No percolator for me," Lizzy said, joining them at the table. "I boil mine … just like we do at the truck stop."

Lizzy Campbell waited tables on the late night shift at Pearle's Truck Stop out on the interstate. It was also rumored that she sometimes worked an even later shift in the cabins the truckers would sometimes rent, so they could get a full night's sleep. This usually left Beth to her own devices.

Lou fought back the urge to get down to business, and let the two women keep it light, sensing that Lizzy needed it that way.

Lola sensed this as well. "Come on, Mrs. Campbell, there's got to be more to it than that," she said, smiling at the woman until the smallest hint of a smile appeared on Lizzy's deeply disturbed face.

"Well, actually, there is something else," Lizzy said. "Salt."

"Salt, in coffee?" Lou said, sounding somewhat skeptical.

"That's right, you sprinkle a few grains of salt over the coffee grinds before you boil 'em," she said, now beaming. "It helps bring out the flavor."

"Now I will definitely try that," Lola said and meant it.

"Mrs. Campbell," Lou said in a tone that signaled a change of subject, "do you have any relatives that Beth might have visited?"

"Yes," she said, and then the furrow that had been in her brow since their arrival, except for the talk of coffee, magically reappeared, "but I called all of 'em. They haven't seen her."

"Mrs. Campbell, has Beth ever done anything like this before?" Lola asked.

"Like what?" Lizzy responded warily.

Lola hesitated, searching for a diplomatic way of putting it. Thinking of none, she pressed on. "Like, not coming home at night or staying away for any length of time."

"Nooo," Lizzy crooned. "My Beth is a good girl. She would never do anything like that," she lied.

"Mrs. Campbell, would you mind if we took a look at Beth's room?" Lou asked. "You know, to see if there's anything that would give us a lead."

Lizzy Campbell was up from the table like a shot and leading the two detectives down the hallway before she had finished saying "yes."

If the rest of the trailer home was well kept, Beth's bedroom was immaculate. The wall between two small bedrooms had been knocked out to make one large room. Like the rest of the living quarters, the room was cheaply, but tastefully, furnished and decorated. The furniture was white Provincial and the color scheme blue and white.

At the center of the room stood a double bed with matching nightstands, which in addition to two small lamps, held family pictures, a white slim-line telephone, and a bouquet of artificial flowers, blue dahlias. Shear white curtains hung at the small window directly over the headboard.

The blue down comforter on the bed, with white sunray patterns and matching pillows, was turned back in wait of a mistress who had not come. In the left corner of the room, stood a matching chest of drawers and a vanity table with a gold-tone stool and large mirror. At the foot of the bed there was also a metal stand holding a small TV and VCR.

Since the original clothes closet had long since been filled, the entire right side of the room was now used for storage. The closet doors had been removed and racks and tables were added to either side to accommodate the overflow.

Beth Campbell's clothes were arranged better than most department stores. One rack held blouses and skirts, another jeans and slacks, and still another long dresses and coats. The variety of clothes ranged from the simple to the designer, mostly the latter.

Two large racks, which were secured to the wall, held row after row of shoes all kinds – from tennis shoes to glittering rhinestone pumps. In the corner a long table held Beth's bags and purses, many with designer names but all neatly displayed according to color.

Lola slowly shook her head as she looked at a large blue Coach bag, one she had coveted for months, but couldn't afford.

"What is it" Lizzy asked upon seeing Lola's reaction.

"It's nothing," she said.

This is bad, Lola thought. *No girl in her right mind is going to run off and leave a wardrobe like this.*

Lizzy's face turned bright crimson as Lola thumbed through the rack holding lingerie items, all of which put her Victoria's Secrets collection to shame.

"Must you do that?" Lizzy asked sharply. Then she went off like a rocket on the Fourth of July. "Exactly, what are you people looking for?"

"Just for something that might give us a lead," Lou said.

"Look, there's nothing missing. All she had with her was the clothes on her back and her handbag," Lizzy said angrily. "You're looking in the wrong place. Beth is not in this room or I would've found her. You need to be out there on the streets. Somebody's done something horrible to my baby, I just know it." Tears ran down her face as she hurried from the room.

Lou threw up both hands in entreaty. Lola shrugged and kept looking.

"Lou," Lola said, shaking her head. "This is not the room of an ordinary teenage girl."

"I know," he said. "You keep looking. I'll go try to calm her down."

Lou found Lizzy Campbell in her own bedroom. She was crying, now in huge choking sobs.

"Mrs. Campbell," Lou said softly upon entering, "the last thing in the world we want to do is add to your misery, but this is just how we have to do things."

Lizzy slowly regained her composure. She sat up and looked at Lou. "Oh, I know, I'm sorry."

"No," Lou said, "we're sorry. And you're right. We do have to hit the streets to find her, but we need to know where to start looking."

"I know, I know," Lizzy said, wiping her eyes with a tissue from a box on the nightstand. She patted a spot on the bed beside her. "Come, sit."

"Oh, I'm alright here," Lou said. "There are just a few more questions and we'll be through."

"Okay, shoot," Lizzy said. She was beginning to feel a stirring within, staring up at the tall man with the Nordic good looks, tousled sandy-blonde hair, piercing blue eyes, and ruggedly handsome face.

"Did Beth keep a diary?"

"No, she had a small phone book, though. But she kept it with her all the time. She guarded that book with her life. We used to tease her about it," Lizzy said, managing a smile. "You know, the little black book?"

"Yeah, I know," Lou said. "What about a beeper?"

"She had one, but she always kept it with her."

"What about the telephone by her bed? Was it a private line?"

"Yes, and it's unlisted."

"May I have the number?"

"Sure," Lizzy said, and then gave him Beth's private number.

Lola had finished her search, which turned up no smoking gun, only the reality that Beth Campbell, or someone, had spent a lot of money on her clothes. As she walked toward the door, Lola was struck by a familiar sight. Hanging on the back of the door was a large color poster.

A headshot of Beth Campbell smiled down at her. By Lola's professional standard, the photography was not great. But *with a subject as beautiful as Beth, how could he fail?* she thought.

Lola tore off the strip of tape that held the lower right hand side of the poster to the wall, peeling it back in search of what she knew all photographers would leave – especially on a picture this lovely – a name and address. She hastily scribbled the information on her note pad, smiling now as she left the room.

As Lou and Lola walked down the pathway to their car, Lizzy, standing in the doorway of the trailer, called out to them.

"Detectives."

"Yes," Lou said as both of them turned toward Lizzy.

"That girl, Faye, I wouldn't take much stock in what she says. She's such a liar."

Chapter 7

For the rest of the week, during the day, Ginny walked around in a daze since she was getting very little sleep at night. She was trying to avoid the horrible dreams, but with little success. Some nights, however, she managed to awaken in the middle of the dream. But once she reluctantly drifted back to sleep, the nightmare would resume exactly where it had left off. Inevitably, the dream always ended at the hole in Witches' Hollow.

Most of the times, *the girl* would lead her there, but sometimes she would go to the woods on her own. But regardless how they began, the dreams always ended the same. Something horrible would grab her, pull her down into the hole, and then the suffocation would begin.

Then over the weekend, as suddenly as the dreams had started, they stopped. So, for the past few nights, Ginny slept peacefully, although as usual, awakening several times before morning. But was it in anticipation of the dreams that no longer came? Ginny wasn't sure whether she felt a sense of relief or disappointment that *the girl* and her dreams seemed to have abandoned her.

Ginny was sure that getting her own car, however, would solve most of her problems. The morning bus ride had become more palatable since Cha-Cha came to town. Her former tormentors had switched to Cha-Cha on her first day riding the bus, but they soon proved to be no match for her. She could curse like a sailor and play "The Dozen," talking about your mama, with the best of them.

By the time the bus reached Ginny's stop, Cha-Cha would have them so far in the dozen that they had little time to bother with her. One of the boys would later become so intimidated by the hefty girl with the fowl tongue that he would stop riding the bus altogether.

Ginny still skipped the bus ride home after school and usually took the shortcut through Simpson's Woods so she could start dinner as she had promised her father. After checking up on his finances, Charlie said they would be able to get the other car in about a month, and Ginny surely wanted to keep him happy until then.

Cha-Cha must've also been too much for *the girl*. She had stopped riding the bus, too. Ginny convinced herself that *the girl* had just been a figment of her imagination. Maybe her mind had played tricks on her due to the stress of the breakup with Sonny James. But it didn't matter now, they were having fun and things were back to normal.

Ginny began to take pleasure in her classes, including the most boring one, American History. Even she was shocked that she enjoyed one of Mr. Chester's lectures. It was about Crispus Attucks, one of the patriot mob that was fired upon by the British troops in the Boston Massacre of 1770. Attucks, the first to die in the American Revolution, was a free black man. The very thought of a black man giving his life for truth and justice made her so proud.

And most importantly, during the entire week, Ginny had been able to steer clear of Sonny James. *Thank God, it was finally over between the two of them*, she thought. Evading Sonny during football season was not a Herculean task since he devoted his heart, body, and soul to the sport. In part, this was what made him so good at it.

In its first game, the Big Blue Wave had easily rolled over Wildwood Academy, a tiny school from the next county, 45 to 0. Sonny had led the way, throwing three touchdown passes and running for two additional scores before sitting out the second half. Joe Meriwether came in and showed that he had not lost his form, passing for two more touchdowns.

Then Coach Dixon called off the dogs and put in the third and fourth string.

"This was just a warm-up," the coach had said. "We're definitely looking toward the State Championship."

As they sat around the conference table, Mr. Robinson called the newspaper staff meeting to order. "Well, gang, how're we coming with the assignments?"

"We have three new teachers," Sarah said, and then coyly added, "one of which, I think you know *very well*."

Jerry Robinson was a bachelor by choice, not by chance. Since his wife left Madison County for greener pastures, taking their two children with her, he had just decided to give up on the fairer sex, that is, until Ellie Benson arrived.

Mr. Robinson grinned shyly and his face reddened. "Ah, hem, I see you're doing okay, Sarah. Anybody else?"

"I'm doing great," Dewey said excitedly. "I'm doing, like, a top fifty players of all time."

"Great," Mr. Robinson said. "That really sounds good."

Dewey pulled out an old yearbook and opened it to the sports section. "And we've had some great ones. "Look, Ginny. This is your uncle."

Ginny slowly looked at the picture of a black boy, holding the football high as he crossed the goal line. The caption read, "Billy Westbrook Scores Again!" She looked at the picture again, and then lowered her head.

"What's wrong, Ginny?" Mr. Robinson asked.

"It's nothing," she said. "I never really knew him. He was killed in Vietnam."

"Oh, Ginny," Sarah said, "I'm so sorry."

"Yeah, me, too," Dewey added.

"We all are, Ginny," Mr. Robinson said compassionately. "That was a terrible war, with no winner."

"And," Ginny said, then paused, "my assignment isn't going well at all."

"Why?" Mr. Robinson asked. "What's wrong?"

"It's Mr. Chandler. He keeps putting me off. I've called his office twice, but it's as if he doesn't want to talk to me."

"Well, you keep after it," Mr. Robinson said.

Suddenly Ginny smiled. "Hey, everybody, I know where we can find some real news."

"Where?" Dewey asked.

"*Let's find Beth Campbell*," she said deliberately, and in a tone of voice that might have been similar to Wilbur Wright's when he told his brother, Orville, "Let's build an airplane."

They all looked at Ginny with mouths agape.

"What?" Dewey said.

"I said, let's find Beth! She's been gone for over a week."

"I really don't see anything newsworthy about a little trollop who stayed out so late with one of her boyfriends that she's afraid to come home," Sarah said flightily. "From what I've heard, she might be living with one of 'em."

"Sarah, don't say that," Mr. Robinson said.

Sarah angrily shot up from the table. "What! Are you people blind? Didn't you see how that little trailer trash threw herself at every man on this campus, including the teachers?"

Sarah Steele knew Beth Campbell's reputation all too well. Last year, she had fallen victim to the beautiful girl from the wrong side of town, whom Sarah now hated with a passion. She not only took Sarah's spot as cheerleader captain, a position that was voted on among the squad, but also for good measure, Beth Campbell stole her boyfriend, Joe Meriwether. That was when Sarah quit the cheerleaders and turned to more serious pursuits, citing that she was joining the newspaper staff to enhance her college portfolio.

Relationships between the upper class and those of lower status were supposed to take place at night, under the cover of darkness. It didn't seem to matter to Joe that he was a Meriwether and had certain standards to uphold. He rubbed Beth Campbell into the faces of the Madison

County aristocracy. And, judging by the "puppy dog" look on his face as he followed her around, Joe enjoyed every single minute of it.

"I don't know about that, Sarah," Mr. Robinson said, and then turned to Ginny. "But, Ginny, if something has happened to Beth, it is strictly a police matter."

"But they're not doing anything," Ginny fired back.

"She's right," Dewey said, coming to Ginny's defense. "The Atlanta newspapers ran the story for a few days, but now, nothing."

"That's right," Ginny said. "We ought to at least be searching or something, like they did up in Atlanta when those little boys were missing."

"The police searched Simpson's Woods all day, Saturday," Mr. Robinson said.

"So," Ginny said questioningly.

"So, maybe Sarah's right," Mr. Robinson said, now in a voice intimating that it was time for a subject change. "Maybe she doesn't want to be found."

"Oh, alright," Ginny conceded.

Dewey raised his hand. "Mr. Robinson, if you give me a note to leave school during study-hall, Mr. Bradley said he would let me go through old newspapers for my sports story."

"Sure, Dewey, that's a good idea," Mr. Robinson said.

"Me, too, Mr. Robinson," Ginny said. "Maybe I can find something on the Chandlers."

The yellow pages of the Atlanta telephone directory declared the Dabolaini Modeling Agency to be "Your Stairway to the Stars." The ad went on to say, "We provide professional consultants to begin your career in photographic and runway modeling, television commercials, pageants and more."

As they pulled into the parking lot of the strip mall – located in one of the seediest parts of Atlanta – Lou and Lola took one look at the dilapidated storefront office and knew right away that the real professional was the person who wrote the copy for the advertisement. No one could accuse whoever did it of not having an active imagination.

Lola readily identified Dabolaini's as being one of those mine-the-miner agencies, which are widespread across the country. Outfits such as these, lure the parents of hopeful young girls and boys – sometimes from the age of three or four years old – into paying huge sums of money for portfolios and modeling courses, which served as little more than decoration for a bedroom wall and a way to spend a Saturday morning. Although she had to admit that the modeling and makeup courses could raise the self-esteem of a young girl, that is, if taught by a capable instructor.

Unlike Ford, Casablanca, and other model agencies of their ilk, these low-lifes made their money from the hopes and dreams of children and their parents, not from the ad industry, where they had few if any contacts.

There were two rules of the game that Lola shared with more than one aspiring model. Rule number one: do not pay them; make them pay you. Rule number two: always follow rule number one.

It was not uncommon, in Lola's experience, to hear of photographers who talked teenage girls into stripping for the camera, whereupon the pictures were either sold to a smut magazine or posted on a web site on the Internet.

The receptionist was a brunette, in her early twenties, with makeup too perfectly applied to a pretty face and a too-cute-to-be-real nose.

"Can I help y'all?" she asked in a deep southern drawl.

After a formal introduction, with the necessary badge flipping by Lou and Lola, Lou took the seat that was offered, and the girl disappeared down the hallway. Lola walked around the office, inspecting the pictures that were prominently displayed on the walls. There was a variety of types and sizes, from black and white 8x10s to large color posters, like the one on Beth Campbell's wall.

As she perused the collection of headshots and full-length poses, Lola raised the mental grade she had previously assigned to Dabolaini's work from D to C+. Although the faces of the subjects were young and amateurish, she could discern a pattern of competency in the photographer.

With a larger sampling of his work available, she could now discern that he had once been a pro – like those she had worked with at the Ford

Agency. But it was obvious from his low rent accommodations that it must have been a long time ago.

Appearing out of nowhere, the receptionist said, "Mr. Dabolaini will see y'all now."

Lou led Lola down the narrow hallway toward the man standing near the door at the end. Ray Dabolaini was a small man who might have been considered handsome thirty years ago, but now his jaws were sagging and his hair graying and thinning. "Come on back," he said, smiling. "I've been expectin' you."

"Is that right?" Lou said rhetorically, walking past the man into the office with Lola close behind. That day, she had forgone her usual pantsuit in favor of a tailored blue-serge skirt-suit, giving the aging photographer full view of her curvaceous figure. Through the sheer fabric of her blouse, he could see the outline of her bra and the roundness of her breasts.

"Mumh, mumh, mumh," Dabolaini grunted as Lola passed. "If I didn't know you were here about the missing girl, I'd swear you were here on business. Y'all have a seat."

Dabolaini took a seat behind his desk and Lou and Lola sat in the two chairs provided for them.

"I could fix you up with a real nice portfolio, young lady," Dabolaini said, looking Lola in the eye. "And with *your* body and *my* connections, we could work wonders."

"Thanks, but no thanks," Lola said. "Been there, done that."

"No kidding," he said. "Where ... when?"

"The Ford Agency," she stated somewhat proudly, "a long time ago."

Dabolaini whistled. "High cotton. I should've known. Maybe you could come up some Saturday mornings, you know, give my girls some pointers."

"Maybe," Lola said, actually considering the informal offer, sensing that the man was no real crook, but just down on his luck. The modeling business could do that to you. You could be at the prime of your career, and then one blink and it would all be over.

Lou interrupted the conversation, placing a picture of Beth on the desk and turning it toward Dabolaini.

"We know you've photographed her. When was the last time you saw her?"

"Aw, man, that's a tough one. It's been awhile," he replied, scratching his balding pate. Dabolaini leaned back in his chair, steepling his fingers together as if in deep thought. "It's been over a year."

"Over a year!" Lou said, then cursed silently, sensing that his most promising lead was quickly headed down the drain.

"Yeah, it must've been summer before last. She came to town full of high hopes, just like so many others. She was waiting tables out at the Colonial Restaurant. It's right down the street from here ... over on Piedmont. And she was living in a boarding house not far from there.

Beth saved her pennies, and I put together a portfolio for her and made a few calls. We got her a few jobs, but she was too impatient. You know how hard it is to make it in this business with no formal training," he said, looking toward Lola. "She lacked poise and confidence."

"Yeah, I know what you mean," Lola said, reflecting back to her early days in New York.

"I tried to get her to take one of the modeling classes, but she wanted everything, bam," he said, slamming his hand to the desk, "right now. I'd never seen a girl with such big dreams, but so little patience. The money was just coming too slow for her."

"Can you remember exactly when you saw her last?" Lou asked impatiently.

"No, not exactly," he said, shaking his head. "I don't remember when, but I *sure* remember where. The last time I saw Beth ... she was at the Moulin Rouge."

The Moulin Rouge was one of Atlanta's premier nightclubs that catered to the refined gentleman, offering illegal Havana cigars under the table, and champagne and nude dancing on top of it. The shift was just changing as Lou and Lola sidled up to the bar. The Italian-looking man behind it shoved a bowl of mixed nuts in front of them as he continued to count the money from his cash register.

"Help yourself," he said over the sound of loud disco music, "shift change ... it'll be a minute."

Lou took him up on his offer. He scooped up a handful of nuts and took in the lay of the land. "Wow, is this heaven, or what," he said gleefully before remembering the gender of his partner, who by now was doing some looking of her own.

Darn! Lola thought, stealing glances around the room. *Is this what we have to compete with? If it is, I surrender.*

There were two large stages, one at the front and another in the back, and four smaller ones, two on either side of the cavernous room. There were three dancers each on the front and back stages, and two each on the smaller ones.

This didn't count those who pranced – in their birthday suits – in front of, or on top of tables. Lou mentally counted at least ten.

"This your first time in a nude club?" he asked Lola.

"No," she lied. "Is it yours?"

Lou took a long sigh. "First time I've been in one like this."

There were girls of all kind, white, black, Asian, blondes, brunettes, redheads, Afros, and anything that might fall in between. No matter the race, creed, or hair color, these girls had one thing in common – they were all drop-dead gorgeous. Lola had not remembered seeing so many beautiful women in one place since the cattle-calls for models, back in the old days.

When Lola turned back to the bar – deciding that if she stared too long at the beautiful girls, someone might get the wrong idea – a new bartender had taken the place of the Italian-looking guy. The tall, dark-skinned, black man, with a handsome face and a weightlifter's build, smiled when he saw the pretty black woman.

"What can I get for you, my sister?" he said with a toothy grin.

"Ginger Ale" she said.

"I'll have scotch and water," Lou said when he turned to join them.

"Sure thing," the bartender said, and then he was off.

"You can't take a drink, Lou, we're on duty."

"Not by my watch," he said looking down at the Timex on his wrist. "It says five-thirty, which makes us thirty minutes overtime."

"In that case, I'll have one, too," she said, pointing to Lou's shot glass when the bartender placed the drinks in front of them.

"Sure, no problem," the bartender said, and was off again to the center of the bar where the liquor was stashed. When he returned, Lola exchanged Beth's picture for her scotch and water. "Do you know this girl?"

"Let me see," he said, taking a closer look at the picture he'd just picked up from the bar.

"Yeah, sure, everybody knows her. She's on TV every night."

"I know that," Lou said. "But do you know her from here … in the club? She used to work here."

"Nah, I don't think so," he said with a shrug. "But you know, they come and go."

"What do you mean, come and go?" Lola asked.

"Marty, the boss, he's got three more of these clubs – in Dallas, Miami, and Boca Raton. The girls make the circuit, you know, a change of scenery for the gents," he said, chuckling.

"So your boss would know her," Lola said. "Is he around?"

"Yes and no," he said. "Yes he would know her, but no he ain't here. He's gone South for the winter. You know how old folks are."

"No, I don't," Lou said, growing impatient. "What about the girls?"

"Yeah, maybe, but before you talk to them, you'd have to clear it with the assistant manager," he said.

The bartender introduced Lou and Lola to the assistant manager, another muscleman with a husky well-tanned body and a shaved head. *They all must double as bouncers,* Lou deduced silently.

After proper identification was shown, the manager – albeit reluctantly – led Lou and Lola back to the dressing room. "Heads up, girls we've got company," he said as they entered. "See if you can help these people out. It's about the missing girl."

The stunningly beautiful girls were in varying stages of undress, causing Lou to blush.

"What's wrong, honey?" a leggy blonde asked laughingly, in a deep southern accent, while casually stepping out of her panties and into her costume bottom. "It's alright to look. You're gonna see it all anyway when I get out there."

"No, no, I'm okay," Lou said, his face now beet red.

"Well, y'all hurry up with this po-lice business and you come watch me," the blonde said, moving toward the door. Suddenly she stopped and turned to Lou. "Oh, and make sure you bring lots of cash."

The blonde winked her eye at Lou, lowering her top just enough to give him a glimpse before she turned and laughed her way out of the room.

Like the blonde, who had just scampered out the door for a waiting table dance, none of the girls in the dressing room had known Beth, but they all hoped she was still alive and wished Lou and Lola good luck in finding her.

Suddenly the music stopped and the dancers who were onstage piled into the dressing room, while others scampered out to take their places to perform in this den of dancing for dollars. There were doors at either end of the dressing room. Lou was stationed at one and Lola the other.

The answers these girls gave, when accosted by the two detectives, were more of the same. No one knew Beth Campbell, but like their counterparts who had just taken the stage, they, too, had seen the news, hoped she was alive, and wished good luck in finding her.

Three hours and many more scotch and waters later for Lou and Lola, the daygirls began to leave and the night shift began to drift into the dressing room. Again, Lola worked one entrance and Lou the other. Around eight o'clock, when the last of the night shift dancers had arrived, they struck gold.

Sitting among the throng of girls, chattering as they came and went, all at once Lou was captivated by the most intoxicating scent he had ever smelled before, Lola's Faberge notwithstanding. A petite exotic beauty, with sparkling dark eyes and waist length black hair, walked up to him.

"I've seen you on TV," she said, smiling, and then turned deathly serious. "It's about Beth, isn't it?"

Her name was Elba, and she was carrying a large tote bag that was about as long as she was tall.

"Yes," he said, almost jumping out of his socks. "Do you know her?"

"Yep. She was my roommate."

Pulling up a stool and lighting up a long gold-tipped cigarette, Elba revealed that she was born in Puerto Rico but was raised in the streets of Brooklyn. She was a vivacious woman, with a bubbly personality, who chattered on-and-on about any-and-everything. Lou thought that Elba resembled a little doll – a pretty little doll. He was intrigued by the woman, but needed to get down to business, badly.

With Lou's prodding, Elba finally got around to saying that the two of them had met on Beth's first night of work. Marty, the owner, had assigned her to teach the newcomer the rules of the game and the method of the con: how to maintain a modicum of modesty onstage while baring your butt; how to entice men to watch, but never allow them to touch; and most importantly, how to make sure that the house got its cut, $100 a night for the privilege of dancing and $20 for the deejay.

What a way to run a business, Lou thought. *You actually make the workers pay you.*

She went on to say that after a week or two, Beth moved out of the boarding house and in with her, although she always told her mother that she was living at the YWCA.

"Did she have any boyfriends?" Lola asked when she was finally able to get a word in edgewise on the talkative little imp, whose impression upon Lou she definitely did *not* like.

"Nah, nobody special. She went to parties and stuff. We all did. But when you're one of Marty's top girls, you work the night shift, you know, when the big tippers come in. Eight hours on your feet and you're not really good company."

I can imagine, Lola thought, but didn't say.

"Beth didn't play around. She had her head on straight. She was saving her money to pay cash for a car, and then she was going to drive to California and get into the movie business. She used to have a saying, 'If it ain't about money, it ain't about nothin','" Elba said with a chuckle. "And I believe she can make it. She's pretty enough. Marty put her on the night shift when she first came. That never happened before. You have to work your way up."

"Do you think there was something going on between her and Marty?" Lola asked.

81

"Yep, the same thing that me and the rest have going on with Marty, money. He leads 'em to the water and we make 'em drink."

They watched as Elba bowled over in laughter, though neither Lou nor Lola saw the humor.

"How is it that the other girls rotate, but you stay here?" Lola asked, now with an edge to her voice.

"My regulars, honey," Elba replied firmly, finally getting the message that the tall handsome Nordic king she was flirting with was more than just a work partner to the Nubian queen who glared at her from time to time. "One year, Marty sent me to Dallas for six months, and they screamed bloody murder."

"Oh, I see," Lola said.

"Well, when was the last time you saw her," Lou asked, sensing that another lead was headed toward drain-city.

"The night the crap hit the fan."

"What crap?" Lou asked.

"The night her mother came and dragged her out of here."

"What happened?" Lola asked. Her annoyance had subsided now that she was sensing a break.

"Well, it all started one Saturday night. Beth came running back into the dressing room and refused to go back on stage. She thought some guy from her home town had seen her, but couldn't be sure."

"And?" Lola urged her on.

"That Monday night, her mother barged into the club and demanded that she leave. Marty tried to stop her, you know, all he could see was dollar bills flying out the door. The guys loved Beth."

"Go on," Lou pleaded.

"Her mother said Beth was underage and that she would be back the next day with the police. That was it. One word about the cops, and Marty kicked her out. When I got home, all of her things were gone. But I hope you find her, that is, if she wants to be found."

"What do you mean?" Lou asked.

"Beth might be in one of Marty's other clubs. She's eighteen, now, you know. I could see her high-tailing it away from home. She hated her mother, and I think the feeling was mutual. Something about who caused the daddy to leave home."

"Yes, we've heard there was some hostility," Lola said.

"And," Elba said, smiling coyly, "there's been more than a time or two when a sugar daddy has asked me to drop everything and fly away. I did it once. That old man took me around the world and back."

The two beautiful women, Elba and Lola, finally smiled at each other. They had made a connection. In this department, the two women had striking similarities. Seeing her reluctant smile, every one of her five senses told Elba that Lola had heard an offer-or-two of her own. She wondered if the shapely detective had taken any. *Probably so*, Elba thought.

"Okay, let's wrap it up," Lou said.

Lou's life had not gone untouched by this spur-of-the-moment phenomenon, he had made such an offer himself, and the pretty girl had taken him up on it. She was now his wife.

"If you think of anything else, give us a call," Lou said, handing Elba a business card.

"Yeah, sure," she said, taking the card and sticking it into her bra. "Wait, there is one more thing."

"What?" Lou asked, his heart racing.

"I was kind of glad that Beth's mother took her away." Elba said with a look of concern she had not shown before. "There was this guy, he just wouldn't leave her alone."

Before leaving, Lou and Lola heard a spine-chilling account of a middle-age man who had fallen hopelessly in love with Beth Campbell. He showered her with gifts and money. Beth returned the gifts, but kept the money. Lola wrote down the description that Elba gave.

"He was tall, pale, and always immaculately dressed, like a banker or something."

Too hard of a day's work and too many scotch and waters sent Lou and Lola in search of the nearest Holiday Inn.

Chapter 8

Ginny's reflection stared back at her from the mirror on the dressing table as she sat and tirelessly brushed her sandy brown curly hair. Her hair straightened with each brush stroke, but then recoiled to its original curliness. She was performing part of the nightly ritual her mother had taught her as a child. Brush your teeth, up and down, floss gently, and then one hundred strokes with a stiff hairbrush before going to bed. The face in the mirror scowled back in frustration.

"Aw, shucks! I can't do anything with this mess."

All at once, a transformation began. With the next stroke of the brush, her hair straightened, but did not shrink back this time. Surprised, but not troubled, Ginny pulled the brush through the hair on the other side of her head. The result was the same. Now, not only did her hair fall straight, it was also growing longer and lighter.

At first, Ginny became frightened, but the sensation passed. She slowly placed the brush down on the table and sat transfixed. Her gray-green eyes had changed to a vivid green and her facial features were transforming, ever so slightly. Though the bone structure remained the same, the face was smaller now and Ginny's once golden-alabaster skin was becoming a ghostly pale white.

Then Ginny was gone altogether, and the face now staring back from the mirror belonged to *the girl* with the long blonde hair and fringed leather jacket. Again, *the girl* was surrounded by that eerie luminous glow as she methodically and purposely walked down the stairs.

Although it was the pale figure of *the girl* that walked to the front door, when it opened, and then closed, Ginny Westbrook stepped out into the darkness. The chill of the night air was unlike that of any in early September, more akin to the colder nights of late October. Although wearing only a thin nightgown, she did not shiver.

As if she were wearing blinders, Ginny stared straight ahead and walked serenely down Cherry Lane. At the house across the street, the big Rottwieler growled and barked loudly, jumping up and down at the front door.

"Duke, oh, no, not tonight," a voice boomed from the living room.

With eyes fixed straight ahead, Ginny continued down the street. When she passed the house on the corner, the tiny Chihuahua howled mournfully, scratching at the front door and barking noisily. A squeaky voice called out from the other room. "Well, *go,* already! I'm not up to it, tonight."

The Chihuahua sprang through the trap door and loped down the street behind Ginny. Silently now, there was no barking. With the little Chihuahua in tow, Ginny walked through the rear entrance to Simpson's Woods. Within minutes, she had disappeared into Witches' Hollow.

Unable to sleep, Miriam tossed and turned restlessly. On a premonition, she shot straight up in bed. Without a sound, she got up, put on her robe and slippers, and then hurried down the hall to Ginny's room. When she peered inside, a wave of fear washed over her.

"Charlie, Charlie, wake up," Miriam screamed, running back into the bedroom. Charlie rolled over to see what was causing such a commotion.

"What? What is it?" he asked.

"It's Ginny. She's not in her room!"

"Oh, she's probably just getting a midnight snack," Charlie said, rising up from the bed. "Fact is, I think I'll join her."

"No, I've already checked." Miriam screamed, now at the top of her voice. "She is *not* in this house."

Charlie drove slowly through the neighborhood, both his and Miriam's eyes strained to scan the darkness.

"Oh, Charlie, do you think it has anything to do with the other girl that's missing?"

"No, don't even think that," Charlie said with tears in his eyes and fear in his heart. He could think of no plausible scenario for his daughter's disappearance. *Maybe I'm dreaming,* he thought.

"I don't know, Charlie, maybe we ought to call the police."

"No! My little girl is not missing. When we find her she'll have a perfectly good explanation for--"

"Charlie, over there," Miriam shrieked, pointing toward Simpson's Woods.

Before Charlie could stop, Miriam had bounded from the car and was running toward Ginny, who was nearing the front gate. Her white nightgown glistened in the moonlight as she walked toward them, the tiny Chihuahua still at her feet.

"Ginny, Ginny," Miriam cried. Tears of joy were rolling down her cheeks when she reached her daughter.

Ginny stopped in her tracks and stared straight ahead, but did not speak. Miriam shook her by the shoulders.

"Wake up, Ginny! You're walking in your sleep!"

Ginny's heart was pounding and her breathing shallow. "What? Oh, ah, where am I?" she asked.

"Oh, Baby," Charlie said, hugging his daughter as if there were no tomorrow.

When Charlie pulled the Taurus onto Cherry Lane, he stopped in front of the house on the corner. Ginny opened the car door and placed the Chihuahua on the ground, and the little pup skittered toward the trap door in the center of the front door of the house, yipping happily as it went.

Dr. Jessie Turner had been practicing medicine in Madison County since the early '60s, back in the days when doctors made house calls at ten dollars a visit. Since opening his practice, the entire Westbrook family had known no other medical man.

Once, when Charlie's mother took sick at a family reunion up in South Carolina, she wouldn't allow another doctor to touch her and insisted that the family cancel the affair, so that Charlie could drive her back to Wrightsburg to be treated by Dr. Turner.

The certificates on the wall, behind the desk in his cramped office, gave testament to study at Tennessee State College, then Maharry School of Medicine. There were several citations, including one for Rotarian Man of the Year in 1980.

Charlie, Miriam, and Ginny were seated facing the desk where the thin mahogany man sat placidly. He had a mane of stark white hair, and was closer to eighty than any other multiple of ten. After examining Ginny and drawing blood for further tests. Dr. Turner was ready to announce his diagnosis and lay out his plan for solving the problem.

He clasped his hands together, drawing them close to his chest, and speaking in a resonant voice, said, "Folks, from all indications, Ginny is suffering from Somnambulism."

Miriam gasped, placing a hand to her mouth. Then she said, "What in the world is that?"

Dr. Turner went on. "Somnambulism is sleep walking or performing other motor activities that are not recalled while awake."

"We know that, already," Charlie said, "but what can you do to make it go away?"

"Well, we need to get at the root cause," the kindly old doctor replied, now sounding more assured in his ability to get the job done.

This made Miriam feel better. She moved to the edge of her seat. "What do you think caused it?"

Dr. Turner leaned back in his seat. "That's hard to say, right off. Sleepwalking is a rapid-eye movement, behavior disorder occurring in the dream stage of sleep. During this phase, a chemical is released that paralyzes the body so that it can rest. Sleepwalkers don't have this chemical, or there's a shortage of it."

"But, Doctor, I was *not* sleeping," Ginny said sharply. "The last thing I remember was sitting at my dressing table, brushing my hair."

"Ginny, the last thing you remember was *dreaming* that you were brushing your hair." Dr. Turner said resolutely.

Ginny shot up from her seat. "No, I tell you, I was not sleep!"

Miriam rose to comfort Ginny. "Now, now, Baby, you remember those bad dreams you've been having. Do you remember how real they seemed?"

"Yes, I remember."

"Now sit down and listen to the Doctor," she said to Ginny, and then turned to the doctor. "She's been under a lot of pressure, lately, and this missing girl thing has got us all upset."

"Well, there you go," Dr. Turner said, seizing the moment. "Stress could definitely account for it."

They sat quietly while he wrote a prescription, tore it from the pad, and handed it to Ginny. "Take two of these before bedtime, and I *guarantee* you won't be going anywhere. You won't even dream."

"Oh, thank God," Ginny said. "That'll be wonderful. My dreams have been so crazy lately."

"Don't worry, folks, we'll get to the bottom of this," the doctor said.

They all rose to leave, but Dr. Turner pulled Charlie aside as Miriam and Ginny walked toward the door.

"Charlie, there *is* something you can do," he whispered.

"What, Doc?" Charlie whispered back. "Anything."

"Until I can get these tests back from the lab, I've just given her something to knock her out. But this is dangerous stuff. You're going to have to lock the windows."

Charlie's eyes widened and his body stiffened. "What, lock her in?"

"That's a crude way of putting it, but, yes. Oh, and put locks on the doors that can only be opened with a key."

Later that night after she had seen to it that Ginny was sleeping soundly, Miriam sat up in bed watching the *Late Show* while Charlie attended to his unenviable duties. She looked up when he came into the room, flipped a switch on the remote control, and then the TV screen clicked off.

"Did you do it?"

"Yes," Charlie said, handing her a key. "Don't lose it."

Miriam took the key, looking at it as if it were the vilest piece of metal she had ever seen. When Charlie took off his robe and joined her in bed, she snuggled close to him. "Charlie, did we do the right thing?"

"You mean about the locks?"

Miriam disengaged herself and sat up. "No, Charlie," she said, more harshly than she had intended. "You know what I mean. Do you think it might have something to do with the problems she's been having?"

"No. How could it? Now look, Miriam, what we did was best for all involved. And it's worked out just fine."

"But, Charlie, you said you were going to talk to her about it. When?"

"When the time is right," Charlie said before turning the lamp off and drifting into a deep sleep with the full awareness that his daughter was safe and sound, at least for the night.

Wrightsburg, Georgia, was typical small town America. The county square, which also served as its business hub, sprang up around the Madison County Courthouse in the early 1800s. At first there was only a tavern, a general store, and a livery stable. But over the years it had grown substantially, adding three office buildings – used mostly for housing lawyers and bonding companies – two department stores, and three restaurants.

Ginny and Dewey walked at a brisk pace along Courthouse Square, as it was called, but then Ginny slowed as she turned to Dewey. "Do you believe in ghosts, Dewey?

"Yes, don't we all," Dewey said, playfully raising his arms in a ghost-like motion as he circled her. "Ooooooooooo!"

"Stop it, Dewey. I'm serious. Something awful happened two nights ago."

Dewey stopped in his tracks when he detected the seriousness in her voice. "What happened?" he said.

As they continued down the street toward the newspaper office, Ginny revealed the whole sorry mess, including *the girl* on the bus and her own midnight march through the park. By the time she had filled him in on all the gory details, they were standing at a storefront office with a sign that read, "The Wrightsburg Herald."

"You must be imagining these things, Ginny."

"No, Dewey, I'm not. And I'm beginning to have thoughts that don't belong to me, so they must be hers."

"Look, I believe you. Just take the medicine like the doctor says, and we'll try to figure this thing out."

"Oh, Dewey, you really believe me," she said, giving him a big hug and a kiss on his cheek.

"Of course."

She kissed him again. "And you don't think that I'm crazy?"

"No."

"Oh, Dewey, I--"

Ginny aimed another kiss at Dewey's cheek, but he turned to meet her lips full on. As they kissed passionately, the door sprung open and Mitchell Bradley snarled as he stared at them. "Dewey Colton, do you have any shame? Is that what they're teaching up at that new school?"

"Oh, Mr. Bradley, I'm sorry," Dewey said. "It was nothing."

Mitch Bradley continued to give the two of them a look that could surely maim, if not kill. Nonetheless, he stepped aside, and Dewey ushered Ginny into the building.

Once inside, the two of them stood uncomfortably in front of the old man.

"Ah, er, this is Ginny Westbrook," Dewey stuttered. "She's my girlfriend."

Totally embarrassed, Ginny playfully pushed Dewey. "Dew-ey," she exclaimed. Dewey was laughing, but Mitch failed to capture the humor. "I know who she is," he said. "Do you have a note from Mr. Robinson?"

"Oh, yes," Ginny replied, opening her purse.

They both handed him their notes.

Ginny had never visited the newspaper, so she eagerly scanned the surroundings as the old man verified the notes as if they might have been passports to a new world.

There were four desks in the old office, two on either side of the room. Stacks of newspapers cluttered three of the desks, whose occupants had long since been handed pink slips, narrowing the paper's employees to a staff of one, Mitch Bradley.

Ginny flinched and recoiled when she stared up at the huge Confederate flag that covered most of the back wall. She hunched Dewey with her elbow, pointing toward a replica of the old St. Andrews Cross, a relic from the past that stirred pain and suffering in one segment of the population and pride and jubilation in another.

"Alright, you two," Mr. Bradley said grumpily, "follow me."

Though his size had diminished through the normal deterioration of body mass that accompanies old age, you could discern that Mitch Bradley had been a stout and sturdy man in his day. They followed the old newspaperman, who was now in his seventies, through the office and down a stairway into a small dungeon-like storage space that was filled with more stacks of old newspapers and several small reading tables.

These stacks, however, were sorted by month and year. The now faded labels were scripted with black markers on strips of cardboard that were tacked to the tops of wooden stands, which lined the rows of newspapers like telephone poles on a highway.

"Alright, you have one hour, then I'll be closing for lunch," Mr. Bradley said, and then turned to leave.

Ginny shakily clutched Dewey's arm. "Are you sure I should be here?"

"Oh, the flag," he said, chuckling. "Mr. Bradley *is* a die-hard, but he's mellowed with age. Daddy said he was a real thorn in the side, though, back when they were integrating the schools. ... Well, let's dive in."

Dewey went to a stack labeled, September 1950, and Ginny began with a stack so old that it had turned completely brown. It was the oldest stack of newspapers in the building and was labeled January 1930.

Thirty minutes later, Ginny rushed over to Dewey. "Look at this."

Dewey looked up as she pulled a chair up to the table and sat beside him.

"What is it?"

Ginny placed a yellowed newspaper in front of him and read the headline aloud. "Anna Marie Jennings, Madison County Student, Still Missing." Then she placed another paper on the table. "And look at this. … Still No Word On Missing Teen," Ginny continued reading.

The story went on to say that Armanda Lockett, a Madison High senior, did not return from a weekend trip to a traveling carnival.

"But what's the point?"

"The point is," Ginny announced, "that we have a pattern of girls going missing in this town."

After finishing their research, Dewey and Ginny climbed the stairs to the newspaper office. Ginny walked outside while Dewey went over to Mr. Bradley's desk to thank him for the use of the stacks. Mr. Bradley looked up from an article that he was proofing with a large magnifying glass.

"Thank you, Mr. Bradley," Dewey said.

"No problem. Did you find what you were looking for?"

"Yes, sir. We have more than enough information."

Dewey turned to leave, but Mr. Bradley called out to him. "Dewey."

Dewey stopped and turned. "Yes, sir?"

Mr. Bradley hesitated, choosing his words carefully before he spoke. "You could say it's none of my business, but do you know that what you and that girl are doing is morally wrong?"

Dewey stood with his mouth agape as Mr. Bradley continued, angrily now. "The Bible says 'Each tribe unto itself.' You just ought to stick to your own kind."

Dewey, turned and stormed out the front door.

Stanley Mitchell Bradley was born in poverty, but pulled himself up by his own bootstraps, moving up from delivering newspapers on his bicycle to becoming the owner and editor of the Madison Gazette, now called the Wrightsburg Herald. Along the way he set a sterling example for his son, Constance Bradley, who went on to become Wrightsburg's most successful lawyer and a member of the Georgia State Senate.

While Wrightsburg had flourished after integration, bringing Constance and his law firm much success, it had brought nothing but hardship to the Herald and newspapers in general. Even the mighty Atlanta Constitution, the morning paper, had to merge with its afternoon counterpart, the Journal, in order to survive.

The trouble started when Ted Turner, who owned a billboard company up in Atlanta, bought a TV station. Initially, Turner's station was actually a newspaperman's friend. Not only did his station not carry the news, but also ran its most popular sitcoms during the six o'clock news hour, causing many frivolous-minded people to rely heavily upon their morning paper for the news.

When this approach thrived to the extent that he became a multimillionaire, Turner bought a cable TV station. Then Old Ted had an epiphany. Flipping the script, he started carrying the news twenty-four hours a day. No one thought he had a chance of succeeding with such a crazy idea, but along came the Persian Gulf crisis, and his station, CNN, broadcast Dessert Storm – live and in living color.

Then the interlopers came, one twenty-four hour station after the other, and that was before Internet usage became widespread, giving full reports of the news in a matter of seconds.

"Nothing but old news," Mitch heard someone say of his newspaper. It had almost killed him. These days, a newspaper was little more than an afterthought to some. In recent years, the Herald had cut back from daily publication and became a weekly rag. Now, it was a struggle to maintain the one edition each Saturday.

A few local businesses still placed ads with him, more out of loyalty than necessity. His readers were now those like himself, die-hard segregationists. They gobbled up the weekly articles he wrote with an angry passion. The pieces were skewed with racist ideology and were quintessential examples of yellow journalism. Then a few years ago, his wife of thirty years died, leaving Mitch Bradley a bitter and broken man.

The very next day, Ginny walked down the sidewalk toward Ty Jr.'s office, which was situated at the main entrance to the food processing plant. She was well familiar with the Chandler plant. As a young girl,

Ginny and her playmates had spent countless hours roller-skating on the concrete sidewalk that ran the full length of the main building, which was the largest structure in the three-county area, occupying over two city blocks.

Ginny's third telephone call to Ty Jr. had been the charm. His secretary told her that if she could come by right after school, he would have fifteen minutes to give, but not a minute more, because Mr. Chandler was a busy man and it was the middle of the harvesting season.

Ginny had rushed right over after the final bell. As she thumbed through a magazine, Ginny looked at the expansiveness of the finely decorated office – with its luxurious Italian leather sofas and chairs, exquisite oil paintings and bronze sculptures – and mentally compared it to the newspaper office she had visited the day before.

"No comparison … money does make a difference," Ginny said aloud, thinking back to her earlier observations of Sarah Steele.

Then the secretary – a nicely dressed and attractive brunette in her thirties – pointed Ginny toward a large double door and said, "He'll see you now."

Before she could reach the door, it opened and a smiling Tyson Chandler, Jr. stood in the doorway. From afar Ginny already knew that he was good looking, but up close Ty Jr. was strikingly handsome. His clothes and demeanor furnished the final brushstrokes needed to complete the painting of the glorious picture of success.

Ty Jr. wore a tailored blue suit, white shirt, and a deep burgundy British-styled tie with bright white stripes – the kind executives routinely wear to "power lunches" where major deals are struck.

"Oh, good afternoon, Miss Westbrook," he said, giving Ginny a firm but polite handshake. "Come on in. Please, have a seat."

"Thank you, Mr. Chandler."

Ginny sat in a deep-cushioned leather chair that was so vastly overstuffed she had to sit near the front so as not to be swallowed up by its cushioning.

Ty Jr. settled down in his luxurious high-backed seat, and Ginny took out a note pad.

"I'm so sorry it took so long for us to get together," he said. "I'm sure you know this is a busy time for us. Why didn't you let 'em know you were Charlie's daughter?"

"Oh, I don't know. I just didn't think about it."

"Well, I don't mind telling you that when I found out who you were, I gave it to 'em, but good, for not putting you straight through to me. There's nothing I wouldn't do for Charlie and your mother. We've been through a lot together, both good times and bad," he said, now smiling.

"Oh, really," Ginny protested good-naturedly, "it was not a problem." There was something about *this* white man that Ginny definitely liked.

"Well, where do we start?" he asked.

"At the beginning," she said, now with a broad smile on her face.

"Well, in the beginning, my great granddaddy started out with a fruit stand ..."

By the time Ty Jr. had told the full story of the Chandler's rise from rags to riches, the clock on the wall showed that two hours had elapsed. Somewhere between the fruit stand and the general store, he took an important phone call, but after that, Ty Jr. told his secretary to hold all others.

Finally, Ginny rose from her seat as Ty Jr. opened the door.

"Well, thank you for your time," she said before turning to leave. "I can see that your father was a kind, generous, and wonderful man."

They exchanged other pleasantries, and Ty Jr. told her that she was to feel free to call if she needed further information, and then Ginny left.

Ty Jr. had enjoyed talking about the past and wondered why no one had bothered to inquire before. He and his family had done a lot for the people of Madison County, and even for the country. During the war, the Chandler farms provided fruits and vegetables for the troops at deeply discounted rates.

Maybe it would make a good newspaper article. No, maybe a magazine story. No, maybe even a book, he thought as his mind raced wildly.

But those were the good things.

Then Ty Jr.'s face hardened as he came back to reality and his thoughts drifted back in time. The Chandlers were always accommodating to others, but that was in order to get at the mighty dollar. However, when it came to their own kin, well that was another story.

His mind returned to one of the most tumultuous times he could remember. It was twenty years earlier, and he had just turned twenty-seven. His father's health was failing and he was contemplating retirement. Ty Jr. had just taken over the construction of the new addition to the food processing plant, and things were not running smoothly. The two men constantly disagreed on a full range of concerns, from the direction the business should be headed to private matters of the family.

That day, father and son were in the ornately paneled study of the Chandler Mansion, having their after-dinner sherry, and they were in the midst of the most violent of their arguments.

"Mama would roll over in her grave if she knew what you've done!" Ty Jr. said.

"You're right," the grumpy old man yelled back. "She'd roll over and clap her hands, because she would know that I'm right, and you're *wrong*. *Dead wrong!*"

Ty Jr. threw up his arms in disgust as he pleaded with the old man. "Look, Poppa, you know I love you, but what you did to Baby Sister was just wrong!"

Tyson Chandler became even more enraged. "No! I'm not the one who did something wrong, it was her. What she did was totally incomprehensible and despicable. There can be no forgiveness for it. Besides," the old man said, now in an almost condescending tone of voice, "only God knows where she is now."

Sensing a chink in the old man's armor, Ty Jr. smiled. "God and *me*," he said. "Let me call her, Poppa, please."

The old man hesitated for a long time before breaking the uneasy silence. "Well, maybe."

"Al-right!" Ty Jr. said, with exuberance.

"I said ... maybe!"

Ty Jr. sprinted to the telephone and dialed a number from memory. The telephone rang and rang on the other end, but there was no answer.

"You see what I mean," the old man said before leaving the room with his head in the air.

Ty Jr. shook himself from his revelry, dusted off memories from the past and punched a button on his office intercom.

"You can put my calls through now," he said.

A medicine bottle and a glass of water sat on the nightstand beside the bed. Ginny reached up from where she lay and shook a single pill from the bottle. She quickly swallowed the huge capsule, washing it down with water. She hesitated, and then took another before turning out the lamp beside her bed.

Downstairs, Charlie slowly checked the locks on the living room windows, and then stuck a key into the front door lock. The tumbler in the lock made a loud clicking sound as it turned, converting a home into a prison.

The computer printer hummed, dispensing a flyer with a picture of Beth Campbell under a heading that read, "Have You Seen This Girl?" Ginny sat at the computer terminal, adding final changes to the flyer, Dewey stood beside her, and Mr. Robinson worked at another station. The popped door opened and Sarah Steele bounced in. "Hi, everybody."

"Hi, Sarah," Ginny said, without looking up.

"Hi, Sarah," Dewey added.

Mr. Robinson looked up from his computer. "Hello, Sarah. Why are you so late?"

"Had an interview with your favorite teacher," she said with an insinuative smile.

"That's alright, Sarah," Mr. Robinson said, playfully, anticipating the line of her comments. "I'm sorry I asked."

His budding romance with the new English teacher was becoming the talk of the teachers' lounge, and Jerry Robinson didn't mind when his students jibed him about it. In fact, he rather enjoyed it.

Sarah walked over to Dewey and Ginny. "Well, if it isn't Agatha Christie and Sherlock Holmes. How's the search coming?"

"Don't start, Sarah," Ginny said, still not looking up.

Sarah looked down at the computer screen. "Oh, lord, not more flyers. They're already plastered all over town."

"Joe and some of the football players plan to place them in every store within a fifty mile radius," Dewey said.

Sarah picked up a flyer and held it up to the light. "I still say that the girl is probably up in Atlanta … enjoying the bright lights of the big city," she said sarcastically.

Ginny got up from the computer and turned to her. "Sarah, how can you be so insensitive?"

"I'm not insensitive. I'm just not a drama-queen like you. You're always full of conspiracy theories."

"Oops, my bad," Ginny said mockingly. "Excuse me for being born."

"Ladies, ladies," Mr. Robinson pleaded.

"Mr. Robinson, why aren't the police doing more to find Beth?" Ginny said pleadingly.

"I don't know what more they could do," Mr. Robinson said after getting up from the computer and facing Ginny. "They've searched all of the wooded areas nearby, and divers have even searched the lake."

"I don't mean searching," Ginny said. "I mean investigating. Like, why aren't the other missing girls being mentioned? It might be the same person doing it."

"You know, you're right, Ginny," Sarah said in a loving tone of voice that none in the room had heard before. "A few years ago, my nanny's granddaughter went missing and was never found."

"Who is your nanny?" Dewey asked in a similar tone.

"Who *was* my nanny, silly. I'm grown now," she said, now back to her old sarcastic self.

"Well, who was your nanny?" Ginny asked.

"Aunt Emma," Sarah said.

"Emma who?" Ginny continued prying. "What's her last name?"

"Lockett," Sarah said, "Emma Lockett."

Ginny's eyes widened, remembering the old newspaper story about Armanda Lockett. "Do you know where she lives?"

"Sure, she--"

Mr. Robinson cut in. "Now wait a minute, Ginny. What are you up to? I've told you, leave the investigation to the police."

"But Mr. Robinson," Ginny pleaded, "isn't it strange that nothing else happens in this little town, but three girls go missing?"

"Listen, I knew one of the girls you're talking about. She just left home and didn't come back. People do it every day. Like Sarah said, some girls like the lure of the city. As for the police, they don't like to mention unsolved crimes."

"Why not?" Dewey chimed in.

"It makes them look bad," Mr. Robinson said. "Usually the press calls attention to things like that."

Ginny became more excited. "Can't you get Mr. Bradley to do a story on it, you know, just to refresh some memories."

"No," he said. "Look, you've got to stop this! Let it end right here!"

Chapter 9

"It's one of your whores," Betty Brazell told her husband, shoving the telephone receiver, hard, against the sleeping man's ear.

"Aw, that hurt," Lou yelped in pain.

She angrily turned her back to him as Lou sat up and placed the receiver to his ear. "Hello."

"Sorry to call so late," said a soft sultry voice.

It was Elba. Lou would have known that voice even if it had been rising up from depths of hell.

"It's about the man, you know, the one who was following Beth?" Elba continued.

"Yes, what about him?" Lou asked with excitement in his voice and now in full command of his faculties.

"He came into the club, tonight, and I followed him to his car. I wrote down his tag number. Do you want it?"

"Yes," Lou almost screamed, opening the nightstand drawer and searching desperately for a pen. "Give it to me."

Hadley Frazier walked out of his office and spoke to his secretary, sitting at the reception desk. "Ina, I'll be gone for the rest of the day."

"But, Mr. Frazier, what will I tell Mr. Rakestraw when he calls?"

"Tell him that whatever it is … I'll deal with it Monday."

"And what about your appointments?" she asked, now with a look of distress crossing her face.

For the better part of a week, his secretary had helped Hadley fend off angry clients. Now with him leaving, she would be on her own to try to salve their wounds.

"Tell them the same thing," he said before walking through the double doors and vanishing down the hall.

Hadley Frazier had paid his dues in the world of high finance. He had enjoyed a privileged East Coast upbringing before matriculating at Yale, where he graduated near the top of his class. Being among the "pick of the litter," he went directly to Wall Street, there serving an apprenticeship as a buyer, on the floor of the stock exchange, for one of the most prestigious firms in New York.

This was where he learned that part of the business no university would dare teach. From there he easily slid behind a desk at Smith Barney, where he excelled, rising to the top of the pile and making millions for his clients while doing so. Therefore, when the top position became available in the new Atlanta office, it was to no one's surprise that Hadley was named to the post.

Five years as head of Smith Barney's Atlanta office had been enough. He had made billions for the company, so now it was time to strike out on his own and make a few bucks for himself. That was when he opened Frazier & Associates. He had made it to the top. It was not that Hadley hadn't enhanced himself financially along the way, he was a millionaire several times over and had the lifestyle to prove it.

In addition to the three bedroom co-op overlooking Atlanta's Centennial Park, Hadley Frazier had condominiums in D. C. and New York. His fifty-foot yacht was anchored in a marina down in Panama City, Florida, next to his beach cottage. And his small, but well-appointed, Lear Jet was hangared at the Fulton-Peachtree Airport.

Some called it the largest theft in the history of the world. Others called it the Savings and Loan Scandal. Whichever you chose to call it, Frazier and Associates had been in on it from day one. The rip-off began in 1980 when the government raised the maximum level of federal insurance on savings and loan deposits from forty thousand to one hundred thousand dollars, even though the typical savings account was only around six grand. Further deregulations eased restrictions so much the S & L's could actually lend themselves money, a recipe for disaster.

It was a buyers' holiday. Hadley not only steered his clients into the newly reformed banking industry, but invested heavily himself. It was a win/win situation. Even when these houses of cards began falling in on themselves, there was money yet to be made by buying into the now failing institutions, for pennies on the dollar. There would be but a short wait until Uncle Sam, with his pockets stuffed with taxpayers' money, stepped in to bail out the failing industry in fear of a collapse of the American economy.

The White House had finally stopped the bleeding after last year's election. But now, there was the piper to be paid by owners and investors who had stolen millions. The Justice Department was hunting them down like common criminals and sending them to jail. It had been all Hadley could do to stay one-step ahead of the posse. They had been hounding him for months. He could deal with the *blue suits*, his lawyer was one of the best in the country, but now his investors were turning on him.

Anyway, how was it that as long as he pitched shut-outs for his clients, things were lovely, but when he had to go into extra innings – like now – they wanted to take their ball and go home. *Hell, the game is just not played that way,* Hadley thought, stepping into the penthouse elevator on the sixty-seventh floor of the *One-Thirty-One* building for the express ride down to the parking level. He knew that Barry Rakestraw, his lawyer, had some kind of bad news for him, lawyers always did. But whatever it was would just have to wait. Right now, his body was full of tension, and he needed relief.

Hadley Frazier was a tall man in his late forties. He was not particularly handsome. His once jet-black hair was both graying and thinning, and his eyes were spaced a little too close together and set a little too far back in his head. Additionally, his jawbone jutted out on either side, making his face appear too angular. But his well toned body looked like he had just stepped off the pages of a Gold's Gym advertisement, and he dressed impeccably.

When Hadley turned the key in the ignition of his tomato red Lamborghini, the motor sung like a choir of angels as the eight pistons and thirty-two valves sprang into action – placing the four hundred fifty horses that lived under the hood at his disposal with just a touch of his toe on the accelerator.

The drive over to the Parthenon, a club for the distinguished gentleman, took less than ten minutes. When he drove through the huge arches, which were patterned after the famous old Greek structure, his regular parking attendant, Wiley, was waiting.

"Good evening, Mr. Frazier. Anything special today, wash, wax?"

"Not today, Wiley. I'll only be a minute," he said, peeling back a wad of bills in search of a ten-spot.

"Alright, suh," the short, dark, elderly man, dressed in an attendant's uniform, said, taking the bill and slipping it into his pocket.

"Go easy on her now," Hadley said, looking back at his most prized possession before entering the extra-wide door, which another elderly black man held open for him.

"How you, today?" the man asked. "Ain't seen you in a good while."

"I've been around," he said, peeling off another ten and stuffing it into the breast pocket of the man's uniform.

"Enjoy the show now," the attendant said, sounding grateful.

The evening shift was in full swing when Hadley walked through the door. The waitresses and dancers were dressed in brightly colored mini-sarongs, carrying out the Grecian theme. The dancers, however, soon discarded their tiny flimsy costumes and ended up being very naked. There were three large stages, one up front and one on either side of the building. A polished mahogany bar ran the full length of the back wall of the former ballroom.

Hadley moved through the crowded room and took a table near the front stage. After staking out his territory and ordering a gin and tonic, he walked directly to the front stage, where four girls danced to booming disco music. He walked up to a pretty black girl on the end of the stage and stuffed a twenty-dollar bill into her garter.

Without looking up, Hadley moved to the next girl, a blonde, and did the same. Skipping the third girl, he moved to the Asian girl at the end of the stage, slipping a twenty into her garter. By this time, the third girl, a gorgeous redhead, was fuming. Hadley turned, looked up at her, and then smiled as he stuffed twenty after twenty after twenty-dollar bill into her garter until he had given her a hundred bucks and the biggest smile her perfectly shaped face could muster.

After that dance, the redhead, called Dell, took up residency at Hadley's table and showed her bottom to no one else for the rest of the evening. Although one of Atlanta's most eligible bachelors, Hadley Frazier had neither wife nor girlfriend. He once had a wife, but she only got in his way. If you were married, there would have to be explanations about where and how time was spent, something that could be a deterrent to making money.

At the end of the shift, Dell's garter was greener than Farmer Brown's cabbage patch. It took her less than twenty minutes to change into street clothes and find Hadley's waiting Lamborghini. It took them less than that to drive to his midtown condominium.

Hadley Frazier, the hunter, had captured his quarry for the night. He usually always did. There were some who played hard to get, but the hunter had his own special way of dealing with them.

Around three the next morning, there was a loud rapid knocking on the door of the condominium. Hadley sprang awake and sat up straight in bed as the hammering continued. Handcuffs still attached to the headboard, and a riding crop lying on the bed, were the residuals of a night of sadomasochistic games.

He looked down at the sleeping redhead. She was naked as the day she got her first slap on her beautiful behind. He shook her awake.

"Wake up," he said with a sense of urgency in his voice.

"Who is that knocking on your door?" she asked as the knocking continued, now louder than before. "Why don't you answer it?"

"No, you go answer it," he said.

Hadley had already slipped on a pair of jeans and a T-shirt and was tying the strings of his tennis shoes.

"You have to do me a favor," he said and peeled off a hundred dollar bill and handed it to her.

"Oh, alright," she said, grabbing the money.

Dell wrapped the red silk sheet around her body and ambled barefoot toward the front door. "Alright, I'm coming," she yelled as she neared the door.

Reaching the front door, Dell looked through the peephole. She saw the caricatures of a short, pinked-faced, pudgy man, and a black woman. There was also a taller blonde-haired man standing behind them.

"Who are you?" she asked nervously.

"Police," she heard the man with the pink face say as he held up his badge.

Hadley had sprinted for the kitchen. He swiped up his keys from the table and swung the door open. Two FBI agents stood waiting.

"Going somewhere?" one of them asked.

They both held up their badges with one hand and fingered their guns with the other.

"Got a warrant for your arrest," the other agent said. "Bank fraud, illegal wire transfers, and using the United States mail for illegal activities. And that's just for starters."

Hadley shrugged and stepped back into the kitchen. By the time Lou, Lola, and the pudgy Atlanta Police detective had walked through the house and joined them in the kitchen, Dell had escaped through the front door and was hot-footing it down the front sidewalk, dressing on the run.

Once Lou and Lola had laid out their evidence against Hadley Frazier to the Atlanta Police, the department assigned Detective Chet Stargill, the pink pudgy man, to run interference for them. Then one of Chet's friends from the bureau dropped a hint that they were also closing in on Hadley. Since the FBI was getting ready to serve a warrant, the three of them decided to go along for the ride.

Catching up with Hadley Frazier had been one thing, but getting to question him, however, was another matter altogether. The cooperation from the bureau had dried up like a spot on a carpet from last night's party. The federal charges had to be dealt with first, and there was a laundry list of them.

For the past few years, Hadley and Associates had been operating as little more than an upscale Ponzey scheme. Money from one set of investors would be used to pay off another set. This worked well as long as new investors were to be found. But when the S & L deals went down the tubes, investors picked up their chips from the table and went home, especially now that jail time had been factored into the equation.

Now, there were many hands taking cash from the pot, but none putting money into it. Barry Rakestraw had been desperately trying to contact Hadley for the past two days, the amount of time the FBI had given for him to turn himself in to authorities.

On their third day spent waiting in Atlanta, Lou and Lola were finally sitting across the table from Hadley Frazier and Barry Rakestraw. They were in an interrogation room at the Richard B. Russell Federal Building.

"When was the last time you saw Beth Campbell?" Lou asked, placing the girl's picture on the table.

Hadley's eyes narrowed, even more than their already unnatural spacing, flinching as Lou turned the picture toward him. Lola made a mental note of the facial gesture. Then Hadley turned toward Barry Rakestraw, who silently shook his head.

"I do not recall," Hadley answered stoically.

"Do you know Beth Campbell?" Lola asked.

"I do not recall."

"Have you ever seen her at the Moulin Rouge night club?" Lou asked, growing angrier by the minute.

"Not to my recollection," he said, his face hardening after each question and answer.

And so the questioning went. On the advice of his lawyer, Hadley Frazier milked the Fifth Amendment to the United States Constitution for all it was worth. He dummied up altogether.

"We need to get into that house," Lola said, angrily, as they walked across the parking lot. "I've seem his kind a million times. They figure that with their money and status, everything they see is up for sale and anyone who doesn't go along with the program is in big trouble."

"Fat chance of getting a warrant," Lou replied. "We can't even prove a crime has been committed."

"Let's go home. I've got to see about my daughter," Lola said.

"Yeah, I need to get home, too."

By the time Lou dropped Lola off at the police station to retrieve her car, night had fallen. After a quick stop for beer at the corner store, he headed home – a three-bedroom bungalow in a new subdivision on the east side of town. When he pulled into the driveway, Lou was startled to see every light in the house on and his wife's car missing from the open garage. He became even more concerned when he got out of the car and approached the front door, which was standing wide open. Lou placed the six-pack down, withdrew his pistol, and eased cautiously into the house.

The hand with the gun fell to his side as Lou stared at the carnage before him. All of the furniture had been stripped from the house and all of his belongings were scattered across the floor of the living room. Disgustedly, he silently walked from room to empty room, finding more of the same.

Turning off the lights in each room as he left it, Lou shook his head as he put the gun back into its holster and retrieved the beer from the front steps. Walking back to the kitchen, he found that the refrigerator and stove were still there. "Thank God for small favors," he said aloud.

Lou tore a can of beer from the six-pack and walked to the refrigerator to put the remainder away. Then he saw it. The refrigerator door was covered, from top to bottom, with typed sheets of paper. He pulled the top sheet from the door and read the heading. It was a declaration of war between Betty Jean and Louis Thomas Brazell – divorce papers. In the center of the papers, stuck individually to the door by magnets, was a sheet with large handwritten letters that read, "SCREW YOU!"

"Screw you, too," he yelled, letting loose with a few more choice words before throwing the beer to the floor and stomping each can with his foot until the floor was a mess of metal and foam. Lou had mixed emotions as he stood there looking at the batch of papers. Now, he could imagine how a cancer patient might feel upon approaching death, sad that it was happening, but glad that it was finally coming to an end.

Their marriage had been over for quite some time. So long ago, in fact, they had forgotten when things had turned really sour. However, they both knew what caused the beginning of the end. It is said that, to err is human, but to forgive is divine. Lou was never able to forgive Betty her one indiscretion, which had taken place many years ago, even though he had said as much.

Maybe things might have been different if her lover had not been Lou's best friend. Danny Dalton had been Lou's partner on the Miami police force. He had laughed at Lou's bad jokes, drank his beer, eaten at his table, and ultimately slept in his bed. Lou was brought up on charges for breaking Danny's nose with the barrel of his service revolver. He and Betty smoothed things over and moved to Atlanta, but things were never the same.

Lou and Betty were cut from different molds and never really seemed to mesh. She was quiet and reserved, at first, but changed drastically after they were married. On the other hand, Lou had been quite the opposite. He grew up a free spirit and a beach bum in South Florida.

After high school and two years at Camden Junior College, on a football scholarship, the tall rustically handsome boy with the athletic body, sparkling blue eyes, and sun-bleached hair sat waiting for the University of Miami to come calling. But the Hurricane's coach called his two years of junior college play, uninspiring, and never did.

After that, Louis Brazell knocked around from pillar to post. Primarily, he was a lifeguard on South Florida's endless stretch of beaches, but Lou finally had found his calling in the United States Army – where he spent ten years, mostly as a military police. He was good at police work, and rose to the rank of Master Sergeant.

After mustering out of the Army, Lou changed planes in Atlanta on the way back home. He met a pretty blonde at the airport lunch counter. After serving him up waffles and bacon that morning and super sex later that night, Betty Coglin followed him home to Miami the next day.

Chapter 10

W hen he met Lola the next morning, Lou uttered not a word of his personal situation. Although she, too, knew that the breakup was as sure to come as Christmas. Let the dead past bury itself, Lou had told himself before tossing some of his clothes into a pile against the wall, making a bed for the night. He would shop for furniture tomorrow.

They were late for their meeting with Chief Callahan, who was waiting anxiously at the conference table. Upon their arrival, they all exchanged morning greetings as Lou and Lola took seats on either side of the chief.

"Well, fill me in," the chief said once the pleasantries and explanations for lateness were over.

And they did so.

Russ Callahan was one of the few who had made it out of Orchard Park to live and work in mainstream Wrightsburg. Now in his late thirties, his success was due to a combination of determination, hard work, and education. The sturdy built six-footer, with the ever-smiling red face, played center on his high school basketball team.

Although he was much shorter than the men who usually lined up against him, it was his tenacity that made up for the lack of height – for the position – and which also served Russ well as a linebacker on the State Championship football team. That he was from the wrong side of the tracks made little or no difference to the citizens of Wrightsburg. Blue Wavers took care of their own. The town accepted Russ Callahan in his position, without reservation.

The police chief never forgot his roots and would always go the last mile for one of the park-people, as they were called. This investigation was even closer to him since Beth, under a different set of circumstances, might have been his own daughter. Lizzy Rollins – now Lizzy Campbell – had been Russ Callahan's high school sweetheart, and they had even kept in touch while he was at the University of Georgia, over in Athens.

They continued dating off and on during Christmas and summer vacations until a smooth talking huckster, named George Campbell, came through town. He stopped for the night, but stayed for a season. George sold overpriced burial policies, door to door, for a little while, but soon got bored with the small town and left for greener pastures, leaving wife and child behind.

"I still hope this is a missing person's case," the chief said after hearing the bad news about the jailhouse interview. "Now let's see. So far, we have a jealous boyfriend and a stalker, both of whom had motive and opportunity."

"That's it," Lou said. "But there's still the possibility that she might've gone off on her own."

"I wish I could be so optimistic," Lola said. "It's that pervert up in Atlanta, Chief, I just know it. I won't be satisfied until we can get inside Hadley Frazier's condo."

The chief stroked his chin, musing, and then broke the silence. "Don't give up hope," he told Lola. "I'll get on the phone and see if my contacts with the FBI can help. If some of my old classmates are still with the bureau, we might be able to get a peep at whatever evidence they collect."

"Great, Chief," Lola said, "that sounds good."

"In the meantime," he said, turning to Lou, "why don't you take another crack at the Meriwether boy."

"Gotcha, Chief," Lou said. "I'll bring him down here, on my turf, and if there's anything there, I'll get it."

"No rough stuff, Lou," the chief reminded him.

Just then, there was a soft knock on the office door.

"Come on," the chief said loudly.

Patrolwoman Myrtle Davis stuck her head into the doorway. "Chief, there's somebody I think you need to talk to."

"Y'all come on in," the chief said, ushering the two females, standing behind her, into the office.

Faye Drummond and her mother walked uneasily into the room.

"Chief Callahan, my daughter didn't tell you everything," the short beefy woman said.

"Why don't y'all have a seat," the chief said with his heart beating wildly in hopes of a break in the case.

"We won't be that long," she said timidly. "Go ahead, Faye, tell the man."

"You know, you were asking about Beth's other boyfriends," Faye said, looking at Lou. "Well she *was* kinda like … seeing somebody else."

Lou Brazell and Lola Morgan stood outside the classroom door as Principal Murray walked up to the teacher who was standing at the blackboard. "Mr. Dixon?"

"Yes?" the football coach answered cheerily.

The two men talked animatedly, and then walked outside, where Lou and Lola joined the argumentive conversation.

On the way to the pencil sharpener, a boy stopped at the door to listen. Suddenly he scurried back to his seat as Coach Dixon returned.

"Class, something has come up and I have to leave," the coach said. "Mr. Murray will send someone to keep the class."

After the coach left, the boy dashed to the front of the room and made an announcement. "They're taking Coach Dixon to jail for killing Beth Campbell!"

A collective sigh went up from the students. "Ooooooo!"

Several students ran from room to room shouting, "They're taking Coach Dixon to jail for killing Beth Campbell!"

It had been but a short jump from Faye's revelation of the scandalous affair, to Lizzy Campbell's admission that, yes, she had gone into that den of iniquity up in Atlanta and brought Beth home. And, yes, it had been Coach Dixon who had told her about Beth's whereabouts but, no, she didn't know of an affair between the two of them.

Faye, on the other hand, had been quite explicit about the details of the relationship, which had begun shortly after the strip club incident.

And just like always, once the trickle started, the floodgates opened. Coach Dixon's telephone records showed that a call was placed to Beth's private number on the morning of her disappearance. It also revealed that, over a period of time, there had been many others.

Coach Dixon, who had come to the police station of his own volition, waited impatiently in the interview room. After making him sweat for at least an hour, Lou and Lola entered.

"Hello, lover boy," Lou said. "I told you we'd meet again."

"Cut the crap, Brazell. I've changed my mind. I wanna see a lawyer."

"Lawyer, for what? You said there was no crime committed. Now, if there was ... you let me know, and I'll be happy to get your lawyer. And then I'll go get mine, the county attorney."

Coach Dixon shook his head. "Hey, there's no crime ... that I know of."

"Come on, Willie," Lola said, "just tell us what you know, then we can all go home. We know you were screwing Beth Campbell. She told her best friend everything."

"No, she's lying!"

Coach Dixon became agitated as Lola laughed uncontrollably. "What's wrong with you? When will you men learn? If you have an affair with a woman, she's gonna tell somebody. If it's good, she's gonna tell," Lola said, now rolling with laughter. "And if it's not, she's really gonna tell it."

"Okay, okay," the coach finally relented, "but I don't know where she is, and I certainly didn't do anything to hurt her! I'm not lying!"

"Did you see her that night?" Lou asked with his face so close to Coach Dixon's that he could have counted the strands of hair in the man's neatly trimmed mustache.

"Yeah, yeah, I saw her. I picked her up, as usual, behind the library, and..."

Coach Dixon snored loudly as he lay naked on the bed. Beth Campbell walked out of the bathroom wrapped in a towel, shouting at the sleeping man. "Willie, get up. You're going to make me late."

"Okay, okay," he said, dragging himself from the bed, and then they both struggled to get dressed.

Night had fallen when Willie Dixon pulled his car into the rear of the parking lot. Beth leaned over and gave him a quick peck on the cheek, and then slipped out into the night. She quickly walked around to the front of the building and headed for the library door, but then stopped and looked at her watch. Now cognizant of the time, Beth turned and ran down the street.

"She would normally go into the library for a lil' while, you know, to make it look good, then she would leave," Coach Dixon continued. "But because we were so late, she didn't go inside. The last time I saw Beth Campbell, she was walking toward Barney's Burger Barn. And that's the honest truth, so help me God."

"You don't have to swear," Lou said. "There'll be plenty of time for that. ... Alright, you can go, but don't plan any surprise vacations."

Coach Dixon sprang from the chair and scurried out of the room.

Word of the investigation soon leaked to the Atlanta media, and the strip club aspect of the case whetted their appetites. Several news reporters stood in front of the Wrightsburg Police Station as Lou Brazell and Lola Morgan walked outside. Two of the reporters shoved microphones into the faces of the detectives as the cameras rolled.

"Detective, we hear that you have two suspects in the case, an Atlanta stock broker and a local coach," a reporter said. "When do you expect an arrest?"

"Did you search either of their apartments?" another asked.

"No, no, let me get this straight," Lou said forcefully. "We are investigating Beth Campbell's disappearance as a missing person's case. None of the persons questioned is a suspect since we have no evidence of a crime having been committed. We are continuing the search."

The picture of the interview filled the TV screen, and then the camera cut to a handsome male reporter. His booming voice filled the room. "Sources close to the investigation report that Chandler High School's football coach, William Dixon, has admitted to having an inappropriate relationship with the high school senior."

Then the camera cut to two juxtaposed headshots, one showing the pitch-black football coach in stark contrast to the lily-white cheerleader.

"He, however, maintains his innocence of any crime," the reporter went on. "The superintendent of schools could not be reached for comment."

Just then a finger touched a button on the remote control and the picture on the TV set flickered before disappearing.

The Atlanta press had come to Wrightsburg to get the scoop on the stalking stockbroker. But by giving enough local officers fifty-dollar-handshakes until they found one who would spill the beans, they also picked up the story about Coach Dixon – two for the price of one. The twin stories had been their lead on the eleven o'clock news.

Word spread across Madison County quicker than wildfire on a dry prairie. When Coach Dixon arrived on campus the next morning, he had to reassure his players and friends of his innocence, especially Joe Meriwether, who was livid at the news of the affair until he was convinced otherwise.

The coach also had to fend off the accusing eyes of his detractors – what few there were. After all, this *was* football season. Few, if any, true Blue Wavers would want to upset the apple cart – not now anyway. Finally, the coach worked his way to the Principal's office and signed in at the attendance desk. As he turned to leave, the secretary called out to him. "Coach, don't go to your class. The principal wants to see you."

Mr. Murray looked up as Coach Dixon walked into his office. "Come in, Willie. Have a seat."

Coach Dixon took a seat and spoke apologetically. "Mr. Murray, I know what you're thinking, but I can explain."

"This looks bad, Willie."

"You know me, Mr. Murray. I wouldn't harm a fly," the coach said, raising his arms in entreaty.

The principal, in an even and measured tone of voice, said, "Willie, I'm putting you on paid suspension until this thing gets sorted out."

Coach Dixon sprang to his feet. "You can't do that!"

"Look," Mr. Murray said angrily. "I knew your reputation when I hired you. But for the sake of these football idiots around here, I took a chance on you."

"We've got too much at stake," the coach pleaded. "What about the team?"

"Let me and you get one thing straight," the principal snarled, leaping to his feet. "I could care less about the team. Football is not what schools are made for!"

"They'll never let you get away with this," the coach said. "The association will see to that."

"Listen, mister, you're in so deep, even your precious Blue Wavers can't help you now. Coach Rice will be taking over as interim coach."

"Coach Rice? No! Mr. Murray, this is the year we go all the way," the coach pleaded continually. "And this is all just a big misunderstanding. It'll go away."

"I have no choice in the matter. It's the superintendent," the principal said sternly. "My advice is that you get yourself a good lawyer. You can make an appeal at the next board meeting."

"Well, at least let me coach. The team will never follow Rice. He's a nobody."

"I can't do that."

"Is this what I get for all that I've done for this school?" the coach said angrily.

"I'll tell you what you've done for this school!" the principal said, moving around the desk until the two men stood toe-to-toe. "You've admitted to having sex with a student. According to regulations, I cannot allow you to remain on school property."

"I tell you what! You take your school property and you shove it!"

Coach Dixon turned in a huff, hurling a string of explicatives at the principal as he left the office.

"They *never* learn!" the principal said, slamming the door behind the irate coach.

At precisely eleven o'clock that morning, Mr. Murray walked out of his office and closed the door. Turning to his secretary, Miss Marable, he said, "I'm going to lunch. I'll be back in about an hour."

"Yes, sir," the small gray-haired woman replied as she had done every day for the past five years. The schedule was exactly the same. Each day, Mr. Murray would leave school to take care of his and his mother's medicinal needs and return within the hour. He was a stickler for making sure that he took no more time for lunch than he would've if he had eaten on campus. No matter what his personal or family problems, Francis Murray would *not* be a burden to the school system.

Later, Mr. Murray left his mother's bedroom carrying a food tray. "I'll be right back with your medication," he told her. The television set, which was perpetually tuned to Channel 17, Ted Turner's twenty-four hour station, blared in the background.

He looked down at the untouched food, and then stuck his head back into the doorway. "Mother, you're going to have to start eating more. And Aunt Clara says you won't call and you don't return her calls. Mother, do you hear me?"

He disgustedly turned and walked down the stairs, shaking his head. "That woman. I don't know."

Mr. Murray carried the tray back to the kitchen, dumped the food into the garbage can, and placed the dishes into the sink, along with the plate he had just used. Then he went to his bathroom, took a syringe from the medicine cabinet, and plunged the needle deep into a small vial. He pulled back the plunger, and then watched as the opaque fluid slowly filled the tube of the syringe. He pushed the plunger until a spurt of fluid escaped, testing it for the chore that lay ahead.

When she and Myrtle Davis returned from lunch, Lola Morgan walked straight over to Lou's desk. "Lou, you got a minute?"

"Yeah, sure," he said, looking up from the newspaper advertisement for furniture.

"He didn't do it," Lola said, matter-of-factly.

Lou got up and walked over to the coffee maker. "He, who? Didn't do what?"

"Willie didn't kill that girl," Lola said, joining him at the table.

Lou poured coffee into a cup, and then turned to face her. "Hey, how can you be objective? You used to bang the guy, for Christ's sake."

"That's got nothing to do with anything, and you know it!"

Lou slammed the coffee cup to the table. "No, I don't know it! Do you need to be taken off this case? If you can't do your job, just say the word!"

"I'm *doing* my job! The man does not have a motive!"

"Look, you and every other skirt in Madison County have been chasing that washed up jock ever since the pros kicked him back to town. I say he's getting what he deserves."

"Are you sure this isn't a man thing?" Lola said before turning and angrily walked away.

Lou called out to her. "Maybe she got pregnant! I don't know! I just follow the leads!"

Lola paused. "Think about it, Lou. Beth was seen by several people *after* she left his apartment."

"That's according to him," Lou shot back. "The way I'm seeing it, is Beth went to visit the coach *after* she and her boyfriend fought. One's the coach and the other is a player. Which one do you think would leave practice first? You think about that!"

Chapter 11

There had not been an automobile, so big, so long, or so black, on Cherry Lane since the limousine – from Fowler's Funeral Home – came to pick up Mrs. Flossie Mae Johnson to take her to bury her husband, ten years ago. That Saturday morning, Sarah Steele pulled the Lincoln Towncar into the Westbrook driveway, and Ginny hopped in.

For the past week, things had gradually begun to get back to normal with the help of the large capsules that Ginny took, like clockwork, every night. Miriam even let her sleep an hour later each morning to help get over the grogginess caused by the medicine, and then drove her to school. Still, Ginny walked around in a daze until around noon, when the full effect of the medicine usually wore off.

The pills, however, were doing the trick, holding the dreams in check. Nevertheless, *the girl* was back. There had been two sightings. One day at school, Ginny saw her standing at the end of a long dark hallway and another day, *the girl* followed her through Simpson's Woods, walking step for step behind her all the way home. Ginny was surprised that she felt comforted by *the girl's* presence instead of fear.

"Hi, Sarah, thanks for letting me tag along," Ginny said, pulling the big luxurious car door shut.

"No, thank you for reminding me of Nanny," Sarah said, smiling as she dropped the gearshift into reverse and slowly backed the Lincoln out of the driveway. "It's been awhile since I've visited."

By the time Sarah had driven the seventy miles to Ellenwood, a small town on the outskirts of Atlanta, she and Ginny were laughing and talking like long lost friends. Before they had left the city limits of Wrightsburg, they were already sharing their most intimate secrets. Sarah was appalled at the harsh treatment that Ginny received from some of the black students, and Ginny was equally surprised at the nastiness some of the white students heaped upon Sarah.

It was because they were all jealous of them, because they were bright, beautiful, and sexy they both concluded, laughing their fool heads off. The most shocking of the revelations, however, was the fact that Sarah did *not* want to become an engineer. That had been her father's idea since her brother was either too lazy or too dumb to be one. What Sarah really wanted to do in life was teach kindergarten. She loved children.

Sarah drove through the Ellenwood city limits and traveled down a winding country road for another ten miles before reaching the Rolling Hills Rest Home. Ginny was flabbergasted when she saw the large white three-story, regal-looking, building standing majestically in the middle of a plush garden of trees, hedges, and flowers.

"Wow, are you sure this is a nursing home?" Ginny said. "This looks more like a resort."

"It ought to. It costs Daddy close to a grand a month, but he says, 'Money doesn't matter when it comes to Nanny. She took good care of us, and we're gonna take good care of her,'" Sarah said, mimicking her father's voice.

"That's really decent of him."

"We have to take care of her, you know, all of her people are gone now."

"Gone? Where?"

"Her husband is dead and her two daughters just loaded up the rest of their children and headed for parts unknown. The family just fell apart after Mandy left."

119

The interior of the renovated mansion was just as stately as the outside. After a short elevator ride to the second floor, the two girls found themselves walking down the gleaming white tiled floors of a grand hallway, where artwork hung at strategic intervals and large green plants sprouted out of enormous urns. Sarah carried a large box under one arm and a bouquet of fresh flowers in her other hand.

Emma Lockett's room looked more like a hotel suite than that of a home for the aged and infirmed. The spacious suite had a sitting area, with a plush sofa, matching chairs, and end tables, and the bedroom had a full-sized bed, dresser, and wardrobe.

When the two girls entered, Emma was sitting in a wheelchair, staring out of a large picture window, which gave a marvelous panoramic view of the garden below. She was a small coal-black woman with neatly braided, silver-gray, pigtails. A food tray on a rolling stand, which had been pushed aside, contained remnants of lunch – mashed potatoes, green peas, congealed salad, and baked chicken.

"Nanny," Sarah said softly.

The woman at the window did not move, but continued to stare straight ahead.

"Nanny," she said, a little louder.

Finally Emma turned, looking over her shoulder and straining her eyes to see. "Who is it?" she asked in a shaky voice.

"It's me, Sarah Jean."

A broad smile suddenly appeared on the old woman's wrinkled face. "Lord, girl, you come here and give your old Nanny a hug."

Sarah leaned down and cradled Emma's tiny frame as a mother would her child. When she rose, Ginny saw a single tear roll down Sarah's face.

"Mama sent you something," she said, placing the box on Emma's lap. In a moment, Sarah had gotten hold of her emotions and was back to being her whimsical self. "And I brought you some flowers. I'll put 'em in some water for you."

"Alright, honey, they sure look pretty," Emma said, and then looked up at Ginny. "Who's that you got wit' ya'?"

Sarah turned to Ginny. "Oh, this is my classmate, Ginny Westbrook."

"Hello, Mrs. Lockett," Ginny said, taking the old woman's hand.

Emma's eyes squinted as she looked up at Ginny. "Westbrook, Westbrook," she pondered. "Who is yo' people?"

"Charlie and Miriam Westbrook," Ginny replied. "Mama's a nurse at the hospital, and my Daddy drives truck for the Chandlers."

"Yeah, I know of 'em. But I didn't think they the had no children."

Sarah took Emma's hand. "Nanny," she said softly. "I know you don't like to talk about it, but Ginny wants to ask you about Mandy."

A frown creased the old woman's forehead and her mouth pulled back in a grimace. "Oh, Jesus, no," she gasped.

"Good lord, Nanny, you don't have a thing to put these flowers in," Sarah said flightily, looking up at a shelf lined with potted plants. "I'll be right back. I've got something in the car."

"Okay," Emma said.

Ginny pulled a chair up close to the wheelchair, and then sat beside Emma. "Mrs. Lockett, you know that there's a girl missing now?"

"Yeah, it's been all over the TV. Sure got me to thinking about my grandbaby."

"Mrs. Lockett, the paper said that some thought Armanda had argued with her family about a boyfriend, got angry, and then she ran away."

"Mandy didn't run nowhere," Emma said emphatically. "We argued alright enough. And she got mad … we all wuz, but it was the white people that killed her."

Ginny's eyes widened. "Killed her, why?"

"She was going with that white boy. I tried my best to warn her, but she wouldn't listen to nobody. Some say it was his people that did it."

"Who was the boy?"

"Connie Bradley. He's a lawyer now, and his daddy runs the newspaper."

For a second Ginny felt faint, but when she regained her composure, made a mental note to look up the state senator. "But how do you know she's dead, if they never found a body?"

"I know she's dead ... because sometimes," she said, almost whispering now, "sometimes she comes to me at night."

Fright rose up in Ginny, and for a moment, she was horrified. "Are you saying there are such things as *ghosts*?"

"No ... I call 'em visitations."

Ginny froze ... in stunned silence. "What do you mean?" she finally managed to say.

Emma looked up at Ginny. "Look at you, child. You're trembling."

When Emma took her hand, a strange magnetism ran the length of Ginny's body.

"Oh, my lord," Emma said. "You haves 'em, too."

"I've had some bad dreams," Ginny stuttered, "but..." Her voice trailed off.

Emma patted Ginny's hand as she spoke in a whisper. "Don't be afraid, child. Sometimes when a soul gets lost ... they comes back ... to places they know and to people they love. They won't hurt you, though."

Ginny shuddered, still frozen with fear.

Emma squeezed Ginny's hand as she spoke even softer. "Because they still love you and they just need your help."

Ginny drew her hand away and looked at the elderly woman in astonishment. "Help? What can I do to help?"

"That's what you have to find out," Emma said sternly. "You have to do it, girl, 'cause I'm too old."

"But, I--"

"Only you can do it. When you find what you're looking for, Mandy will be free, too. Go, now," she said, now smiling. "God'll be with you."

As Sarah drove down the highway, Ginny stared ahead blankly, but did not speak.

"Nanny is certainly looking well," Sarah said gingerly. "Did you get your information?"

When she noticed the dumbfounded look on Ginny's face, Sarah snapped her fingers. "Hello … Ginny … anybody home?"

All the way home, Sarah carried the conversation. Ginny answered in grunts and nods, but uttered not a single word.

Chapter 12

Being an athlete, Sonny James learned early on that – more times than not – you had to play with pain. There would always be a nick here or a ding there, but last year he had been constantly plagued with ankle and knee injuries. Though not serious enough to sideline him, a knee twist or an ankle sprain always took a little something away from his game. Coaches had a way of describing this phenomenon. You might hear them make statements such as, "He's only playing at about ninety percent."

But that was then, and this was now. Things would be different this year. Over the summer, his parents hired a personal trainer to work with him down at the YMCA, and Sonny was in the best shape of his life. Otto, his trainer, taught him warm-up activities to get the blood flowing properly before going into contact drills, which protected him from unnecessary injuries. Without a doubt, this would be the best year of Sonny James' athletic career.

He was hell bent on bringing that State Championship trophy back to Chandler High, as well as a smaller one, with the inscription, "Sonny James, Most Valuable Player." With those two pieces of hardware in hand, he could write his own ticket. The University of Georgia, Georgia Tech, and Auburn University had already come a calling. Nonetheless, Sonny was holding out for the big brass ring that was sure to be extended from South Bend, Indiana, the University of Notre Dame.

Sonny had followed the Fighting Irish, religiously, since he played Pop Warner Football at the age of ten. He could rattle off the names of the legendary coaches from Knute Rockne to Frank Leahy to Ara Parsegan, and was intrigued with their impressive strings of victories, especially the National Championships. Sonny dreamed of the day when he would strap on that Notre Dame helmet, which was said to be coated with paint mixed with real gold.

It was seven o'clock in the morning and the training room at the YMCA was filled with executive-types who truly understood the value of exercise of the body contributing to the functioning of the mind. These young men and women paid professional trainers, handsomely, to hone their bodies to perfection before going out into the world of work. After an early morning at the gym, they were sure to be at the top of their game, so to speak.

Television sets were attached to the walls at various locations so that exercisers could break the monotony of a forty-five minute workout on the thread-mill or a thirty-minute session on the stationary bike. Suddenly the picture of a news reporter filled the many TV screens.

In the midst of his pre-school workout, Sonny was working on the cross-trainer – an elliptical bike with weight resistant handles that allowed you to work both upper and lower body muscles simultaneously.

"Sonny, get over here," Otto called out to him. "You gotta see this."

Sonny brought the machine to a halt, wiped the sweat from his eyes with a towel, and then strode over to where Otto stood, watching the morning news.

"Constance Bradley, counsel for Coach Dixon, said that he will cooperate fully with the investigation," the strikingly handsome reporter said as a close-up of Connie Bradley filled the screen. "This, however, will *not* include a voluntary search of his premises and, certainly, no lie detector test. Mr. Bradley points to the unreliability factor involved in such tests."

Sonny frowned, shaking his head in disgust as he and Otto stared up at the screen.

The reporter continued. "In other related news, pending investigation by the Professional Practices Commission, the Madison County School Board has placed Coach William Dixon on paid suspension. It has also been rumored that the former pro wide receiver might return to the Detroit Lions as a scout for the team."

Sonny slammed his elbow into the wall. "Damn it! There goes the season!"

The next time Lou and Lola interviewed Coach Dixon, he had taken the principal's advice and hired a good lawyer, in fact, the best that Wrightsburg, Georgia, had to offer, Constance Bradley. The firm of Bradley & Post consisted of Constance, Billy Post, the other part of the company's namesake and senior partner, and two junior partners.

There was no doubt, however, as to which lawyer was the crown jewel in the stable of barristers. Constance had only taken a partner after he was elected to the Georgia State Senate. Now he had to be up in Atlanta three months out of the year – taking care of the people's business.

Constance was the spitting image of his daddy, Mitch. He had taken the newspaperman's curly hair, dark eyes, and muscular build. The two men also shared political and religious ideologies. Constance was a card-carrying member of the Madison County Heritage Society. He paid his dues religiously, though he no longer attended the meetings, not wanting to alienate his black constituents and clients.

Since he had taken over Willie Dixon's defense, things were much different. Today, there would be no interrogation room. The meeting would be held in Chief Callahan's office, and it would be Lou and Lola who would do the waiting.

"Is this really necessary?" she asked, anxiously swinging one crossed leg over the other.

They had been waiting for Coach Dixon and Constance Bradley for almost an hour.

"Take it easy," Lou said, turning to Lola, who sat beside him at Chief Callahan's conference table. "There's no rush."

Lola shrugged.

Then they heard the clicking of footsteps coming down the hall. Suddenly the door opened and Constance Bradley stood in the doorway. "Sorry, folks. I didn't mean to keep you," he lied to the detectives before turning to the coach, who was standing behind him. "Right this way, Mr. Dixon."

Coach Dixon entered the room and walked with Constance to the conference table, but said not a word. Lola couldn't help from noticing the lawyer. Constance was a tall handsome man, well into his thirties, with a magnetic personality. He had a full mane of curly black hair and still wore long sideburns and a mustache, a throwback from the 70's.

The two men sat down across from the detectives, and then the interview began.

"Basically," Lou said, "we're here to coordinate a time for the search, which Mr. Dixon has already agreed--"

Constance cut in. "Ah, er, that has changed. While my client has absolutely nothing to hide, it would be a blatant violation of his constitutional rights for his home to be invaded, since there is no evidence of him having committed a crime."

"I understand," Lou said without argument.

Lou Brazell had come prepared for just such a turn of events. When he found out that Constance had taken the case and heard his comments on TV, Lou knew that the voluntary search was history. Emory Shepard, the county attorney, was already on the case. Judge Iverson had been out on the golf course when Emory got him to sign the warrant, therefore, they just had to stall until the courier arrived with the official document. Lou and Lola continued with the perfunctory line of questioning.

Constance Bradley proved to be just as good a coach as Hadley Frazier's lawyer, Barry Rakestraw, had been. Coach Dixon's answers were well rehearsed and interspersed with, "On the advice of my attorney and I'd prefer not to answer."

Finally, there was a knock on the door. Lola stepped outside, took the envelope from the courier, and then returned to the table.

"I think you will find these papers to be in order," she said, handing the search warrant across the table to Constance, who seemed no more surprised than Lou had not been, earlier. It was just how the game had to be played.

Ultraviolet light illuminated Coach Willie Dixon's kitchen as Brian Pollard, the crime-scene investigator, Lou Brazell, and Lola Morgan scanned the floor and walls with magnifying glasses. Brian had sprayed them down with Luminal, a chemical that was used to clean toilets before someone discovered that even the scantest trace of blood would be revealed when exposed to ultraviolet light. Brian was on his hands-and-knees examining the floor beneath a cabinet. He suddenly looked up at Lou, who was working a nearby wall.

"Lou," he called out excitedly.

"Yeah," Lou answered.

"Bingo," he shouted, sounding like an expert player of the popular game.

The Fab-Five, as they called themselves – Fab for fabulous – consisted of Sonny James, his best friend and the team's star running back, Luther Bagley, the Abdullah twins, Kaleed and Hassan, two burly linebackers, and Leon Pope, a massively built white boy. Leon was the best defensive tackle in the State of Georgia, and he loved the ground that Sonny James walked on. The gang stuck together like glue. Wherever Sonny went, the other four were sure to follow.

On Fridays before really big games, the pep rally was moved to the noon hour, so that parents and other Blue Wavers could stop by to join in the festivities. And this game was *huge*. The Blue Wave was to have its first real test of the season.

The team would travel over to Barnesville, where their archrivals, the Richmond High Titans, lay in wait for a Saturday afternoon showdown. It was billed as the "game of the year," and it was a foregone conclusion that the winner of this grudge match would have a cakewalk into the state playoffs, for sure.

When the Fab-Five entered the gym, the band was playing the Blue Wave's fight song, and the cheerleaders, dressed out in their scant blue-and-white outfits, were prancing in time to the music – stopping intermittently to lead the crowd in a rousing cheer. The gymnasium was a sea of blue and white. Streaming banners and other signs spelled out the impending doom of this week's opponent, the Titans.

The bleachers were filled to the rafters with students, parents, and other community members, who had taken off from their jobs to attend. Workers from every segment of the industrial population were present, that is, all except Chandler employees. There were only three times a year when the Chandler machines and trucks sat idle, Thanksgiving, Christmas, and New Year's Day.

Some of the crowd cheered as Sonny and his boys – wearing their blue and white varsity letterman's jackets – walked the full length of the gymnasium floor to get to the risers at the other end of the building, where their teammates and coaches, except for Coach Dixon, sat. The crowd applauded when the cheerleaders performed their last routine and moved to the sidelines.

When the music stopped, Principal Murray walked to the podium. He cleared his throat, and then spoke into the microphone. "And now, our acting head coach, Johnny Rice."

Most of the students booed, but there was some scattered applause as Coach Rice, a mountain of a man, at three hundred fifty pounds, walked to the podium and took the microphone into his beefy hand. The freckled faced coach had pallid white skin and a shock of red hair. The big man had been expecting some opposition to his appointment, therefore, large beads of sweat ran down his face, soaking his blue football jersey as he spoke.

"I know that we all feel a great sense of loss for Coach Dixon, and we wish him all the best," he said, wiping his brow with the sleeve of his jersey. "But we must move on."

"No!" a single voice rang out across the gymnasium.

Sonny James could take no more of this foolishness. All night long, he had wrestled with the decision, but finally decided that there was but one thing to do. He rushed toward the microphone, screaming as he came. "We want Coach Dixon back, and we want him *now*."

"Stop him!" Principal Murray said, looking over at the coaches.

The students booed and shouted taunts as Coach Rice and the other coaches tried to restrain Sonny.

"Get him off the stage," the principal yelled.

Bedlam ensued as the rest of Sonny's boys rose from their seats and joined in the fray. The rumbling stopped and the building went silent when Leon snatched the microphone from Coach Rice's hand and spoke into it. "If Sonny goes, we go, and that means for the game as well!"

The coaches reluctantly released him, and then Sonny took the microphone. "We won't play another down until Coach Dixon is reinstated!"

A hush fell over the crowd.

Sonny turned to his boys and the rest of the first string players. "Let's go, boys! Let the second string team play for the second string coach!"

The Fab-Five and most of the other first stringers left the stage, storming out of the building to the applause of the crowd, some of which followed them.

Madison was a dry county, which meant that no alcoholic beverages could be sold – legally, that is. After walking out of the pep rally, the boys piled into Sonny's royal blue Ford Explorer, and then headed for the liquor store. The County Line Package Store sat on the border of Marion County, thirty miles away.

There, they stocked up on beer and bourbon whisky, in which to drown their sorrow. They also bought an array of chips, dips, and other goodies, which rounded out the refreshments for their pity party.

After driving back to Simpson's Woods, Sonny turned the tape player up to maximum volume and opened the back gate of the Ford, converting the Explorer into an mini-nightclub. The boys settled in for an afternoon of skipping school, eating, drinking, and moaning and groaning about the loss of a coach and the death of a championship season.

Leon had some trepidation as to what they were about to do. He was in line for a scholarship to Georgia Tech and desperately wanted to play in Saturday's game. He was about to drink from a tall cup of Jack Daniels, but stopped and turned to Sonny. "Are you sure we're doing the right thing?"

"Look, man," Sonny said angrily, "don't you go freakin' out on me."

"Alright," he said, sounding like the loyal follower he was, "I just asked."

Leon lifted the plastic cup to his lips and chugged down the entire contents.

The party was on.

Up at Chandler High, it had been a tumultuous day. Principal Murray was being pressured from all quarters. By two o'clock, he had gotten so many threatening telephone calls from parents and other Blue Wave loyalists that he took the receiver off the hook for the rest of the day.

The more distressing calls were from school board members, demanding that he clear up the situation – immediately – or else. And then there were the anonymous calls threatening bodily harm if Coach Dixon was not reinstated.

Sonny James' actions had neither surprised nor concerned Ginny in the very least. She knew that it would be just like him to pull such a childish stunt. Nevertheless, she was surprised that in a strange way, she felt sorry for him. After all, he was human, and it is human nature to want to achieve your goals.

Further, she had to admit that Sonny was an outstanding athlete, and she had heard that Coach Dixon was just as good a coach. Ginny still pulled for Sonny James and the Blue Wave, although they didn't see eye-to-eye on the romance thing.

Mr. Robinson and the newspaper staff spent most of their time that day making flyers for a candlelight vigil that would be held in Simpson's Woods, the following Sunday night. Ginny left school early with a backpack full of flyers, which she would stuff into mailboxes on the way home and in other parts of the black community.

Sarah and Dewey were doing the same in their respective parts of town. She made several stops, placing flyers into the mailboxes of the houses along the way, and then Ginny slung her backpack over her shoulder and headed for her shortcut home.

When she reached the entrance to Simpson's Woods, Ginny slipped through the ever-open gate and followed the trail, deep into the forest. As soon as she reached the clearing, she heard the loud hip-hop music that blared from the back of Sonny's Ford. Ginny could see Sonny and the other boys, each with a beer bottle in hand, dancing crazily to the music. Sensing trouble, she pulled up short, and then tried to move across the clearing without being seen.

She had almost made it past the partying boys, who were so drunk that they seemed oblivious to any and everything. Suddenly Leon sprang from behind the foliage, blocking her path.

"Sonny, look who's here," the big drunken boy called out.

Ginny attempted to sidestep him, but one of the Abdullah twins blocked her path. Then Sonny came, and now they had her surrounded. They were all laughing and taunting her, especially Sonny. "Look at the half breed!" he said.

"We can have a real party, now!" said one of the Abdullah twins.

"Let's do her, man, all of us!" said the other.

Then the oddest thing happened. Further down the trail, two squirrels scampered up a tree. It was Ginny's favorite tree, where she had spent endless hours as a child daydreaming about things to come.

Back in the clearing, Sonny stepped forward. "Stand back," he said to the others. "I got this."

He taunted her as the two of them circled each other, Ginny looking for an opening to run.

"You little slut, you're all alike," he yelled in Ginny's face. "Like that tramp, Beth, she couldn't keep her legs closed. Now she done run Coach Dixon away."

He stopped and angrily shook his head. "I hope she's *dead!*"

Sonny James was losing it.

Down the trail at Ginny's tree, hornets now swirled around a nest high up in the treetop.

Back at the clearing, Ginny suddenly bolted past Sonny. She raced toward the path home, with Sonny and the boys in hot pursuit. When she felt her backpack slipping from her shoulder, Ginny snatched it off and ran with it in her hand. But as she approached the tree, Sonny took a running dive and clipped her heel with his outstretched hand, sending Ginny sprawling and her backpack flying. In a second, he had straddled her and was holding both hands above her head as he continued his tirade. "Who do you think you are?"

Ginny valiantly struggled with Sonny, but she was no match for the star athlete. She then tried to appeal to his sense of decency. "What's wrong with you, Sonny? This is not like you. Let me up, please," she cried. "Sonny, Stop!"

"What's up with you, hoe … you think you too good for me? You little half-white --! I ought to--"

By this time, the other boys had surrounded Sonny and Ginny and were shouting, "Do it. Do it. Do it..."

High above in the tree, a branch snapped as one of the squirrels scampered across.

The day of anger and alcohol had taken its toll on Sonny James. He seemed to be out of his mind and carried on like a wild man. Ginny screamed as he tore her blouse away from her body, exposing her bra.

"Sonny, please, don't," she whimpered and began to cry.

The other boys passed a bottle of Jack Daniels around the circle, each one taking a swig as they spurred Sonny on with their chant. "Do it! Do it! Do it..."

Back in the tree, the branch broke when the other squirrel scampered across, which set things in motion. The falling branch knocked the hornet's nest loose from its mooring, and then the angry insects swirled and flew high into the air before diving – in formation – toward Sonny James. The forest reverberated with the sound of buzzing as the hornets honed in on the boy, now looking up in horror.

"Aw," he screamed as the first one hit his neck. He released Ginny to slap at the insect with his hand, but another hornet struck the side of his face, then another, and then still another. Soon they were all over the screaming boy.

"Help, help! Get these bees off me!"

Sonny rose to his feet and swatted helplessly at the hornets, which were now also attacking the rest of the boys. They all screamed like frightened children on Halloween night as they flailed helplessly at the hornets and ran to the Ford. Once they had all piled in and he had the engine going, Sonny slammed his foot down on the accelerator, and the Explorer reared up high into the air before its spinning wheels dug deep ruts into the earth as it roared out of the forest.

Ginny cried and cried as she attempted to pull the torn blouse back over her exposed upper body. Sensing that it was useless, she crawled over to her backpack and pulled out her physical education T-shirt. As she pulled it over her head, Ginny looked up just in time to see her.

The girl waved and smiled at Ginny, and then disappeared into Witches' Hollow. Although she didn't know how, Ginny knew deep inside that it was *the girl* who had saved her, and that she would never have to fear her again.

It was her day off and Miriam Westbrook had a date with Aretha, her beautician. After leaving a Yankee pot roast slow cooking in the crock-pot, she drove down to the New Look Beauty Parlor, which was located in the Ashley Street Shopping Plaza. This was the home of the foul-smelling scalp-burning chemical hair straightners and the sizzling-hot ear-searing curling irons.

There, Miriam spent the better part of the day catching up with the local gossip, adding a few tasty tidbits of her own to the mix, and getting her frizzy hair fried into greasy locks. She spent the rest of the afternoon grocery shopping.

Miriam arrived home around five o'clock, carrying two bags of groceries. She placed the sacks down on the table. And then, noticing that Ginny had not finished dinner, she looked around the kitchen and called out to her. "Ginny, where are you?" Getting no response, she walked into the living room. "Ginny?"

Hearing the clothes dryer going, Miriam just knew that Ginny was in the washroom. But when she opened the door, there was nothing. "Ginny, where are you?" she called out again. Still getting no response, Miriam walked upstairs to Ginny's bedroom. She tried the door, but it was locked. She knocked lightly. "Ginny?"

She waited, but there was still no response. Miriam shrugged, and then turned to leave. *Growing pains*, she said to herself as she went back to the kitchen to finish dinner.

Ginny, who had been crying since she locked herself in her room, was lying in a fetal curl on her bed. The telephone rang and rang until she slowly picked up the receiver and placed it to her ear. "Hello," she whispered.

Ginny was overcome with emotion when she heard the familiar voice on the other end of the line. "Oh, Dewey," she said, and then broke down and cried uncontrollably.

Later that night, Roy Mills, one of the black coaches accompanied Coach Rice over to the Rib Shack Soul Food Café, where they both downed substantial helpings of fried chicken, candied yams, and collard greens before convincing Sonny and his dad that he should play the next day. Finally, they reached an agreement whereby he and the other boys would play, but Sonny would call his own plays.

Essentially, Sonny and Coach Mills would run the offense, leaving the defensive effort up to Coach Rice and the other assistants.

That Saturday, the Fab-Five had traveled with the team over to Barnesville, Georgia – bee stings and all – and beat the tar out of the Titans, 40 to 0. On this day, it also became known that Roy Mills, not Willie Dixon had been the brains behind the operation. Some said that the precision, with which the Big Blue Wave's offense dissected the Titan's defense, had never been witnessed before.

But it was upon the team's arrival from their victorious mission that the firestorm hit. Charlie and Miriam Westbrook were waiting at the Rib Shack for Sonny and his daddy, Bob, to get there. Unbeknownst to Miriam, Charlie had his pistol in his hip pocket. Ginny had cried all that Friday night and well into Saturday morning before Charlie finally coaxed the truth from her.

When the team bus pulled up and let them off, Charlie and Bob had a violent confrontation, almost coming to blows. A cook was about to call the police when Miriam and Sonny's mother, Sylvia, brokered an uneasy truce between all parties concerned. There was agreement that there would be no recrimination of Sonny, but he would apologize to Ginny, and after that, he wouldn't come near her again, ever.

After the Simpson's Woods fiasco, Ginny was under strict orders never to go there again. Moreover, until the following Saturday, when they would go up to Atlanta and pick up the new car, Miriam had made arrangements on her job, which would allow her to drop Ginny off at school in the morning and pick her up in the afternoon. Additionally, Charlie bought three pagers, one each, for emergencies.

Chapter 13

A group of students milled around the entrance to the building, but quickly scattered, clearing a path for Sonny James and the rest of the Fab-Five – all with swollen faces – as they strode down the sidewalk. Suddenly a leg extended onto the walkway, tripping Sonny.

"What the hell," Sonny yelped as he lay sprawled on the sidewalk. Then he looked up into the grimaced face of Dewey Colton.

"Let's see how you do with somebody your own size," Dewey screamed angrily down at him.

"You're dead!" Sonny said, pointing at Dewey while scrambling to his feet. Then, with his head down, he charged like a bull that had just seen red, but Dewey deftly sidestepped him. Then Sonny took a wild swing, which Dewey also ducked.

Now Sonny's gang gathered around the two boys as they circled each other, each one seeking an advantage. The gang, sure of a mismatch between Sonny and the highbrow brainy boy, started to chant. "Go! Go! Kill 'im! Kill 'im…"

The other students quickly gathered around, creating a carnival-like atmosphere. Once more, Sonny charged Dewey, who sidestepped him again. This time Dewey landed a judo chop behind Sonny's ear, sending him sprawling to the pavement again.

Sonny, rising to his knees, looked up at his boys. "Don't just stand there! Help me!"

As Leon, Luther, and the Abdullah twins moved toward Dewey, Joe Meriwether and the second string players pushed their way through the crowd, all carrying baseball bats "I don't think so," Joe said.

Joe and the second teamers stood arm-to-arm, forming an impenetrable human-arena. Big Corley, a three hundred pound black boy, who played on the second string offensive line, stood nose-to-nose with Leon. "Let's jes' keep it fair," he said, crossing his massive arms with his baseball bat extended high.

Now Dewey was taking the offensive with several swift kicks to the midsection and chops to the head. As Sonny slumped to the ground, a voice rang out. "You guys, break it up!"

"It's the assistant principal," a student yelled.

Within seconds, the crowd had scattered like leaves in a fall wind.

Students in the Advanced Placement literature class responded as Mr. Robinson called the roll.

"Benson?"

"Here."

"Bostic?"

"Present."

Just then, Dewey walked through the door and handed Mr. Robinson a note. Taking the note in hand, Mr. Robinson looked up at Dewey. "Well, you look none the worse for your morning's activities."

Dewey smiled and the class chuckled.

"Yeah," Dewey said, "but you should see the other guy."

The students rolled in the aisles with laughter.

"Well," Mr. Robinson said, looking closer at the note, "it looks like you don't have anything that detention for the rest of the semester won't cure."

The students groaned.

Dewey slipped into the seat behind Ginny as Mr. Robinson continued with the roll.

"Carter?"

"Present."

Ginny turned to Dewey. "Oh, Dewey, I'm so sorry," she whispered. "I shouldn't have told you."

"Don't worry. It was worth it … trust me. I'll enjoy every minute of detention."

Ginny smiled and squeezed Dewey's hand.

Jerry Jones, the class clown, rose from his seat and pantomimed a kiss. "Oooh, my prince," he said facetiously. "My knight in shining armor."

The students roared with laughter, now with Mr. Robinson joining in.

"Tap, tap, tap, tap," a yellow number-two pencil beat a steady rhythm on the table top.

"Must you do that?" Lou asked.

"Do what?" the man said.

"That pencil thing. You're driving me nuts."

Emory Shepherd was serving his second term as the Madison County Attorney, and was up for re-election next fall. Chief Callahan, Brian Pollard, Lou, and Lola sat across from the little round man, in his early fifties, as he nervously drummed a pencil on the table while silently scanning a stack of papers.

Looking up at Lou, Emory dropped the pencil, and then addressed the group. "Okay, folks, we wanna talk about the pros and cons of indictin' Willie Dixon," he said in a deep southern accent, "and if so, what for?"

Emory was noticeably shorter than the average man, barely standing five feet tall, if that. In a futile attempt to overcome his Napoleonic complex, he wore shoes that were slightly elevated and spoke in an artificially deep booming voice. He was also a nervous man who attempted to structure every activity of his daily life down to the minutest detail. In doing so, Emory had developed a nervous habit of drumming a pencil on the desk or table as he formulated each plan, turning it over repeatedly in his mind.

Lou spoke first. "Well, he admitted to having an affair with the girl."

"But she was eighteen," Lola countered. "His having an affair with Beth might be a fire-able offense, but it is *not* a crime."

"Well, maybe it should be for some folks!" the county attorney said. He then leaned forward on his elbows and spoke directly to Brian. "What about the blood spatter found on the kitchen floor?"

The lanky young man, in his mid-twenties, pushed his black-plastic thick-lens eyeglasses back on his nose with his finger and cleared his throat before he spoke. "The State Crime Lab results prove conclusively that the blood found on Mr. Dixon's kitchen floor *was* the same type as that of Beth Campbell."

"Good," Emory said.

"Not so fast," Brian came back. "There *is* something that troubles me."

"What is it?" Chief Callahan asked.

This was Brian Pollard's first real case. Like Lola, he had ridden into the department on the Chief's latest grant. Additionally, like Lou and Lola, he had not worked a real investigative case other than helping to identify the crystal-meth in the big drug bust. Usually his days were spent mainly shuffling papers, getting coffee for those above him, and surfing the Internet.

They all knew that the Madison County Police Department was just a stepping-stone for the tousle haired boy-man who lived in a boarding house during the week and drove home to his mama's house in Macon on the weekends. Brian knew that, because of his age and inexperience, he did not have the respect of those in the department, therefore, he chose his words carefully. "It's not that blood was or was not found since Mr. Dixon has acknowledged the girl's presence at his home on numerous occasions."

"Go ahead," Emory impatiently urged him on. "What's your point?"

"Mr. Dixon alleges that Beth cut her hand on a broken glass, and the place where blood was found corresponds to the location he pointed out, the kitchen floor near the cabinets."

"So?" asked Chief Callahan, now becoming impatient himself.

"It's not where the blood was, but where it wasn't," Brain offered in a technical sounding voice. "There was no castoff."

Lola's eyes widened. "That's right," she said, remembering a lecture she and Lou had recently attended while at the State Crime-fighters Convention over in Augusta. "If he killed her with a knife, blood would be not only on the floor, where it would pool under her body, but also specks would be cast off on the walls and maybe even the ceiling." She motioned up and down with her hand, now holding a phantom knife.

"Exactly," Brian corroborated. "Every time the knife was drawn back, a spray of blood would be strewn."

"You know, his explanation just might be plausible," Lola said. "Once I had to go to the emergency room when I cut my hand reaching down to pick up a broken glass."

"Come on," Emory said, "you've got to be kidding."

"No, really," she went on. "The glass had a sharp edge sticking up. I misjudged the distance from the floor, causing my finger to strike it too hard. It was a bloody mess."

"We have the girl's blood type all over the place," Lou said. "And I know he admits she was there. But what about the two other girls who admitted to having affairs with him at his last job site?"

"That proves he's a creep, not a murderer," Lola said.

"You're right, Lola," Chief Callahan added. "All of this evidence is going to get him good and fired, but where is the corpus delicti? Without a body…" His voice trailed off as he shrugged and threw up his hands.

Lola rose from her seat and turned toward the table that held the coffee pot. "You're right, Chief. It's back to the drawing board."

"Not so fast," Emory Shepherd said. "Sit back down."

Lola returned to her seat, and Emory leaned forward. "Have any of you heard of the Mark Crew case?"

Everyone sitting at the table, except Brian, looked at each other blankly.

"It happened last year in Santa Clara, California," Brian said methodically. "Mark Crew was convicted of killing his girl friend, Carrie Johnson, although her body was never found."

Emory Shepherd was jubilant. "Chief, I don't know where you got him from, but he's a smart boy."

"But this case is entirely different," Brian continued.

"How so?" Emory asked roughly.

"Crew had a track record of abusing Carrie. Once, when he caught her with another man, he beat her badly and was arrested for it. Plus, Carrie was last seen in Crew's car."

"So what's that got to do with the price of tea in China?" Emory said.

"So he had a motive. I've got to warn you," the young criminologist said, in his firmest tone of voice, "if you don't have a body, the motive had better be overwhelming."

Emory could take no more. He sprang to his feet and pounded the table with his fist. "Well I don't know about all 'a the details," he said angrily. "Then again, it ain't for me to know, it's for a jury to find out. All I know is that we got this joker dead to right, and I ain't lettin' him go!" Emory was pacing the floor now. "And another thing, if I find out that he blackmailed that girl into havin' sex with him, I'm gonna string his black butt up."

Lola gasped so hard that the breath almost left her body. Her eyes narrowed and her brow furrowed as she stared at the chubby little man with incredulity.

"Oh, ah, I'm sorry, Lola," Emory stuttered apologetically.

"You mean you didn't mean to say it in front of me!" she fired back. The county attorney's puffy white face was now crimson red, and they were both on their feet.

"People, let's settle down," Chief Callahan pleaded.

"I can't settle down," Emory went on. "This town is in a frenzy and if we don't do something, they'll never let us forget it."

"Yeah, we've got to do something," Lou added.

With a puzzled look, Lola gazed around the table from face to face. "I am *not* hearing this conversation," she said, standing toe-to-toe with Emory Shepherd. "And you guys wonder why black people have no faith in the system!"

"This is not about race," Emory shot back. "It's about survival! I bring a big case like this and don't convict, I'm a goner. On the other hand, if I sit by and do nothing, it's the same thing. Unlike you people, *I* have to face the voters."

"So what are you gonna do?" Chief Callahan asked.

"The only thing that I can do," Emory said firmly.

"And what, may I ask, is that?" Lola said sarcastically.

"Put it into the hands of the people. I'm sending this case to the *grand jury*," Emory said.

He picked up his papers from the table, stuffed them into his already bulging brief case, and then strutted – like a little fat peacock – out of Chief Callahan's office.

It had been a full Sunday for Lola and her daughter. After church, her mother had made the usual soul food dinner for the three of them, and Lola, as usual, had eaten herself silly. Before coming over to the vigil, she and Janie went by the Timberlake Mall to do a little shopping and to walk off the double helping of Hattie's banana pudding.

By the time they left the shopping center, it was dark, and for the third time that week, the mysterious car lights appeared. Lola seldom felt angst, especially when she was not on duty, but for the past month, someone had been following her. This was the final straw. She intended to find out who was stalking her and why they were doing it, *right* here and *right* now. The car lights followed them until she pulled the Camry to the curb in front of the entrance to Simpson's Woods. Then Lola peered at the line of cars that pulled past, but recognized none of the drivers.

It was a cool star-filled night and the hundred or so lit candles, carried by the participants who stood in the clearing around the statue of Colonel Simpson, seemed to be no more than a reflection of the sky. On this night, however, the somber reality of the occasion seemed to contradict the peaceful ambiance of the heavens.

Although United Methodist where Lizzy Campbell was a member, was sponsoring the candle light vigil, the service was actually an interfaith venture among several churches. Reverend Jennings of Antioch Baptist was the first speaker. In the flickering candle light, the tall black man could only be discerned by the triangle formed by the whites of his eyes and the tiny bit of white clerical collar that showed at his neck. His voice crackled from the speakers that hung high above the crowd on tall stands.

"Dear, Lord," he began, "we are assembled here tonight … to humbly beg your assistance in helping to find our lost sister…"

As the preacher invoked both the presence and participation of the divine one, Lola and Janie stood near the back of the crowd, each with candle in hand.

"Come on Janie, let's move to the other side," Lola said softly.

"Why, Lola?" the girl asked in like tone of voice. "I can see alright from here."

"Because I said so, young lady," Lola said, now in an irritated tone of voice. She was not angry at her daughter's reluctance to move, but her flat-out refusal to call her mother or mom. "Let's go."

It was obvious that Janie might have forgiven Lola for running off to New York and leaving her with Grandma Hattie, but she had not *forgotten*, and was not about to let Lola forget either. As the two of them made their way through the crowd, Lola could still sense the presence of the eyes behind them, which had been staring at her since their arrival.

Later, Lola sensed that the eyes had followed her and Janie to their new position on the other side of the statue, and were still glued to her back. As Reverend Clark, the pastor of the United Methodist Church, ended the service, Lola turned abruptly, staring into the sternly rigid face of Mitchell Bradley.

That Monday night, the monthly meeting of the Madison County Heritage Society was held at the Meriwether Mansion – home of Abigail Meriwether, the ninety-year-old matriarch of the Meriwether family and the Wrightsburg community. Carlisle Chester, the president, had drawn the business meeting to its conclusion and was about to reconvene the assemblage in the main parlor for finger sandwiches and punch when a red-faced Mitch Bradley rose from his seat. "Wait a minute, we can't leave yet. We've got more pressing business."

"What?" Carlisle asked.

"We've got to take our state back," he yelled, his face growing redder by the second. "We just stood idly by while those nigger lovers up in Atlanta took it away."

"Amen," a portly woman in the back of the room added. "Now you're talking."

"I've told you, we're not going there tonight, Mitch," Carlisle countered. "That's not what this organization is about."

"That's right," said a man sitting near the podium. "We are here to restore the historical sites of Madison County. This is *not* a hate group!"

"Well maybe it should be," added the woman in the back of the room. She was on her feet now. "They've taken our schools and our neighborhoods."

"That's right," another man said.

This man bore a strong resemblance to Colonel Sanders, of Kentucky Fried Chicken fame. All that was missing was the white suit. He had stark white hair, a handlebar mustache, and a Van Dyke beard. "Our forefathers must be turning over in their graves," he said emphatically.

Then Mitch Bradley stood and faced the rest of the twenty-or-so men and women, pacing slowly as he launched into his tirade. "This whole idea of multiculturalism, which has been promoted by the government and the media, has destroyed the racial basis of civilized society. Everyone involved in it loses. We all lose our biological heritage and it has caused the moral deterioration of our way of life."

"We're not trying to say that we don't agree with you," Carlisle said pleadingly. "That's just not the function of *this* organization."

"Function of this organization?" Mitch exclaimed facetiously, "This organization has no function!"

"Tell 'em, Mitch," the portly matron said.

"When we were running things, this society was about something," Mitch said.

"When you were running things, this was no society," Carlisle countered angrily. "It was the Ku Klux Klan!"

Mitch was now seething with anger. He turned and shook his finger in the air in the direction of those assembled. "You are no more than antique collectors of worthless junk and paraphernalia. To hell with you all," Mitch yelled, and then turned and angrily stomped out of the room.

The following Wednesday, the first edition of the *Chandler High Chronicle* hit the stands and the newspapers were distributed to the student body during lunch. However, it had taken until Friday for the mail man to deliver Ty Jr.'s personalized copy from Ginny. He beamed as he read the handwritten message under the headline, "Chandler Family Gives Back to Community."

It was a personal note from Ginny, thanking him for his help with the article. The piece was well written and showed the Chandler family and businesses in the most positive light. Its prose was far beyond that expected from a high school student.

I like her. She's a smart girl. Ty Jr. mused. *I could use someone like her ... here in the office.*

Ty Jr. made a mental note to call Ginny regarding a summer internship, but then his eyes drifted down the page to the other article, also under Ginny's by-line, "Missing Girl Could be One Among Many." He quickly scanned the article, shuddered, and then turned away. Standing there in a daze, Ty Jr. was seemingly looking out the gigantic picture window, but he was really looking deep into the portal of his very soul as memories of his sister came flooding back over the years.

After the morning roll call, where he handed out the day's assignments, Chief Callahan met with Lou and Lola for an update of the Beth Campbell case.

"Did either of you see this?" the chief asked, shoving a copy of the *Chandler High Chronicle*, which was folded to show Ginny's article on the missing girls, across his desk toward them.

"No," Lou said, picking up the newspaper. "Let me see."

"I saw it," Lola said. "My daughter brought one home, but I didn't think anything of it."

"Maybe you should check it out," the chief said. "I remember one of those girls."

Then the telephone rang.

"Callahan," the chief announced after placing the receiver to his ear.

When he heard a familiar voice from the past, Russ Callahan cradled the telephone between his neck and shoulder, reared back in his seat, and smiled broadly. "Tommy, how's the boy?"

Then the two old friends made small talk for more than a short while as Lou and Lola sat impatiently.

"Good," the chief said, finally, before flashing one last beaming smile. "Thanks … and Tommy, give the wife my regards."

The chief hung up the telephone and leaned across his desk. "That's my boy with the bureau, Tommy Brunson. He's sending us a fax."

"What's it about?" Lou asked.

"He didn't say," the chief said with a shrug. "He just said it would probably be something we would be interested in."

Russ Callahan had been an honor student at the University of Georgia's School of Criminal Justice. One of his strong suites was writing term papers. Therefore, near the end of each semester, he always had a line of classmates outside the door to his dormitory room seeking help. Now, Chief Callahan was calling in some of those favors

Shortly, Carolyn Chestnut, the chief's secretary, came into the room and handed him a fax.

"Thanks, Carolyn," he said, taking the sheet of paper from her outstretched hand. He took a quick glance at the fax, and then placed it down on the table in front of Lou and Lola.

"Well, how do you like that?" Lou said, looking down at the facsimile of the front and back of a company check that was drawn on the account of Frazier and Associates. It was made out to Elizabeth Campbell, and her signature was affixed to the back of the check.

Evidently the relationship between Hadley Frazier and Dell, the stripper, was still going strong. When Lou and Lola arrived at the condominium in Midtown Atlanta, the stunning redhead was backing out of the driveway in a gleaming white Cadillac convertible that was every bit as eye-catching as she was – even at eight o'clock in the morning. When Dell recognized the two of them, she gave them "the finger," uttered a profanity, and then quickly sped away.

Hadley, who had walked Dell to the door, ventured onto the porch to retrieve his morning paper. He had turned to go back into the house when he spotted Lou and Lola walking up the curving sidewalk. "I have nothing to say to you two," he yelled out as he stood with newspaper in hand.

"Chill out, man," Lou said. "We'll only take a minute of your time."

"You have my lawyer's number. Why don't you use it? Let him earn some of that ton of money I'm paying him."

"Just take a look at this," Lola said, holding out the faxed sheet.

"What's with you people? Why don't you go away? I've got problems of my own."

And indeed Hadley Frazier did have problems, big ones, but some were not unsolvable. His bond had been set at an outrageous one million dollars, an amount tough to raise for most people, but no big deal for Hadley. It had not been easy, but by liquidating most of his foreign accounts, he had posted bail and even paid back some of his investors. They were so glad to see any of their money – although pennies on the dollar – that some had actually dropped the charges against their former financial consultant.

After seeing the copy of his company's check, Hadley looked up and said, "Y'all come on in."

As they walked through the sprawling townhouse, Lola asked, "Do you mind if we tape this interview, for the record?"

"Naw, go ahead," Hadley said, pulling up a stool to the kitchen bar and waving Lou and Lola to seats across from him. He was nursing a huge mug of steaming coffee. "You want a cup?" he asked.

"No, we've had ours for the morning," Lola said as she placed the tape recorder on the bar. After speaking into the microphone to give the pertinent information regarding the interview, Lola nodded, and then Lou popped the question.

"What was the purpose of this check, and when and where was it written?"

Hadley took a sip of coffee, and then exhaled deeply. "Back during the summer, Beth called my office and said she wanted to see me. Well, I think you already know I was attracted to her, and … it's happened before."

"What?" Lou prodded him. "What's happened before?"

"The girls, you know … some of 'em play hard to get, but that's just their ploy. Anyway, I won't lie. I drove down to Wrightsburg, hoping to get together with her. You know what I mean."

"Yes," Lola said contemptuously, "go on."

Hadley Frazier was trying both Lou and Lola's patience.

"I picked her up from the trailer park and we drove across the county line to a café, the Blue Bird, I believe was the name of it."

"Yeah," Lou said, "it ain't much for atmosphere, but the food is filling."

"Well, after dinner, she said she needed my help, and I told her to name it," Hadley continued with a shrug. "Said she needed money to get away from Wrightsburg. Some old dude, she was fooling around with, was hassling her. It was the schoolteacher, I guess. Anyway, Beth wanted to break it off, but he didn't. He even threatened her. Boy, was he ever stuck on her? But … we all were."

Lola shook her head. This was not what she came to Atlanta expecting to hear.

Hadley took another long sip of coffee, and then went on. "Beth wanted to borrow five thousand dollars to buy a car. She was going to drive to California to get into the movie business. She could've made it … I mean, she still can … if that's where she is. Well anyway, five grand might seem like a lot of money to some folks, but it was just chump change to me. But at the time, I didn't have that much cash on me," he shrugged again, "so I wrote her a check."

Hadley leaned into the back of his plush leather stool as the two detectives stared him down.

"And," Lola said, "what happened?"

"Nothing happened. We kissed and all that, but didn't have sex. Beth was supposed to pick up a used car, and then just drop out of sight. That weekend, she was to come up to Atlanta so we could spend some time together before she left. But she never made it. I thought she had just taken me for the cash, but I wasn't that concerned … if you know what I mean."

"Yeah," Lou said facetiously, "it all comes out in the wash, doesn't it. You could say you're like a modern day Robin Hood. You steal from the rich to--"

"That's it, man!" Hadley said angrily, climbing down from his stool while motioning toward the exit. "Unless you've got a warrant stuck up your butt, this interview is over!"

Lola flipped the switch, and then the red light on the tape recorder went dark. The trip she had thought might clear Coach Dixon would probably serve as the last nail in his coffin.

As Lou and Lola walked down the sidewalk, Hadley mentally disrobed the Nubian princess – as he had named her in his earlier fantasies. Maybe he would make another trip to Wrightsburg ... real soon. He had certainly made more than the one, of which he had just spoken.

As Lola's hand reached out to open the car door, Hadley Frazier wondered what her silky black body would look like when splayed across his bed with its red silk sheets, and what would his sterling silver handcuffs look like when they were secured tightly around her dark slender wrists.

In the living room, a large TV screen showed two lawyers facing each other as they sat behind the news desk.

"Down in Wrightsburg," the female lawyer said, "the Beth Campbell grand jury has been in session for over a week. But as you know, the proceedings are closed."

"That's right, Marion," her male counterpart acknowledged. "We don't know what physical evidence has been presented, but we do know that Coach Dixon *has* testified."

"Yes," the woman said, "but some would say that an indictment without a body would certainly be a long shot. Does the prosecution have a chance?"

"Not a ghost of a chance," the man said.

"I believe you're right, Chuck," she said. "It'll be the classic case of show me the body or it's going to be sayonara for the prosecutor."

He looked up from his seat on the sofa, but neither spoke nor moved as the two onscreen lawyers babbled on about the legal mumbo-jumbo surrounding a murder case without a body. A copy of the *Chandler High Chronicle* lay on the coffee table. Ginny's article about the string of missing girls was circled in red.

Some people were born to cure the ills of the world, and he was surely one of these. For a while now, he had known that his mission on God's green earth was to be one of those chosen to right the wrongs of the world. All it had taken was that one incident, long ago. It served as a sign of what he had to do, and why it had to be done. His, was a heavy burden.

As with anything else, the first time was the most difficult. Not that any of these horrid affairs was easy on the stomach, but over time, the work had become more palatable. And as it was with a parent disciplining their insolent child, it hurt him just as much as it did them. He did not asked for the job. It had been thrust upon him.

But now that he had taken on the mantle, he would continue to do his best to answer the call, whenever it came. *Men had their weaknesses,* he thought, *but it was the daughters of Lillith, the mother of she-demons, the ones who gave birth to Satan and his horde that were the worst offenders.* Therefore, the she-devils – the purveyors of sex and sin – had to be punished. He had recently heard the call, and it would soon be time to answer again, for he was the **Angel of Death**.

Chapter 14

L ou hung up the telephone and turned to Lola, sitting at the desk across from his. "Get your hat," he said. "We've just got a break."

"I don't wear hats," she said while springing to her feet and matching Lou stride for stride down the hall to pick up Brian Pollard. Then they all piled into Lou's car and headed for Simpson's Woods.

Lou had driven the unmarked car as deep into the forest as he could, but then they had to travel on foot to the heart of Witches' Hollow. An hour after they found the location, revealed by an anonymous telephone call to 911, the body had been exhumed. A bright yellow tape cordoned off a section of the forest and uniformed officers guarded the perimeter from a few onlookers who had followed the exodus of police cars from town.

Emory Shepherd, Chief Callahan, Lou, and Lola, all looked on as Milton Hicks, the county coroner, forced the eyelids shut on Beth Campbell's anguish filled face. Her once rosy cheeks had turned a dull ashen gray, as had the rest of her naked body.

A face that was stunningly beautiful – while she lived – was now a shockingly grotesque caricature in death, left frozen in fear with empty dead eyes and mouth agape. The coroner was about to force her mouth shut when Brian Pollard called out to him. "Not yet, I need a sample of the contents from in there."

"Oh, alright," Milton said tersely, looking up scornfully at Brian. "You make it snappy, you hear. The last thing in the world I need is some amateur under my foot."

This was the first time that the two of them had worked together. The idea of a crime scene investigator was a relatively new phenomenon, so Brian's instructors had prepared him and his classmates well for just such confrontations – with detectives, medical examiners, and coroners.

The CSI is a support person for the investigator in charge, which in this case was Lou Brazell. His main job was to document, identify, and collect physical evidence at a crime scene. While most of the investigator's job was away from the body, he or she also had to attend autopsies and assist the pathologist with physical evidence from it. This was where most problems occurred.

The CSIs were usually younger people in a new profession that overlapped other people's duties to the extent that they seemed to step on the toes of both, men of medicine and crime fighters alike. Sometimes, neither group wanted younger eyes looking over their older more experienced shoulders.

"I'm sorry," Brian said. "It'll only take a minute."

He slipped his hands into plastic gloves and removed soil samples from the dead girl's open mouth with a small plastic spoon. True to his word, it had only taken the CSI a minute, and in another second, he was back to his original point of inquiry – tiny white particles that seemed to cover the girl's entire body.

The coroner knelt back to his work, examining the body in great detail. It had just begun to decompose.

"Talk to me, Doc," Emory Shepherd said as he approached. "Tell me something."

"You know it's too soon for that," the coroner said, without looking up.

"You've got to tell me something," Emory said, anxiously. "I've got to get a warrant."

Milton Hicks was a tall spindly man with gaunt features. Only wisps of white hair remained on his long pointy head, reflecting his seventy odd years of living, forty of which had been spent either at the Mortuary, which had been in the Hick's family for over a hundred years, or in the coroner's office, sometimes both.

Milton turned to look up at the son of his oldest and dearest friend. "He might not be your man, Sonny," he said, calling Emory by his much hated childhood nickname. "The body has no cuts, no bruises, not even a broken fingernail. And there *is* an old wound on her hand that's consistent with the coach's broken glass story."

Lou became agitated. "That doesn't mean a thing! He might've strangled her."

The coroner shook his head. "Nope. No bruises or ligature marks on her neck. But there *were* indentations where handcuffs were used to restrain her wrists and her right leg had deep cuts from some kind of leg iron or shackle."

"What?" the chief exclaimed.

"That's right, the bastard had her tethered like a dog," the coroner said disgustedly.

"Did you see the anguish on her face? He might have poisoned her," Lola said.

"Could be. That's the first thing I'll be looking for."

"That's good enough for me," Emory said, turning to Lou before leaving. "I'm headed to Judge Iverson. I'll call you when I get some paper."

"Don't worry, we'll be ready," Lou said reassuringly.

True to the details of the phone call, a team of officers had to use weed-eaters to hack through the tall grass and underbrush for almost a quarter-of-a-mile before they came upon a partial clearing where odd-looking statues still stood, and rock formations were deeply embedded into the ground.

Earlier, teams searching for the missing girl *had* ventured into the much dreaded Witches' Hollow, but not nearly this far in – whether out of trepidation or inconvenience. Beth's shallow grave had recently been dug beside a fallen statue of a ram's head with a man's body. Nearby, there was another toppled statue with the opposite orientation, a man's torso sat atop an animal's body.

"Let's hurry up and get out of here," Lola said, wrapping her arms tightly around her body. "This place gives me the heebie-jeebies."

"Me, too," Brian said. "Do you think there's any truth to the rumors?"

"About what?" the chief asked.

"Blood sacrifices," Brian said.

"Come on," Lou said, "get real."

"Yes, please do," the chief said.

Somewhere in the middle of the crime scene investigation, Mitch Bradley showed up with his trusty camera. A chill ran down Lola's spine when she saw him. After taking several shots, he ambled over to Chief Callahan. "You wanna fill me in, or do I have to make up my own story."

The chief pulled him out of earshot of the crowd of onlookers, which was getting larger by the minute. Like wild growing Kudzu, Emory Shepherd had eagerly spread word of the body's discovery around town when he went back in to get the warrant.

After the body had been bagged, tagged, and cleared for removal, Mitch Bradley took a picture of it being carted out by two ambulance attendants. In his mind's eye, he was already having visions of *it* as a lead-in photo on the Atlanta television's evening news. Mitch reveled in the knowledge that he would make the stations pay through their collective noses for his pictures.

One station would pay dearly for an exclusive, and could have them all, or he would peddle smaller groups of pictures to all three, on a sliding scale of prices. The highest bidder would get their pick for the six o'clock news, the next highest could pick over what was left for an eleven o'clock showing, but the low man on the totem pole would have to wait until the next day to run whatever pictures where left. That's how things were done in this business.

As soon as he developed the pictures, he would high tail it up to the city. This would be the first time that Mitch Bradley had scooped the Atlanta media since the Armanda Lockett and Anna Jennings stories.

After the others had left, Chief Callahan kept the investigative team at the crime site for debriefing. "Well, what's your take on things, Brian?" the chief asked. "Do you think it was poison?"

"No," Brian said without thinking.

"Why not?" Lou asked gruffly, hoping against hope that they could tie Coach Dixon to the murder, let him get on with his life, and buy himself some furniture.

Not wanting to say anything stupid that would reduce his newly gained status, Brian hesitated before he spoke.

"I can't say right now. I'll send some tissue samples up to the state lab, but something's not right about this case," he said. Not that he had any real cases for comparison, but the scholarly young man had read a million case-studies.

"What?" Lola asked.

"I can't put my finger on it right now," Brian said. "Check with me later."

As they all walked back to their cars, Brian reiterated the few conclusions, upon which he and the coroner had both agreed. The deep gashes around her wrists and ankles and the lack of decomposition indicated that Beth had been held captive before her murder. The State Crime Lab would help delineate the timeline from abduction until death. Additionally, although the body was nude, there were no abrasions or contusions in the pubic region.

In fact, there had been no outward sign of sexual activity at all, and once again, the lab would be more conclusive. And finally, although there were no markings on Beth's neck, there was still the possibility that asphyxiation could be the cause of death.

"What's up with the white stuff?" Lou asked as they trudged through the woods.

"I think I know what it is, but I have to check with an expert."

"The crime lab?" Lola asked.

"No, the hardware store," Brian said before getting into Chief Callahan's car.

Lou shook his head as he started the engine and looked over at Lola. "Modern crime fighting techniques, it's for the birds."

Lola smiled half-heartedly and sat back in her seat, her mind awhirl. "Lou?" she said.

"What?" he asked, taking his eyes off the road and looking over at her. Even in the short time that he had known her, Lou could always tell when something was bothering Lola, and this was one of those times.

"Nothing," she said.

Lola wanted badly to tell Lou about the man who was stalking her and the possibility that it might be the newspaper publisher, but thought better of it. If she told him, would he perceive her as being weak or afraid? This was always a concern for female law officers.

And what about Willie Dixon? Lola still had not reconciled herself to the fact that her former lover might be a murderer. Although they had attended high school together, stolen glances at each other, and exchanged small talk, the difference in their ages wouldn't allow the two of them to date. Willie was a senior and the star of every athletic team, but she was just a child in the eighth grade. But they had stumbled upon each other up in New York.

Willie was in town with the Detroit Lions, who were there to play the Jets. He had seen Lola's picture on the side of a bus. It was her famous Calvin Klein's jean ad, the one that some said made her have "the world's most famous behind." Thanks to that one advertisement, Lola's beautiful butt was shown off on all five continents.

Willie went to every modeling agency in the city until he stumbled upon Ford's. After slipping a secretary a five hundred dollar bribe, she gave up Lola's address, and within the hour, the handsome black Adonis of a wide receiver was standing at her apartment door. For a while, they carried on a long-distance love affair, which came at a really good time for her, but a horrendously bad time for him.

She would meet Willie in whichever city the Lions were playing and, after the game, they would go out on the town for a show and an extravagant meal, talk about their days in Wrightsburg, and then make love until the morning sun washed over the elegant suite that Willie would have taken for the weekend.

For Lola, Willie became the soothing balm that helped salve the wounds of a badly directed love affair. She tried, unsuccessfully, to help him cope with a phenomenon that all star athletes had to face eventually, the loss of a step or two and relegation to the bench.

That next year after a severe injury, things quickly went downhill for Willie Dixon and he was cut from the Lions. He tried to catch on with the Saint Louis Cardinals, but things were never the same. A man's body was simply not designed to crash into other bodies while running at top speed. It soon became a chore just for Willie to get out of bed each morning.

Then Willie stopped calling and Lola stopped waiting for his calls to come. They soon lost track of each other, and both were surprised that they ended up back where they had started out, Wrightsburg, Georgia.

Nevertheless, Lola owed Willie, big time, for helping her get over her misguided love affair, and for this she would repay him, but only by seeing to it that he got a fair shake from the law. If in the end, Willie Dixon had really killed Beth Campbell, she would take him down herself, hard.

Another thing Lola still had not gotten over was the nagging feeling she had when Brian mentioned the handcuff marks on Beth's wrists. Instantaneously, her mind flashed back to the pair of silver cuffs hanging from Hadley Frazier's headboard.

Lola never did believe everything he had said. After all, this man made a living out of telling lies. *But if Hadley killed her,* she thought, *why would he bring the body back to Madison County? To deflect attention away from himself,* she answered her own question. Maybe Lou was right about her inability to be objective in this matter. *Maybe Willie did do it.* Anyway, she hoped not.

Lou looked over at Lola, who had ridden speechless all the way back to the station. He wanted to ask what was bothering her, but he knew that if it were important, in time, she would tell him. *We all have our secrets,* he thought. Lou had not even told Lola that his wife had left him.

Chapter 15

Emory Shepherd was waiting at the station when the convoy of police cars pulled into the parking lot. "I've got it," he said, waving a folded sheet of paper high above his head. "Let's go!"

"Gimmie a minute to get organized," Chief Callahan said as he walked past the county attorney into the building. "Wait in my car. It'll only take a minute."

Emory sullenly got into the front seat of Chief Callahan's Chevy Caprice as the chief and the rest of the officers disappeared into the police station.

It took all of twenty minutes for the Wrightsburg Police Strike Force to return to their cars, but when they did, they were armed to the teeth and ready for battle. They were wearing black Kevlar helmets and bulletproof vests, all of which were courtesy of one of the chief's federal grants. One of the officers stowed a battering ram in the backseat of his car, and then they were off to the Spring Valley Apartment Complex.

The Valley – as it was called – was an upscale community for upwardly-mobile young professionals. There, lived young doctors, lawyers, and construction engineers who, like Brian Pollard, were in

Wrightsburg, Georgia, for one reason only – to get on-the-job experience, which would soon transport them to Atlanta, Chicago, or even New York City. And had it not been for the substantial retirement check that he received from the National Football League Pension Fund, the sizable monthly rent would have been far beyond Willie Dixon's means.

The townhouses looked identical, but were not joined at the hip as were all of the other apartments in Wrightsburg. Each unit had its own little piece of green grass around it with enough space for a barbecue grill and a couple of chairs for sunning and the like.

Emory Shepherd watched from the safety of the Caprice as Russ Callahan and the rest of the officers scampered from their cars and surrounded the townhouse. Some of the officers went to the back of the building while others covered the sides where there were downstairs windows. Two officers, carrying a battering ram, followed closely behind Lou, Lola, and Chief Callahan, all with weapons drawn, as they approached the front of the building.

The chief pounded on the door. "Coach Dixon, open up …. This is the police!"

There was no answer.

"Coach Dixon, come out with you hands up!" he said again. "We have a warrant for your arrest."

Still no answer.

The chief looked back and nodded to the officers with the battering ram.

"Wham!" the ram banged against the door, and it popped open like the top of a sardine can. Within seconds after entering the luxury apartment, it became abundantly clear that Willie Dixon had flown the coop.

Indeed, Emory Shepherd had spread the news. When word of the body discovery hit the ears of Mary Brewster, a waitress at Pappas' Drive-in and Willie Dixon's latest bed partner, she gave the coach a call. After throwing a few things into the back seat of his classic convertible, a 1966 Cadillac, Coach Dixon headed for Atlanta. He drove through the intersection of State Highway 216 and Willoughby Road about five minutes before the Georgia State Patrol received Chief Callahan's call to set up a roadblock. So far, he was one-step ahead of the posse.

The coach pulled the convertible into the general parking lot of Hartsfield Airport, grabbed his bags from the car, locked the doors, and then headed for the terminal. After taking a few steps, the coach turned and blew a kiss at the gold Cadillac that he had purchased for $20,000 and had used another 50-grand to restore to mint condition. Today's market value of the classic car was nearly $200,000. Before he reached the terminal, the coach unceremoniously dropped the gold plated car keys into a nearby garbage receptacle.

Willie Dixon had no idea where he was going. That would all come later. Soon he was standing under the Delta Airline departure board, scanning the destinations as he searched his memory for places, times, and *women*. Back in the day, when he was with the Lions and in town for a game, there would always be groupies awaiting the players as they checked into their hotel. And Willie Dixon, the former all-pro wide receiver, certainly had his share of one-night stands.

Today, however, he was searching his memory for one of those few relationships that had lingered longer to become a friendship, of sorts. Then the name "Mary Tilloston" popped into his mind. Having made a mental-match, he joined the other travelers in the long line at the ticket window. Later, when it was his turn, the smiling woman asked, "May I help you?"

Willie peeled off five hundred dollar bills from his wad and plopped them down on the counter before he spoke. "One way, to Green Bay, Wisconsin."

By noon the next day, Coach Willie Dixon was wanted for questioning in the death of Elizabeth Campbell, and the Madison County Police Department issued an all-points bulletin for his arrest. More damning evidence was added to his flight-to-avoid-prosecution charge when they found that he had not only closed his bank account, but had also drawn down all of the cash from his NFL retirement fund. Willie Dixon had already been planning to reinvent himself.

While at the bank, checking up on the Dixon account, Lola found that Beth had not purchased a car with Hadley's five thousand dollar check, but had deposited it into her savings account, bringing the balance to a little over ten grand. The money came in handy. Since there was no life insurance, Lizzy Campbell used it to pay for Beth's funeral.

All that next week, an ominous cloud seemed to follow Ginny wherever she went. Each day her mood had grown drearier, and soon her effervescent spirit and quick sense of humor deserted her, altogether.

It began that Saturday at Beth's funeral. The sad occasion made the dismal rainy afternoon even more depressing. By the time Charlie dropped her off at the United Methodist Church, the sanctuary was already overflowing with mourners.

Ginny joined many of her classmates in the church cafeteria as they listened to Reverend Clark's words of comfort over the public address system. She found very little consolation in his words, however, and sunk even deeper into her blue funk.

The following Monday, Ginny passed another uneventful day, avoiding her friends for the most part. She had long since stopped eating lunch with them, going to the library to read instead. When Dewey made one of his boyish attempts at humor, designed to bring her out of her bad mood, Ginny had been short with him, more so than she had intended.

The prescribed medicine was no longer effective and she had slept fitfully the night before. In addition, *the girl* was back. When Ginny awakened that morning, she was sitting in the chair at the foot of the bed, smiling as she rocked back and forth. Ginny was no longer afraid of her, but *the girl's* presence was an annoyance that seemed to place her at the edge of insanity. Sometimes it even seemed that she had total control of Ginny's body and mind.

Three forty-five, the wall clock finally read. This had been the longest day of Ginny Westbrook's young life. Additionally, it was also the darkest. But, somehow, she had made it to its end. Margo and Cha-Cha tried desperately to lift Ginny's sprit as they all sat at the bus stop in front of the school, where Ginny also waited for Miriam to pick her up each day. She did chuckle a bit when Cha-Cha told one of her off-color jokes, but soon went back to the novel she was reading. Eventually, the school bus came and went, and Margo and Cha-Cha were gone. Ginny was alone.

Ever since the ugly sleepwalking incident, Miriam – still working the 3 'til 11 afternoon shift – had made arrangements to go in an hour early, so she could pop over to the school and take Ginny home during one of her breaks.

Becoming a bit concerned with the lateness of the hour, Ginny looked down at her pager. There were no calls. She walked back into the building and used the pay phone to call the hospital. The receptionist answered after the first ring. "County General," she announced.

"Is that you, Mabel?" Ginny asked.

"Yeah," the woman said jovially. "Your mama said you'd probably be calling."

"Where is she? She's late coming to pick me up."

"Honey, they just had a code-red, and you know she's on that cardiac-arrest team. But they're almost through. She said to tell you she'd be right on."

"Okay," Ginny said, and then shrugged as she angrily hung up the telephone and walked back to the bus stop. *I could've been home already,* she thought. *I hate being treated like a child.* She leaned back and again became engrossed in her novel.

The two electrical paddles thudded loudly as the doctor held them to the patient's chest. "Once more," she yelled to the team assembled around her and the patient. "Clear!"

Once again, the paddles bounced off the man's chest after sending a measured flow of current into his heart muscle.

Miriam, like the others in the room, wore a green surgical gown with a matching cap and facemask. She looked up at the machine that monitored the patient's vital signs. This was her assignment on the Code-Red Recovery Team.

"We have a pulse," Miriam exclaimed. "We've got him!"

"Thank you, people, and once again, you've been marvelous," the doctor said, dismissing the team members.

As she left the resuscitation room, Miriam stripped out of the green garb, which made her and the other team members look like creatures from outer space, and headed out the door. As she walked past the reception desk on the way out, Mabel was making a pointing motion at her own head.

"What?" Miriam asked, and then thought about the green plastic cap that she still wore. "Oh, thanks," she said, snatching it off.

"Miriam," Mabel called out. "Ginny just called. I told her you were on your way."

"Thanks a million, Mabel," Miriam said before disappearing down the hallway and sailing out into the parking lot.

When Miriam arrived at Chandler High, she was more than an hour late and feeling terrible about it. *I'll take 'em out to dinner at Pappas', tonight,* she thought as she turned into the long curving driveway, which ran the full length of the gigantic building. When she saw the empty bench where Ginny would always be waiting, Miriam Westbrook panicked. A million thoughts began to race through her head. *Maybe she went back into the building to call the hospital again. That's it, exactly,* Miriam assured herself, pulling the Taurus to the curb and sprinting toward the main office.

The front door was locked.

Miriam tried the door again, shaking and pulling at it, but to no avail. Fear and anger began to rise up within her. She began to fear that Ginny had wandered off again, or perhaps even worse. Now she was angry. But with whom? Was it the man ... for having that stupid heart attack that caused her to be late to pick up her daughter? No, that's crazy.

Then she saw Mr. Harris, the custodian. "Mr. Harris, Mr. Harris," she blurted out, "have you seen my daughter, Ginny?"

"Yes, Ma'am," the old man said congenially.

"Whew! Thank God," Miriam said, wiping her brow with a sigh of relief. "Where is she?"

"She's out front ... sitting at the bus stop, just like always."

"No! No!" Miriam said. "I just left there! She is *not* at that bus stop."

"Well," the old man said, "settle down. She's around here somewhere. I'll help you find her."

"Thank you, thank you so much," Miriam said, trying her darnedest to be calm as she followed him down the hall.

While they searched wing after wing of the school, with no sign of Ginny, Miriam stopped at a pay phone and called the hospital. No, Ginny had only called that once, Mabel told her.

Finally, they checked the after-school detention room. Detention had long since been over. The room was empty. Leaving the kindly old custodian shaking his head, Miriam rushed back to her car. First, she drove around to the football field. No one there had seen Ginny either.

Then it hit her. *It's that blasted shortcut,* Miriam said silently. Then she drove like crazy to the front entrance of Simpson's Woods, and then jumped out of the car. Leaving the key in the ignition and the door standing wide open, Miriam ran through the gate, following the trail deep into the forest. "Ginny, Ginny, where are you?" she called out as she probed deeper and deeper into the woods.

In addition to being distraught, Miriam was now becoming disorientated. It had been years since she had gone into Simpson's Woods, and even then, it was never alone. She also had not eaten lunch, and with all of the unexpected activity, her blood sugar was running precariously low. Miriam was already a bit dizzy. It was only after getting totally lost for several minutes that, off in the distance, she saw the outline of houses.

Miriam realized now that she had followed the trail all the way home. Then it came to her. *That's what Ginny did. She got tired of waiting and took the shortcut home. She's probably in the kitchen, fixing her daddy's dinner.*

"I'm going to give that girl a piece of my mind," Miriam said aloud as she regained her composure and walked out of Simpson's Woods toward Cherry Lane.

Then she remembered that she had left not only her car, on the other side of Simpson's Woods, but her keys as well. Miriam quickly found a ladder that they kept in the garage for just such emergencies. She placed the ladder against the back wall, quickly climbed it, and then ran her fingers across the top of a ledge until it touched a small bit of metal.

Miriam hurriedly took the spare key and opened the back door. She was surprised to find the kitchen empty, but not alarmed. Ginny was probably in her bedroom, pouting, since Miriam had been so late that she had to walk home. Well, she would be woman enough to take her medicine and would go straight upstairs to Ginny's room and apologize.

Miriam, a little tired now – it had been years since she had done this much walking – made her way up the steps and walked to the end of the hall to Ginny's room. The door was standing wide open. Her blood ran cold when Miriam stared heart-stricken into the *empty* room.

"Oh, no," she cried out.

Suddenly a wave of dizziness washed over her, and then everything went dark.

It had been a hard day for Charlie Westbrook. The trip to Chattanooga was always difficult. On such days, he had to leave earlier in the morning and return home later in the evening. On top of the long trip, he also had a bad headache, which had been with him almost all day long. All Charlie longed for when he got home was a hot dinner, an even hotter bath, and a place to lay his aching head.

It was around six o'clock when he dropped Jay Dee off at his house, over on Mulberry Street, and then headed home. When Charlie made the turn onto Cherry Lane, his heart almost flew up into his mouth. There were flashing lights all over the place, especially in front of *his* house. His jaw dropped.

"It's Ginny," he shouted to himself. "Something's happened to Ginny!"

Charlie swerved the truck to the curb, jumped down from the cab, and then took off running as fast as he could. When he reached his driveway, two paramedics were lifting a stretcher up into their emergency vehicle.

"Wait," Charlie yelled. "Where're you taking my daughter?"

He pushed through the crowd of neighbors to the ambulance and got in through the back door. The man attending to Miriam adjusted the drip bag of glucose that slowly seeped into her arm. When Charlie looked down at the stretcher, Miriam opened her eyes and whispered hoarsely, "Charlie, it's Ginny … she's gone."

"She's gonna be alright, Charlie. It's just an irregular heartbeat," a voice called out to him from the front seat of the ambulance. It was their neighbor, Flossie Mae Johnson. "I'm goin' to the hospital with her, but the police need you here. You gotta help 'em. They can't find Ginny."

Torn in two directions, Charlie looked down at his wife, and then back at the police officers waiting for him on his doorsteps.

"Go, Charlie, find my baby," Miriam whispered.

Charlie kissed her on the cheek, and then backed out of the ambulance. Chief Callahan, Lou, Lola, and another young officer, Don Henley, were waiting for Charlie at his front steps.

"Mr. Westbrook, I'm Russ Callahan, Chief of Police," he said, extending his hand.

"I know, Chief," Charlie cut in, ignoring the hand. "What happened?"

"I was on patrol near Simpson's Woods," Officer Henley began. The young patrolman quickly related how he and his partner had found the Taurus awkwardly parked in front of Simpson's Woods with the driver's side door left wide open and the keys still in the ignition. The two of them had followed the trail into the woods in search of the driver, but not finding anyone, they returned to the car. After finding the address on the key chain, Officer Henley's partner followed him in the squad car as he drove the Taurus home, still in search of its driver

"When we got here," the officer continued, "the paramedics were already working on your wife."

Lola went on to tell how Miriam, along with the shock of her daughter wandering off, had suffered a bout of hypoglycemia and blacked out. When she awakened, she was lethargic and knew that she needed medical attention, so Miriam made the call. When the paramedics arrived, they discovered that she had a mild arrhythmia, so they decided to take her to the hospital for observation.

Then Chief Callahan stepped in to discuss matters that were more pertinent, the missing girl. Under normal circumstances, he would not have been as concerned. However, with the murder of Elizabeth Campbell fresh on everyone's mind, the game had to be played by a different set of rules.

"Your wife told Officer Henley that your daughter wandered off before, and that you'd know what happened," the chief said.

"Yeah," Charlie said hesitantly. "She suffers from some kinda sleep walking sickness."

"Somnambulism?" the chief asked.

"Yeah, that's it," Charlie said, and then laid out the whole story about Ginny's escapade into Simpson's Woods, the doctor, the medicine, and the horrid tale of locking her inside the house at night.

"Well, at least we know where to start," the chief said. "I'll call in more of my men and have them meet us at the edge of the woods. We'd better get going."

"You're right," Lou said. "We've only got an hour or so of daylight left."

Before joining the police officers, Charlie went into the house and called Jay Dee.

They all drove to the back entrance of Simpson's Woods, although it was in walking distance. In a few minutes, they were joined by most of the Wrightsburg police force. Shortly thereafter, Jay Dee arrived on the scene. He had rounded up most of the drivers from Chandler Enterprises along with several other men from the neighborhood.

Charlie was overwhelmed with emotion at the show of support from his friends and neighbors. He was certain that they would soon find Ginny and be back home in time for a late supper.

Chief Callahan had the duty-officer patch a telephone call through to Principal Murray's home. When made aware of the situation, Mr. Murray immediately took charge, mobilizing the coaches and football team. The chief sent him a walkie-talkie for communication. The plan was simple.

The principal would lead the football team in a thorough search of the school grounds, and if they didn't find Ginny there, they would begin another search at the front entrance of Simpson's Woods. Whichever group found Ginny, would call the other, and if, heavens forbid, neither group found her, they would all meet up at Witches' Hollow.

In the beginning, the chief, as everyone else, was sure that at the next turn or step, a dazed Ginny would be found – wandering aimlessly. On the other hand, maybe she had fallen and sprained an ankle, and would be lying there writhing in pain, but happy to see her rescuers. However, when night fell and they had not found Ginny, much of the optimism vanished.

The police officers were well equipped with large flashlights. On the other side of the park, however, the football team was searching in the blind. Mr. Murray went back to the school, took the cash from the Coke machine funds, and then bought out Ace Hardware's entire stock of Eveready flashlights – all sizes and all shapes.

Now, both groups of hunters were equipped to take their search far into the night, if necessary. In all, more than a hundred men participated in the search. When viewed from high above, with their flashlights shining into the black darkness of the woods, the searchers resembled a bizarre nighttime invasion force, moving ever closer toward each other.

Charlie was beginning to panic. His heart pounded loudly with each step. Like the others, he, too, was confident that they would find Ginny right away. Then the two of them would go home and clean up before going to the hospital to see about Miriam. Another thing that Charlie had decided was that – right then and there – he was going to have Ginny admitted to the hospital, and there she would stay until somebody found out what was wrong with her and fixed it.

It was now well after midnight, and the two groups had long since met and merged at Witches' Hollow. They were now searching deeper into the Hollow than anyone ever remembered going, well past the spot where Beth's body had been found. There, the going got rough and the progress slowed tremendously. The weeds and underbrush were unforgiving. Each forward step had to be earned.

Finally, the Chief could take no more. "Alright, men, let's call it quits for the night," he said.

"No! No!" Charlie said. "We can't!"

"He's right," said Sonny James from back in the pack. "Let's keep going."

They went on for another hour, and then Jay Dee caught up to Charlie. "Charlie, we hongry, man," he said pleadingly. "We ain't had nothin' to eat. Let us go. We'll come back in the mornin', fust thang."

Charlie shook his head and sighed long and hard before turning to Russ Callahan. "Chief, let's call it in."

Without going home, Charlie rushed straight to Miriam's hospital bed. The two of them cried – well into the morning – until they were both rescued from their misery by merciful sleep.

And the next morning they *were* back, and more came, too. If there were a hundred searchers last night, there were almost five hundred that morning. Chandler High School had been stunned by the news of Ginny's disappearance, especially on the heels of Beth's horrible murder. Many of the students joined in the search, but others found the whole experience too much for their young hearts to bear, so they returned home.

Margo and Cha-Cha led all of the bus riders from Ginny's neighborhood down to the woods to join the search. Dewey and Sarah also led a group of their friends to help. Dewey, especially, was overwhelmed, somehow feeling that if he had not engaged in that silly fight with Sonny James and gotten detention, he would have been there with Ginny and none of this would've happened.

Mr. Murray left the Assistant Principal, George Willis, in charge of the school and, once again, he joined Chief Callahan in coordinating the search. Those who passed by the Chandler processing plant were probably shocked at the silence of the heavy machinery, which had ground to a halt, so that men who maintained and serviced the strainers and cookers could join the search.

The going was much easier today, since the mayor had sent in the heavy metal. There were tractors; with long blades that cut through the tall grass like a hot knife through butter; bulldozers that pushed through the limbs and dead trees as if they were kindling wood; and backhoes to cart away the debris. The big machines blazed a path for the searchers as they marched shoulder to shoulder through Witches' Hollow and far beyond.

Even with the sunlight and the clearing of the land, Ginny was still not to be found. Therefore, around noon, the search was over. At least the city finally delivered on its promise to finish clearing Simpson's Woods for a picnic area – as if anyone would be attracted to such a place once this whole sorry mess was over. The sight of Principal Murray leading his band of disheartened students back to school, with their bowed heads and without their classmate, was more than the heart could take. The students spoke not a word as they disappointedly returned to their classes.

Before leaving Simpson's Woods, Chief Callahan, called an impromptu meeting of his investigative team. The beleaguered lawman – now at wits end – peered at Lou and Lola across the hood of his Caprice. "Where do we go from here, folks?"

"Back to Atlanta," Lou snapped. "I'd like to know where Mr. Hadley Frazier is, along about now, and his whereabouts for the past few days."

"I don't think so," Lola injected.

"Why not?" Lou snapped back, perhaps, stronger than intended. "The man is a professional liar. He does it for a living, and if he came here once--"

"That was to see Beth," Lola cut in. "Comparing Beth Campbell to Ginny Westbrook would be like judging saints against sinners."

"She has a point, Lou," the chief said. "And we don't have a minute to waste."

"Alright," Lou conceded, "you're the boss."

"Here's the official line. We treat Ginny Westbrook's disappearance as a missing person's investigation, but with an eye toward foul play. While I'm not ready to link Ginny's disappearance to Beth's murder or to any of the other missing girls, we do have to take precautions."

"I guess you're right," Lou conceded further. "What's next?"

"I'll get a team over to search the lake," the chief said, "but you two come with me."

"Where to?" Lola asked.

"Back to school," the chief said, turning to get into his car.

"Chief," Lola called out.

"Yeah," he said, turning back to her.

"I ... ah," she sputtered, searching for words.

"Come on, spit it out. We've got things to do," the chief said.

"I think we should have a little talk with Mitch Bradley."

"Mitch Bradley?" Lou asked in astonishment. "What in the world for?"

Then Lola laid out her suspicions that Mitch had been following her and about the stare-down at the candlelight vigil."

"Absolutely not," the chief raged. "Why, that man is one of the finest citizens of this town."

"I know," Lola said, "but he sure has been acting suspicious."

"Suspicious, how?" the chief ranted on. Then he looked Lola up and down. "Look at you, Lola, you're a pretty woman. *All* men stare at you!"

Lola admitted to herself that the chief was probably right and she was stupid for thinking such a foolish thing. "You're right. I just feel so helpless."

"We all do. Let's go," the chief said before getting into his car.

And, at this point, they were helpless. As they retreated to their car, Lou and Lola, both had sneaking suspicions that, before long, Simpson's Woods would be giving up another dead body. They all held their collective breath, hoping-against-hope that they would *not* receive another anonymous telephone call.

Chapter 16

After sending the diving team – instructors from a local diving school – to Lake Blackshear for an underwater search, Chief Callahan, Lou, and Lola headed for Chandler High School. The chief could no longer take chances with the lives of the citizens of Madison County, especially its young women.

Principal Murray's voice crackled across the intercom system as he sat behind his desk and spoke into the microphone.

"Students, once again, I have disturbing news. It pains me to no end … to have to be the bearer of such bad tidings." He paused briefly, but then went on. "But we have been unable to find Ginny Westbrook, who wandered away from school yesterday. However, let me make this perfectly clear, we are *not* giving up the search."

Applause could be heard across the school building.

"And I would like to thank those who participated in the search, both yesterday and this morning. I would also like to thank Chief Callahan and …"

Suddenly the principal's voice lost its deep resonance, and its pitch rose to a shrill whisper before it faltered, and then failed him altogether. With the back of his hand, he wiped away a tear, trickling from the corner of his eye and down his face, and then sighed as he struggled to regain his composure.

Francis Murray was an affable man and a caring principal who was never too busy to give a student a smile, a hug, or an encouraging word. However, the stress of leadership was getting to him now, what with the loss of one student and possibly another. "I'm sorry," he said. "Before we go any further, let us have a moment of silent prayer for Ginny's safety and an expedient return to us."

There was a pause. The building fell silent for a moment, and then he continued. "Chief Callahan would like to say a word about Ginny's disappearance and the safety of others."

The principal passed the microphone to the chief, now sitting in the chair beside him where Lizzy Campbell had so recently sat. Lou and Lola stood by watching silently.

The chief took the microphone from Principal Murray, cleared his throat, and then spoke in the most reassuring voice that he could muster under the circumstances.

"As Principal Murray has already said, we will continue the search for Ginny, but we need your help in doing so. If there is anyone who saw Ginny after school yesterday, please let Principal Murray know as soon as possible. ... You should also know that Ginny suffers from a medical condition that might have caused her to have a lapse in memory. Her doctor said that under stress, she is liable to lose track of time, reality, and location, so it is possible that she might not be fully aware of her surroundings."

A collective gasp could be heard across the building as the students took in the astounding revelation.

When contacted by the police, Dr. Turner substantiated the Westbrook's story involving the sleepwalking incident. He also said these kinds of occurrences could, indeed, take place during daylight hours and that Ginny might have walked off in a state of amnesia.

"She might very well have hitched a ride out of town with one of the truckers," he had said.

Pearlie's Truck Stop would be the next stop for Lou and Lola when they left the school.

"At this time, we have no reason to think that Ginny's disappearance had any connection to the horrible thing that happened to Beth Campbell," the chief continued. "I don't want to alarm any of you, but until we find out exactly what happened to Ginny, we must exercise caution."

The chief paused to choose his words carefully. "Just to be on the safe side, I'm asking that you stay close to home or school, especially you young ladies. If you must be out, remember that there is always safety in numbers. And it goes without saying that you should never accept rides from strangers."

After placing the school into virtual lockdown, with a police officer stationed at every entrance, Chief Callahan headed to the Chandler plant, where he deputized the security guards that Ty Jr. had released from their regular duties in order to help patrol the streets of Wrightsburg.

That afternoon, the school became even more gloomy when it was announced that Saturday's football game with Upton County was in danger of being postponed or cancelled, so that residents, especially females, could remain close to home.

In the school newspaper office, it was the most somber and uncomfortable time Mr. Robinson and the others had ever known. They had barely spoken to each other since their arrival. He sat at his desk, staring blankly at the computer screen while Dewey sat idly by, in deep solitude. Sarah sat hunched over with her head resting on the desk.

Dewey looked up when he saw the familiar figure standing in the doorway. It was Sonny James.

"Oh, I hope I'm not interrupting anything," the team captain said. For the first time that any of them could remember, Sonny James was alone.

"No," Dewey said, looking up at the boy who had been his nemesis since the infamous onstage kiss. "Come on in."

"Well, I just thought that, ah," Sonny stuttered as if lost for words, but he walked into the room. "I was just thinking. If y'all was gonna make some of them flyers, you know, like you did for Beth. Well … me and the boys, we'd like to help put 'em out."

"Yeah," Dewey said, getting up from his chair. "That's a good idea. We should be doing something. You know Ginny would be."

"Sorry, man," Sonny said to Dewey, looking him in the eye.

"Yeah, me, too," Dewey said, taking the out-stretched hand that Sonny James extended toward him.

While the other searchers had called it a day, Charlie Westbrook might have been giving out, but he was nowhere near giving up. And although Miriam was released from the hospital, she had not been freed from her pain and suffering. She was still inconsolable, a nervous wreck. Charlie, however, realizing that one of them had to remain strong, was as solid as a rock.

After he had retrieved Miriam from the hospital and did his best to assure her of Ginny's safe return home, Charlie left her in the capable hands and under the watchful eye of Flossie Mae Johnson before heading back to Simpson's Woods.

Buddy Rogers, Jay Dee's uncle, was a peach farmer over in Roberta, Georgia, who dearly loved two things, moonshine whiskey and coon hunting. To further his pursuit of pleasure, the ninety-year-old man built the best liquor-still in Crawford County, and bought himself two full-blooded Irish Pointers and three Bloodhounds, making up the best team of tracking dogs in the State of Georgia.

All that it had taken was a call from Jay Dee, and Uncle Buddy had thrown a jug of his finest corn liquor in the front seat of his 1955 Dodge Ram truck – which still ran like a Singer sewing machine – piled the team of hunting dogs into the back bed of the pickup, and then drove the fifty miles to Madison County.

Uncle Buddy, Jay Dee, and the team of dogs were waiting for Charlie at the rear entrance of Simpson's Woods.

"Charlie, this my Uncle Buddy," Jay Dee said.

"Thank you for coming on such short notice," Charlie said appreciatively, waving at the old man instead of shaking his hand.

Uncle Buddy had his hands full just keeping the team in check. He held the Bloodhounds with his right hand and the Pointers with his left. The dogs barked and pawed the ground as he pulled their leashes taut to restrain them.

"Think, nothin' ov it," Uncle Buddy said, in a hillbilly twang as he continually tugged at the leashes. "If she's anywhere in these woods, my dogs 'a find her."

"He's right about that, Charlie," Jay Dee added, chuckling. "I remember last year, when the prison dogs over in Milledgeville lost track of a mean inmate, Uncle Buddy put old Shep and his boys on the case, and they had that sucker cornered 'fore nightfall."

"Thank God," Charlie said with a huge sigh of relief.

"Settle down, Shep," Uncle Buddy yelled to one of the Bloodhounds, the lead dog. Finally, the dogs relented and their leashes went slack. They whimpered and sniffed at Charlie's feet.

"You brought anything with her scent?" Uncle Buddy asked Charlie.

"Yeah, sure," Charlie said, pulling a white blouse from a bag that he held under his arm. "This is hers."

"Give it to Jay Dee," Uncle Buddy said. "He know what to do wit' it."

When Charlie did as the old codger asked, Jay Dee placed the blouse under Shep's sniffing nostril, and then under the noses of the rest of the team. After getting the scent, each dog bucked before turning toward Simpson's Woods. They were "chomping at the bit" with their noses to the ground and their tails pointed skyward.

"They got it," Uncle Buddy yelled as he desperately struggled to hold them back.

"Good," Charlie yelled. "Let 'em go."

"Here goes," Uncle Buddy said. Then he yelled at the lead dog. "Shep, heel."

First Shep, then the other dogs loosened the tension of their leases. Uncle Buddy first unleashed Shep, and then yelled at him. "Go, Shep."

The big speckled dog's paws dug deeply into the earth as he scampered toward Simpson's Wood, barking wildly. In turn, Uncle Buddy unleashed one after the other until each barking dog had been released and was playing follow the leader with old Shep, deep into the woods. Charlie and Jay Dee ran after the dogs, but Uncle Buddy walked at a slow pace.

"I'll see y'all when they find 'er," he yelled after Charlie and Jay Dee as the two men disappeared into the forest behind the dogs. They were moving as fast as their legs could carry them, guided by the sound of steady barking.

Charlie and Jay Dee came upon the entrance to Witches' Hollow and were about to enter when they heard the dogs barking their heads off, but in the opposite direction.

"Whoa, Charlie," Jay Dee said, stooping over to catch his breath. "Them dogs sound like theys on the other side of the woods."

"Yeah," Charlie said, struggling to catch his breath. "They're in the clearing. Let's go."

The two men took off, running toward the sound of the barking dogs. Charlie and Jay Dee stopped short when they reach the clearing. All five of the dogs barked ferociously as they pointed their noses toward the top of an old oak tree. It was Ginny's favorite tree, where two squirrels were perched on a limb. The little furry animals were trembling and shaking, frightened out of their wits.

"Charlie, I don't know where your lil' girl is," Uncle Buddy said, after joining them at the oak tree and attempting to force his dogs further into the woods, "but I sure as hell know where she ain't. She ain't in Simpson's Woods."

Jay Dee and Uncle Buddy rounded up the dogs and headed home, where a jug of moonshine waited to drown their sorrows. Charlie hung his head as he walked back to the house.

Chapter 17

Maryella Leticia Chandler was named after the three granddames of her family: her mother, Eleanor; her grandmother on her father's side, Leticia; and her grandmother on Eleanor's side, Mary. Eleanor had borne a string of boys and was getting on in age, so they could hardly take a chance on her having another girl to be used as a namesake.

Even from its very beginning, Maryella's had been a life filled with turbulence. She was born "under the veil." Medically speaking, this meant that she had been wrapped in her own placenta at birth, which starved a portion of her brain of oxygen for just the briefest of moments.

However, to others, with much darker views, this meant that the baby girl would grow up to be special. Such people were thought, by some, to be in possession of powers that went far beyond the scope of belief and understanding of the normal person, especially when it came to matters of life and death. Those who were born under the veil were believed to have the gift of *seeing* ... the dead.

In the eyes of Tyson Jr., who was eight years her senior, Maryella was an angel and could do no wrong. Their mother had a troubled pregnancy with the baby that many said she was much too old to have, at forty-one.

Nevertheless, she had already given her tyrant of a husband three fine boys, so now Eleanor was hell-bent on having a girl for herself.

Therefore, against the advice of her doctor and without the knowledge of her husband – she had thrown away her diaphragm – Eleanor gave birth to the baby whose delivery would ultimately lead to her own demise. Never fully recovering from the troublesome pregnancy, Eleanor Chandler died a week later from its complications.

Ty Jr. and Maryella had two older brothers, Walter, who was away in the Army, and Logan, who worked with their father in the family's business. After Eleanor's death, the upkeep of the enormous house and grounds was left to the servants. The upbringing of the baby girl fell to a nanny, a small black woman called Miss Ida, and Ty Jr.

As a young boy, Ty Jr. could hardly wait for school to let out each day, so that he could rush home to bounce the little blonde princess on his spindly knobby knees. When Maryella became a toddler and could sit alone, Ty Jr. would place her into his little red wagon and pull her all over the neighborhood.

For Maryella, growing up in a house full of men was not an easy task, especially under a domineering father such as Ty Sr., a man who expected that everything all of his children did should be done to perfection. Maryella was a free spirit and full of adventure and, as she matured, found it increasingly difficult to live up to the high standards set by her father and the other men of Chandler House. They all closely watched her every move and critiqued them harshly.

It was only their mutual love of animals that made Maryella the apple of her father's eye. Some said the old man was the best dog breeder in the Southeastern United States, so he always maintained an extensive kennel of pure breed dogs. Tyson Chandler, Sr. trained Pointers, Setters, and Bloodhounds – for hunting – Rottwielers, German shepherds, and Dobermans – for security.

Additionally, he had a stable of show dogs that participated in exhibitions all across the globe. At these grand affairs, the dogs were tested on obedience, agility, and breed showing. As a young girl, Maryella became just as adept as her father at dog handling and had a shelf full of trophies and loving cups, plus a wall full of plagues and blue ribbons, to show for her efforts.

She had the unique ability to train different breeds at the same time, which was no simple task. Her prized Doberman, Gingerbread Man, won *Best of Show* in London, England, in 1970.

When she entered high school, Maryella was the most intelligent and beautiful girl at Madison High. She had flowing blonde hair, deep green eyes, an outgoing personality, and a pretty face with an always-radiant smile. The fiery little blonde always stood up for what was right and always spoke her mind. She was always in the top ten percent of her class. To that end, during her senior year, in 1972, she was elected President of the Student Government. That same year, Maryella was crowned Madison High School Homecoming Queen.

To the chagrin of the Chandler men, however, Maryella broke with the blueblood dating traditions and, more times than not, went out with boys from the wrong side of the track. Her dates had to be of her own choosing, or not at all.

In the spring of the year, there would be a glorious graduation celebration before Maryella was to spend the entire summer, vacationing in Chicago, New York, and Los Angeles with some of the female family members. The idea was for Maryella to improve her social graces after having grown up in a houseful of men and a Negro nanny. That fall, she was to enroll at Emory University up in Atlanta, where she would study fine arts and foreign languages.

But then it happened.

Ty Jr., as the other Chandler men, felt badly about the incident, but his sister's one indiscretion – if you could call it that – certainly did *not* warrant the cruel treatment meted out by their father. The punishment simply *did not* fit the crime, which after years of thought, Ty Jr. came to realize was not even a crime at all.

Therefore, when his father forbade the members of the family to speak her name under his roof or contact his sister in any way, Ty Jr. completely ignored him. In fact, he had been in constant contact with Maryella most of the time. He was completely devastated, however, that the one time when it had really counted … when he had finally caught his father in a weak moment and convinced him to let her come back home, Ty Jr. could *not* locate his sister.

After the old man disinherited her and sent Maryella packing, it had taken a full year for Ty Jr. to track her down. She was then living on

Ponce deLeon Avenue, in the hippie section of Atlanta. Ty Jr. visited her as often as he could find a reason to go to there. He visited every college classmate he could think of that lived in Atlanta, and once a month, sent her money via Western Union.

Then late one night, he had gotten a call from San Francisco. Maryella had followed some of her hippie friends to the popular Haight Asbury District of the city, where wine ran like water and drugs flowed like a river. Though he never visited her in California, he still wired her money and was able to leave messages for her at a friendly pharmacist who – Ty Jr. could tell from their conversations – had strong feelings for his sister. However, he began to worry about Maryella's wellbeing, considering the drugs and the free-style sex, for which that part of the country was very well known.

Ty Jr. knew for a fact that his sister did not use drugs when she was in Wrightsburg, but he later began to have great fear and trepidation in that regard. Many were the times when she would be incoherent when she called and would break into tears at the sound of his voice. One day Ty Jr. called the telephone number at the drug store in San Francisco, and the pharmacist – whom Ty Jr. had come to know as Jerry – had bad news. Maryella and her hippie friends had taken off for parts unknown.

Then one day at the office, some months later, Ty Jr. got a call. It was Cousin Margaret, a distant relative on his mother's side of the family. While shopping downtown, Margaret had stumbled upon Maryella. She was panhandling on the streets of Chicago.

"Maryella is strung out on drugs, begging for quarters, and only God knows what else," Cousin Margaret had said.

At the time, Maryella was too ashamed to speak with him, but Ty Jr. convinced Cousin Margaret to take her into her home and help with her rehabilitation. The next day, Ty Jr. flew to Chicago for a vacation. He had been working too hard and needed to get away, he had told his father and brother. Their reunion had been a tearful affair, but Maryella was strong in her resolve to get her life back on track. Cousin Margaret talked her husband, Nicholas, into hiring Maryella at the garment factory, where he was a supervisor.

"Blood runs thicker than water," Cousin Margaret had told him.

Then Maryella's rehab began. Although Cousin Margaret had little regard for the wishes of Ty Sr. – an old man whom she deemed to be stubborn and arrogant – together, she and Ty Jr. contrived, clandestinely, to clean Maryella up and get her back home. Ty Jr. worked on the old man down in Wrightsburg, trying to change his mind about his daughter while Cousin Margaret tended to Maryella up in Chicago, attempting to help her break the mysterious spell cast by the venomous drugs.

During the day, Maryella stitched the hems of dresses and skirts and attended drug counseling at night. Sure enough, after a few months, she had kicked the habit, moved into her own apartment, and had – to Ty Jr.'s great satisfaction – her own telephone.

The telephone number at Maryella's apartment was the one that Ty Jr. had called, getting no answer, on that critical day. A few days later, when he called back, the phone had been disconnected. Cousin Margaret said that she had fallen off the wagon and gone back on drugs. No matter, she was still his sister, and Ty Jr. was determined to see to it that, one day, Maryella would come home.

December 20, 1976

As he stood in his office with the telephone to his ear, Ty Jr. could hardly contain himself. A private detective, hired when Maryella dropped out of sight in Chicago, was on the line. It had taken almost a year, but he had found her. She was back in Atlanta, and as far as the detective knew, not on drugs.

Maryella waited tables at a local restaurant and had her own apartment. Ty Jr. hesitated, but then hastily dialed the telephone number that she had given the man. He held his breath as the phone rang and rang at the other end. He was finally going to invite his sister home for Christmas.

The telephone on the nightstand rang and rang. A young woman in her early twenties, with tangled blonde hair, lay in bed sleeping off the deep fog left over from a night of drugs and alcohol. After several more rings, the naked girl sat up in bed and picked up the telephone.

"Hello," she said in a raspy voice, and then listened uneasily. "What? Who is this?"

Then she gathered her wits about herself. "Oh, Junior, is that you?" she asked jubilantly.

Maryella Chandler beamed as she listened carefully to her brother. "So the old man wants me back," she said, now with a bit of arrogance. "Wait a minute."

She placed her hand over the telephone receiver, and then shook the man lying in her bed. "Hey, you, your time is up! Get out of here!"

The man, well into his fifties, snarled at her. "Don't do that."

She shook him again, this time violently, and he turned over. The man unleashed a string of invectives, and then turned his back to her.

"I said your time was up! Now leave," she said, pointing to the door of the dingy furnished-room that somehow the private detective mistook for an apartment.

"Oh, alright!" the man said.

He grudgingly slipped into his clothes as Maryella spoke into the receiver. "Junior, are you still there?"

Suddenly the man grabbed the wad of money from the dresser and turned to Maryella. "Whore," he shouted contemptuously.

As he ran for the door, Maryella sprang from the bed and ran after him. "Hey, you put that back! You son of a-- Oh, no," she groaned as the man bolted through the door and down the hallway.

Realizing that she was naked, Maryella stepped back into the room. Visibly shaken, she momentarily clung to the doorframe, and then slowly slid down to the floor, weeping uncontrollably. Eventually, she crawled back to the side of the bed and picked up the telephone.

"Oh, Junior, I don't think I can make it," she said with tears streaming down her face. "I'm not a pretty sight."

"Yes, I can imagine," Ty Jr. said sadly.

He'd heard every word spoken, so Ty Jr. had a pretty good idea what was going on. Then he spoke more encouragingly. "Look, I don't care what you look like. We can deal with that when you get *home*. You get yourself cleaned up. You're coming home for Christmas. Do you hear me?"

"Yes," she said.

"We miss you."

"And I miss you, too. You and Daddy."

184

"Look, just tell me where you are, and I'll be there in an hour or so."

"No, no," Maryella protested, "you don't have to do that."

"Well, I'm going to send you some money. Are you near a Western Union Office."

"No, don't, Junior," she said, looking sorrowfully up at the dresser where her money had been. Then she lied, "I have enough money for the bus."

The man had taken it all – that which he'd paid her as well as the money she'd earned the night before in her loathsome line of work.

"Trust me, Junior," she said confidently. "I'll be there."

Maryella had been too embarrassed to take money from her brother. She had already taken too much from him. She pulled on an old terrycloth bathrobe, took a towel and a bar of soap from under her nightstand, and walked, barefoot, down the hall to the communal bathroom, which serviced the third floor residents of the dilapidated rooming house. When she reached the tiny bathroom, Maryella turned the shower knob until the water was as hot as she could bear it, stepped inside the stall, and attempted to wash all of her sins away.

Maryella Chandler could not remember why she had started using drugs. As many young people did at the time, it was probably an experiment. However, she knew the reason that she continued was to escape the reality of her misguided life. But she had come closer to making it this time than any other, and this time it had been on her own. She had almost made it when she was with her Cousin up in Chicago, but then an old lover showed up on her doorstep.

The old beau was on his way to Atlanta and talked Maryella into to joining him. In a way, she had thought that being closer to home would better prepare her for her return – if and when the opportunity presented itself. But, as with the best-laid plans of mice and men, things had gone terribly wrong, again. After a few days, the man whose name she couldn't even remember, Jimmy or Jessie, it didn't matter, left her stuck at the rooming house with overdue rent to pay.

Even after then, she had made great strides. The job at Johnny's Steak house didn't pay that well, but sometimes the tips were good and the food was great. She had even gained a few pounds. Then one day after work, she went out for a beer with some friends from the restaurant. Even that had gone well until they all decided to stop by a party before turning in. There, she was reunited with another old friend, heroin. After missing three days of work, old man Johnny gave her the boot, driving Maryella back to prostitution, the only occupation where there are no layoffs and only minor job credentials are needed – just a half-decent face and body.

Maryella turned the water off and toweled herself dry. This would be her golden moment, and she was hell-bent on making the best of it. Returning to her room, she began to prepare herself for the trip home. Standing in front of the tiny mirror on her dresser, she brushed her long blond hair so that it fell down across her shoulders, and put on a white blouse and bell bottomed jeans. Maryella dabbed a bit of Lilac toilet water behind each ear, and then slipped into a brown fringed-leather jacket. She stuffed a few things into a matching knapsack, which she slung across her shoulders, and then left the room.

It had taken almost an hour to walk to the edge of the city, but Maryella was on Highway 19, the road home. It was around five o'clock and the evening traffic was getting bad, but with luck, she would eat dinner Chandler House. After spending the last four years wandering from pillar to post, Maryella Chandler was going home for Christmas. As she waited along the highway, with outstretched thumb, Maryella began to have misgivings about the trip.

Maryella knew in her heart that she had done something bad. However, it was not that for which her father had expelled her from his household, but bad, nevertheless. Was this God's way of punishing her for her misdeed? However, she *was* going back and, if possible, would right the wrong that she had done three years earlier.

Several cars passed as she stood along the highway. Some of the occupants didn't even give her a second glance. Others stared inquisitively, but none stopped. Her spirits lifted when an eighteen-wheeler pulled to the side of the road. Maryella smiled as she ran to the truck cabin and looked up at the stocky driver. "Are you going near Madison County?"

The driver grinned. "Goin' slap through there. Wanna tag along?"

"I sure do!"

"Well, come on, little lady, and climb aboard!"

"Catch this," Maryella said, and then threw her knapsack up to him.

The man helped her into the cabin of the truck, and then pulled the big rig onto the highway.

"What's yo' name?"

"Maryella," she said, smiling. "What's yours?"

"They call me Sam." Then he turned to Maryella. "You wouldn't be headed to Pearlie's, by any chance?"

"Pearlie's Truck Stop? Nah," she said, shaking her head.

"I love that place," Sam said, chuckling. "The food is good ... and the action is hot and heavy."

"So I've heard."

"Say, you 'a pretty lil' thang. You wouldn't happen to be in that line of work, would you? If you are, we can make our deal right here and now."

She smiled but shook her head. "Thanks, but no thanks. I don't do that anymore. I'm going home ... for the first time in a very long time."

"Oh, yeah, what's been keeping you away?"

"Well, that's a long story."

"Well, if you happen to change your mind, I'll be at Pearlie's. I've got a regular room. Room 200."

Maryella smiled widely, shaking her head. "I don't think so."

Then Sam pulled out a cellophane bag full of pot and dangled it in front of Maryella. "Too bad you done gone and got religion. All 'a this is gonna have to go to waste."

That was when Maryella's old demons reared their ugly heads. But pot was just for fun, wasn't it? Pot was nothing like cocaine or that old "white horse," heroin, which she had ridden from San Francisco to Chicago.

"No it isn't," she said, snatching the bag from his hand. "I didn't get that much religion."

Maryella rolled herself a big fat joint, took a hit, and then passed it to Sam. He took to the back roads as the two of them had a rolling pot-party.

It was dark when Sam pulled the truck up to the gates of the Chandler mansion.

"Ooo, wee, I see you a lil' rich girl," Sam said, taking in the panoramic view of luxury.

"No, not really. But thanks ... for everything," Maryella said, and then wobbled down from the cab on unsteady legs.

Sam grinned back, looking down from his high perch. "Don't forget. If you change your mind, I'll be at Pearlie's."

"Okay," she said.

Maryella waved goodbye as the truck pulled away, and then stumbled as she turned toward the house. "Okay, Maryella," she said aloud, "get yourself together."

She walked a few feet down the long curving driveway before stumbling again.

"Come on girl, don't blow it," she said aloud.

Maryella tried to clear her head, and then strode up to the huge polished-oak door. She drew back the big brass knocker, but hesitated before letting let it fall, silently.

Look at you! she said to herself. *After all these years, you're going to screw it up – for sure!* She sat down on the steps and wept softly. Shortly, she got up, slung the knapsack over her back, and then walked slowly back toward the highway.

Chapter 18

Kelly's Roadhouse was located in Marion County, the only "wet district" in the tri-county area of Madison, Marion, and Chattooga, thus, it was the usual point of assembly when college students came home for the holidays. Kelly's menu consisted of simple fare – pizzas, burgers, and hotdogs. Food didn't really matter that much to the students who were now of drinking age. They came for the draught beer and pint bottles of bourbon, gin, and Scotch whisky.

The place was small, a few booths, tables, and a jukebox in the corner. The bar was only lit by the various signs advertising Budweiser, Coke, and Miller High Life, making it an ideal location for the young men to get together to swap school stories and meet girls. The backwoods local girls were sometimes easy pickings. They greatly admired the worldly sounding boys who had traveled afar, chasing their dreams of higher learning and a better tomorrow.

Mojo, Rags, and Peter were the nicknames given to the three boys while they were in elementary school. Mojo was called such because of his eccentric grandmother, Maggie, who some said could put hexes on anyone who crossed her family members. One day after Mojo lost a fight to one of the local bullies, the boy was accidentally struck and killed by a car. Somebody said the old woman had put the mojo on him, and that was it. The name stuck.

Rags was called so for the way his mother dressed him – in his older brother's hand-me-down clothes. They first called him Raggedy Man, then simply Rags.

Peter got his name while he was in the first grade. The boy loved nursery rhymes, especially his namesake, Peter Pumpkineater. He could easily commit a rhyme to memory, sometimes after the first reading. The day he got his name, the children had first read *Peter, Peter, Pumpkineater.* He enjoyed the poem so much that he had a terrible fight with the teacher when she wanted to leave that portion of the lesson and go on to math.

The nicknames stuck with the three boys through high school and into college. While in high school, the close-knot trio was also dubbed, "The Three Musketeers," alluding to their similar height, around six feet tall, and weight, about one eighty. They even dressed alike, usually wearing tight fitting jeans and short-sleeved sports shirts, with rolled up sleeves and upturned collars, Elvis style.

Now they were all finishing their senior year of college. Mojo was the athlete of the group. He had been the quarterback of his Madison High football team, and was attending Georgia Tech on an athletic scholarship. Rags was the talented one. He had a tenor voice that sounded like a budding Pavarotti and studied music at Mercer College. Peter, however, was the scholar among the three, matriculating at Emory University, where his major was pre-law.

Rags, a blonde-haired boy, was nursing a beer in a back booth when Peter, with piles of curly black hair atop his head, walked through the door. Like most boys of that era, both of them wore their hair well below their collars and had long sideburns and mustaches.

"Peter, Peter, Pumpkineater," Rags yelled, flashing a wide grin as he rose to greet his friend.

"Had a wife, but couldn't keep her," Peter replied laughingly, meeting Rags in the middle of the room, and then two of the three musketeers hugged each other.

"How's it going, Raggedy Man?" Peter said.

"Not bad, not bad," Rags said, standing back so he could look Peter up and down. "Hey, man, you're looking good."

"You, too."

Rags turned and sung out to the waitress, "Hey, Mable, Black label," emulating the commercial for a beer that was especially popular with the college crowd because of its low price, thirty-five cents.

Peter joined Rags in the booth and soon Rachel, a tall skinny woman in her thirties with mousey blonde hair, brought over a couple of red and black cans of beer.

"Hey, Peter," she said coyly, "how was school?"

"Hi, Rachel," Peter replied blandly, "it was alright."

Rachel plopped the beers down on the table and left, smiling as she turned to look back at the boys.

"You could do her, man," Rags said excitedly. "The woman digs you."

"Come on, man, too old. I'm looking for a young chippie," Peter said after chugging almost half a beer. "When did you get in?"

"Yesterday. What about you?"

"About an hour ago," Peter said. "Did Mojo get in?"

"Yeah, this morning. I talked to him a few minutes ago. He'll be on."

"Who else is here?" Peter asked.

"Well, let's see," Rags said contemplatively. "Jimmy Conrad and Lewis Mallory are home. They're coming."

"Females!" Peter chided Rags. "I've just finished mid-terms, man, I need wine, women, and song."

"Just funning you, man. Collette McCollum and Joyce Golden said they might be out later."

"Now you're talking, my man," Peter said, holding his hand up for a slap.

Just as Rags slapped Peter's palm, another dark haired boy pushed through the door.

"Mojo, over here," Peter yelled to the third musketeer.

The three boys exchanged pleasantries in the middle of the floor. "Let the games begin," Peter yelled, and then turned to Rachel. "More beer, and keep 'em coming."

As the three boys laughed and talked, exchanging "war stories," the hour grew late and the beer began to take its effect. It was well after midnight, and not only were Joyce and Collette no-shows, but so were the local girls. Only a few came out that night, and those who did, paid little or no attention to the college boys' drunken prattle. As the night wore on, Rachel, the waitress, began to look better and better.

"This joint is really dead," Mojo said. "I wish I'd stayed up in Atlanta. At least they've got the strippers."

"Come on, man, don't be a kill-joy," Rags said. "The night is still a baby and everybody comes home for Christmas. They'll be here. Where else is there to go?"

"Well, let's go to Pearlie's," Mojo said.

Peter playfully grabbed Mojo's big head. "Oh, you're paying for it now."

"I will, tonight," Mojo said.

"Me, too," Rags added. "Boy, am I horny."

"Let's get a little something for the road," Mojo suggested.

"Yeah," Rags agreed, "I could stand something a little harder. What about you, Pete, you want to go in on a pint?"

"Nah," Peter said, dismissing his friend with a wave of his hand. "I don't mess with that grog anymore."

Then Peter pulled out a bag of pot.

"Ooo, I'll be seeing you in jail," Mojo said.

"No way, not a chance." Peter said smugly.

The three boys laughed and talked as they poured what was left of their beers into plastic cups, and Mojo and Rags went together and bought a pint of Old Heavenly Hill from Rachel. They walked outside, and then each boy got into his own car for the drive to Pearlie's.

Pearlie's Truck Stop was named after Pearlie Willingham, a hard-nosed woman who was one of the first females to drive an eighteen-wheel transfer-truck across country. Pearlie, now long deceased, also had a reputation of brewing the best coffee and making the best country-fried steak in Madison County. Therefore, when her trucking days were over, she bought five acres of land, at the crossroads of State Road 5 and Highway 19, and opened a small diner. There was just one pump for gasoline, one for kerosene, and another for diesel fuel, which was the lifeblood of the big trucks. Then the government decided to run Interstate Highway 95 near the other two state roads and – as they say – the rest was history.

Pearlie's had now become one of the best-known truck stops in the United States. A common byline among truck drivers was, "I'll meet you at Pearlie's." The huge dining room still boasted of the best coffee and country-fried steak in the country. There were individual pay telephones situated at each oversized booth – truckers came in all sizes, but mostly extra-large – so the drivers could call home while awaiting their orders of country-fried ham with red-eye gravy, grits, and piping hot biscuits. Pearlie knew what drivers needed. She had been one of them.

For those who didn't choose to stay overnight in one of the cabins out back, there were pay showers behind the dining room, so the drivers could clean up before going back out on the dusty roads. There was also a game room, with pool tables and slot machines, for relaxation and entertainment. Alongside the main building, there was a large repair shop, with both diesel and gasoline pumps, where trucks could be refreshed and pampered while their drivers received the same treatment inside.

It was not unusual for truckers to drive twenty miles or more away from their normal route in order to swing by Pearlie's to partake of its multitude of offerings. Therefore, there was always a steady stream of traffic, twenty-four hours a day and seven days a week. And, where there was any great congregation of men, women were soon to follow, much to Pearlie's annoyance.

Scores of women, some locals and others transients, sat poised to offer "love at first sight" to the truckers – who were well known for carrying large sums of money, some of which belonged to their companies. It was also true that many, well meaning, uncles have dropped nephews off at one of the cabins out back for their initiation into manhood.

The restaurant was filled to capacity when – one after the other – the three boys drifted in. A much younger Lizzy Campbell joked with some of the drivers as she poured them coffee and took their orders. Eventually, the boys were able to get seated at a booth near the back of the room. While they waited for the hamburgers and fries that were ordered, Lizzy brought them tall glasses of soda, into which Rags and Mojo promptly poured liquor from their bottle. The two of them drank up as their eyes eagerly scanned the premises for females. Peter passed on the liquid refreshment, he had smoked a joint during the trip over.

Later, the hamburgers and fries had come, and been quickly devoured by the hungry boys, who were having no luck at all in their search for female companionship.

"One more for the road," Rags said, pouring the dregs from the liquor bottle into his glass. "There's nothing here, tonight."

"You said it," Peter added. "This place is as dead as a door nail."

"Yep, this is hopeless," Mojo agreed. "Drink up, and let's get out of here."

Then Rags looked up into a familiar face as a young woman pushed through the crowd and took a seat at the counter. "Whoa," he blurted out. Then he spoke slowly and evenly. "Hold the phone."

"What?" Mojo asked.

"Look who just walked in," Rags answered.

Mojo and Peter, whose backs were to the counter, turned to look. Mojo's eyes widened in disbelief, and Peter recoiled at the sight of Maryella Chandler as his mind raced back into time. It was as if his whole life was flashing before him, not just its most demeaning and humiliating moment.

Peter's mind quickly hastened back to 1972, when they were all back at Madison High. It was the Friday afternoon, the day before the Homecoming football game, a time when the school's former graduates came out for a grand and glorious reunion. Earlier that week, Maryella Chandler had been named Homecoming Queen. Members of the homecoming committee were clowning around, in good spirits, as they decorated the float, upon which she would ride through the Courthouse Square the next morning.

The boys, including Rags, Mojo, and Peter were nailing the wooden frame to the flat wagon that would hold the throne, upon which Maryella would sit and blow kisses from as a tractor pulled it through the city in the Homecoming Parade. Maryella and a host of other girls sat on the school steps making blue and white crepe paper flowers and cutting out big blue letters that would eventually spell out, MISS HOMECOMING.

They were all taking a Coke break. Mrs. Taylor, the homecoming sponsor, had just let one of the boys bring a case of Coca-Colas from the home economic kitchen. Mojo was popping the tops with an opener and passing the cold drinks around. Most of the boys, however, took this time to turn their attention to female pursuits. Rags was sitting in the tractor seat, sipping his soda and explaining to Karen Hodges how the gearshift lever worked while attempting to entice her to be his date at the Homecoming dance. Mojo popped the last bottle top and sat on the steps beside his girlfriend, Linda Wilcox. Peter and Maryella, the campus lovebirds, stood on the steps above them, talking.

Maryella had been distant all that week, and Peter was attempting to determine what the problem was. "What's wrong, Maryella? You've hardly said a word, all day."

"It's nothing, Peter, really. It's just that I…" Her voice trailed off as she saw a familiar car turn into the driveway.

A black boy pulled the car to the curb, flashing a wide grin as he leaned across the front seat and opened the passenger side door. Maryella turned to Peter. "I'm sorry, but I have to go," she said, turning to leave. She eagerly walked down the sidewalk and got into the car. Peter stood speechless as the car pulled away.

Some of the boys began to laugh at Peter, including Rags. "Well, how do you like that?" Rags said facetiously. "A damned nigger done took your girl!"

When he saw the dejection on his best friend's face, Rags immediately wished that he could recall his words, but the damage had been done.

Mojo, however, was not amused. "Jus' like they say, give 'em an inch and they'll take a mile!" he scowled, looking up at Peter. Anger and bitterness colored his words.

The State of Georgia had finally gotten around to implementing the edits of the momentous decision of Brown vs. Topeka, and Madison High was in its second year of racial integration.

Word of the romance between the homecoming queen and the black boy spread through Madison County as quickly as the wires of Southern Bell could carry it – from Orchard Park to the Chandler Mansion.

That had been the most demeaning and embarrassing moment of Peter's life. Not only was he hurt that his darling, Maryella, would walk away from him, but totally crushed that she would do so in front of his friends – and with a Negro?

Now angrily back in the present, Peter's face hardened and turned beet-red as he brought himself back to reality and rose from the booth. "You guys, go ahead. I've got some *unfinished business*."

Maryella gasped when she turned, looking up into Peter's hateful eyes as he stood behind her. "Oh, don't do that," she said. "You'll scare me to death."

"What are you doing here? I thought this town was through with you," he said brusquely.

Momentarily, Maryella was speechless as she looked up at him, but then she spoke. "Well, don't just stand there," she said, patting the empty stool beside her. "Sit. I won't bite."

"It's been a long time," Peter said tersely as he, reluctantly, sat astride the stool. "How've you been?"

"So-so."

Rags and Mojo walked up to the two former lovers. "Hi, Maryella," Rags said, almost under his breath.

"Hello, Rags," she said, and then looked up at Mojo, who stood stone-faced and didn't speak. "And how're you, Mojo?"

"Fine, until you showed up," he snapped back, still harboring hatred from the past. "Let's blow this place, Rags. All of a sudden, I smell a foul odor."

After the two boys left, Maryella turned to Peter. "Aren't you going to buy a girl a drink?"

"You know this is a dry county." Then he smiled coyly. "But I have something better."

Maryella had come to Pearlie's to find Sam. She had decided to head further South with him in the morning, Florida maybe. She'd figure that out when she got there. The one thing Maryella did know was that she just couldn't face her family. Maybe later, but not right now.

But things were looking up, she thought. So many times before, Maryella had longed to heal the rift between her and Peter, and now she had that opportunity.

They had been parked at the lovers' lane in Simpson's Woods for almost an hour. At first their conversation had been awkward and strained, but as the opiate has done down through the centuries, inhibitions were lowered and old differences pushed aside. Now they talked amiably, even jokingly, as Maryella told tales of San Francisco and spun yarns about Chicago and New York, places that Peter could only dream of traveling to when he finished law school.

Peter lit up the last joint from his stash, took a long draw on the marijuana cigarette, and then passed it to Maryella. She took a long pull, held it briefly, and then exhaled the smoke before passing it back to Peter.

"You know, I thought about you a lot."

"Really?" Peter said, and then took another hit before passing it back to her.

"I'm really sorry, you know, about how things worked out. I was young, and didn't know nothing," she said, almost angrily. Then she smoked the last of the joint and became more relaxed. "But I tell you what, these last few years have taught me a thing or two."

And she really was sorry. Maryella did *not* intend to hurt the boy she had dated off and on through most of their high school days, even over the protests of her father and brothers. Peter was much too poor for the Chandlers' tastes. But the two of them had even spoken of marriage after college.

He would become a famous lawyer and she would teach, maybe at a university. Therefore, she, too had been saddened by the strange turn of events that senior year in school. But sometimes those things happened when you fell in love. Maryella had not planned to leave Peter for the tall black boy – who had come into her life and turned it upside down – but she loved him with a passion.

But that was then, and this was now. Maryella moved closer to Peter, touching his face lightly.

"You were such a cute little boy when we were in grade school," she said, now looking him in the eye seductively

Peter's face flushed. "Aw, go on."

"I had a huge crush on you, even back then," she said, now snuggling even closer.

"Did you really?"

"Yes. I used to love to hear you recite nursery rhymes," she said laughingly. "You were always the first to memorize them."

"Do you really remember that?" he asked, now smiling. "I was so silly."

"Noo," she said. "What's that love rhyme you used to recite to me? Say it for me."

"Aw, I don't remember it. That was a long time ago."

Then Maryella began to tickle him. "Yes you do," she said playfully. "Go ahead. Let me hear it."

Peter playfully squirmed and laughed as she continued to tickle him. "Alright, alright, stop. Here goes."

Peter thought for a moment, his mind searching for the right verse that was long since buried in his adult memory. Then he spoke slowly and lovingly, saying, "There once was a little boy and a little girl. The little girl says to the little boy, 'What shall we do?' ... Says the little boy to the little girl, 'I will kiss you.'"

There in the moonlight, Maryella's beauty dazzled the young man as it had done so many times before. The old flame was quickly rekindling as former lovers kissed, passionately. Then Peter pushed her down onto the seat, tugging at her clothes as they kissed. Suddenly she pushed him up.

"Wait a minute," she said

Maryella climbed over into the back seat and, raising herself to one knee, slowly began to unbutton her blouse. Peter quickly joined her, seating himself in a corner while staring lustily in anticipation of the removal of each piece of clothing. In the moonlight, he saw that she wore no bra as the blouse fell to the floor. The sensual sight of her breasts almost overwhelmed him, evoking the same titillating response as in times gone by. He could already feel his manhood rising. After kicking out of her shoes and striping off her socks, Maryella struggled a bit with her tight jeans, but soon dispensed with them, leaving only the tiniest of white bikini panties.

"No, let me," Peter said, breathing heavily as he greedily took in the view.

"Okay," Maryella said, nibbling at his lips as he slowly eased her panties down and tossed them aside.

Now Maryella was stunningly naked. Her long blonde hair and creamy-white body glistened in the moonlight as she looked at him, seductively, slowly licking her lips. Peter could take no more. He was ready. Hastily lowering his pants and shorts, he quickly mounted her and the two of them began to move rhythmically.

But, then without warning – he froze. They both lay motionless for a second, but now Maryella's pot kicked in. She uttered a low chuckle, which at first sounded as if she were crying. The chuckle swelled into a laugh, and then into a belly laugh. "Ha, ha, ha..."

Peter was infuriated. "Stop it, you little tramp! It's your fault!"

"Ha, ha, ha..."

Then Peter placed his hands around her neck. "Stop it, I said! Stop it!"

When she continued her guttural laugh, his hands tightened around Maryella's throat, harder and harder. Suddenly she gagged and began to struggle with him. "Aaggh! Peter! You're hurting me! Aaggh!"

Now she was fighting back, clawing at him with all her might. But she was no match for the angry man. Peter's eyes widened in rage. He had totally lost it and was now squeezing both hands together around her neck, tighter and tighter. After a few long moments, Maryella's face turned pale, and then blue before, finally, her eyelids shut. Then she went silent ... and struggled no more.

When the full affect of what he had done hit him, Peter panicked and began shrieking, "Maryella, wake up. Wake up!"

He pushed the car door open and placed one foot outside before remembering that he was naked from the waist down. Totally frustrated now, Peter sat beside Maryella, whose body was sprawled across the seat with her head cocked to the side at a very unnatural angle. He was crying now as he rocked, pitifully, back and forth. "It's your fault," he screamed "It's all your fault."

"The wages of sin ... is death," a stern voice bellowed from the television set. The TV preacher ranted on, extolling the virtues of repentance and the penalty for not doing so as the short plump woman, lounging on a threadbare sofa, with her hands draped loosely around her rotund belly, snored loudly. She had long since dozed off, leaving the word of the lord to an otherwise empty house.

Just then Peter burst through the front door, startling his mother awake. "Mother, Mother, wake up! Where's Dad? I need his help!"

The ashen-faced woman slowly stirred. "What is it?" she said.

Wiping the spittle – drooling down her chin – with the sleeve of her worn bathrobe, she said, "Your father's not here. There was trouble at work, and he had to stay late."

"We have to call him," Peter said, staring down at his mother with pleading eyes. "Mother, I've really done it this time. It's Maryella, she's back!"

His mother struggled to her feet. "So?"

"Mother, I've killed her!"

"Killed her?" Her eyes widened. "How? Why?"

"It was an accident, Mother, I swear! We were just--"

"Stop it, boy! Pull yourself together!" she said, grabbing her son and shaking him.

"We've got to call the police," he said, walking toward the telephone on the table beside the sofa.

"No!" she said, blocking his path. "We don't need no trouble. You're too close to graduation!"

"Well, let's call Dad. He'll know what to do."

"No. He's got enough problems of his own," she said angrily. "Slow down, let's think this thing through."

She took Peter firmly by the shoulders and looked him squarely in his eyes. "Now, I don't know what happened, but her kind … they deserve whatever they get."

Peter whimpered as he took a seat on the sofa. The woman continually shook her head, pacing nervously. "The minute I laid eyes on her, I knew that little slut was gonna be nothing but trouble for you. Her and her people, thinking they're so much better than the rest of us."

"Yes, Mother, you told me," he ruminated. "I should've listened."

"Where is she?"

"She's in the car. It's parked in the garage."

"Let's pray," she said. "We have to seek the guidance of the lord, and then we'll do what we have to do."

"Yes, ma'am," he said, taking the woman's thick hand and kneeling with her as he had done since a child.

"Never do anything without guidance from the lord," she said.

After a prayer that was much too long and too rambling, the woman finally brought things to a close, and then they walked through the kitchen into the garage. Peter opened the back door of his car. As they stared down at Maryella's nude body, the woman was repulsed. "Cover her up. I don't want 'a see this daughter of Lillith," she said harshly. " It was just such as she that gave birth to Satan."

"I know Mother, you've told me that … so many times."

When Peter had wrapped the motionless nude body in a blanket that he found on a shelf in the garage, his mother turned to him, and then spoke even more sternly. "You see that bag of lime over there?"

"Yes."

"Now this is what you have to do."

It took Peter over an hour to dig it deep enough, but finally, he pulled himself up from the hole and rested on the pile of dirt. After catching his breath for a minute, he dragged Maryella's body to the side of the hole. Then Peter gave the blanket a hard pull, rolling it over into its grave.

There was a loud thud as the body hit the bottom of the hole. Maryella landed face-up and her eyes sprung wide open. She was now gasping desperately for air as Peter threw shovelful after shovelful of dirt into the hole.

Maryella looked up, in abject horror now, as a shovelful of dirt landed in her face. "Peter, don't," she screamed, using both hands in a futile attempt at pushing the dirt away. But there was too much and he was piling on, more and more.

When he heard her excruciatingly loud screams, Peter's heart raced and his breathing shortened. Under the full moon, all he could see were two shiny emerald eyes, staring agonizingly back up at him. He stopped for a moment and started to reach out to her. But something came over him, forcing Peter on. His eyes flashed wildly as he resumed shoveling dirt, but now with a fury. "Die, you little whore, die!"

Then her cries became muffled, and then the night went silent. *Finally, Maryella Chandler had gotten what she deserved. Yes, this had righted the wrong she had done him*, Peter thought as he walked away from the grave with a feeling of euphoria.

Christmas at Chandler House was indeed a grand affair. And Ty Jr. and his brother, Logan, were seeing to it that this year's celebration would be more lavish than any before. The mansion was built at the turn of the century – a golden period in the State of Georgia, a time of money, elegance, and refinement – but it had been renovated and added to over the years.

The main building was large and luxurious. There were three levels, twelve bedrooms, and fifteen bathrooms when servants' quarters were counted. It was a gracious house with a wide center hall and a handsome staircase.

A veranda, spanning the front of the house, held a line of white chairs, in which the family rocked and whiled away pleasant summer evenings. All around the stately mansion, picture windows invited the sunshine and panoramic view inside. The woodwork throughout the opulent structure was magnificent, from the crown molding around the ceiling of its spacious rooms, to the tall columns that held the huge oak crossbeams of the library in place. They were all masterpieces of the wood-carver's art from Holland and Ireland.

The mansion's furnishings were massive, yet elegant. In the library, there was room to sit, converse, and play card games, as well as enjoy tea or stronger beverages. In the living room, a roaring fire blazed in the hearth beneath a terracotta mantle piece, which was lined with trophies and loving cups won at dog shows and other exhibitions.

Two young black women were placing ornaments on the twenty foot Scottish pine that the men had erected in the center hall. However, Ty Jr. had given the women explicit instructions that they were not to place the crowning jewel, the star, on the top of the tree. For the first time in four years, this honor would go to Maryella. This had been her loving duty since she was so small that Ty Jr. had to hoist her upon his shoulders in order for her to reach the highest branch of the tree.

The side tables in the huge dining room – where stately dinners were served on the finest pieces of China and eaten with the purest of silver cutlery – were laden with fruit pies and cakes of all kinds. And the mixed aromas of roasting turkeys, hams, and legs of beef wafted from the kitchen.

Walter, now a major in the Army and stationed at the Pentagon in Washington D.C., was already home and Maryella was expected later that night. Tomorrow afternoon, all of the twenty-six seats at the long table would be filled and several smaller tables would be set up in the wings to accommodate the rest of the Chandler kin that lived within driving distance, over fifty people in all.

The night before Christmas had been far spent. It was well beyond the midnight hour, and Ty Jr. had long since sent the hired help home. Miss Ida, Maryella's nanny, who was now in her seventies and more a member of the family than one of the work crew, had been jubilant all day long as she directed the Christmas fixings, from the food in the kitchen to the linen's placed on Maryella's bed. Miss Ida had come to love Maryella as her own and she, too, had been crushed when Ty Sr. drove her from the house.

Around midnight, however, enthusiasm, changed to doubt, and then disappointment. Nonetheless, before she left for the night, the old woman was still heartened. "Don't worry Mr. Junior, my lil' girl'll be here in the mornin', for sure," she had said before her grandson came to drive her home to her own family – with hopes of seeing her precious Maryella the next day.

That had been two long hours ago. The men of the manor had shared a late-night bottle of Claret with cold beef and cheese, before drifting off to bed, first the old man and Logan, and then Walter – leaving only Ty Jr. and a bottle of Cognac to wait for Maryella.

It was with a sad face that Ty Sr. crept back down the stairs. He walked over to the Magnavox stereo and flipped the switch. The sound of Bing Crosby's "White Christmas," which had been playing much of the night, died. Finally, he walked over to his sleeping son, gently lifted the Cognac snifter from his fingers, and then tapped him on the shoulder.

"Come on, Junior. Let's go to bed," he said softly. "Maybe she'll come in the morning."

With a look of misery on his face and a sense of betrayal in his heart, Tyson Chandler, Sr. guided his namesake, who'd had way too many Cognacs, up the steps. *God forgive me for the pain I've caused my family,* he prayed silently.

Chapter 19

Three days had passed since Ginny vanished – without a trace – and the police were no closer to finding her than they were that Monday afternoon when she just dropped out of sight. The town of Wrightsburg had virtually become an armed camp. Other than the investigators, all of the police officers patrolled the streets. Instead of attending to their regular duties at the plant, Chandler security guards watched over the schools, libraries, and other public buildings.

Charlie thought it best that he return to work. The frequent trips would at least give him and Jay Dee the opportunity to widen the search area. Between the Chandler drivers, Dewey, Sonny, and the football team, flyers with Ginny's picture, announcing the five thousand dollar reward for information that was put up by Chandler Enterprises, were plastered on the walls of every establishment within a two hundred mile radius.

Miriam, however, had not been so lucky. She had mostly taken to her bed. When she was not under sedation, Miriam walked around the house, clothed only in a nightgown, babbling to herself as if she had lost her mind.

"I should've done it, myself," she rambled on.

Several of the women from the Florida side of the family took turns watching over Miriam as she constantly uttered something about a punishment from God.

Chief Callahan had set up a hotline to receive telephone calls regarding the whereabouts of Ginny. Spurred on by the hefty reward, many sightings were reported. There were many leads called in, but none substantial. There were so-called sightings of Ginny from Rome, Georgia, to Tallahassee, Florida. One caller placed Ginny with a traveling tent-preacher – she was supposed to be a member of his gospel choir. Another man insisted that he had seen her shopping at Rich's Department Store up in Atlanta.

Then there was the woman who had seen Ginny somewhere along the Georgia-Florida Parkway. She was said to be traveling with a band of new-age hippies. Without a single hard lead, however, members of the investigative team had to admit that they were stymied.

The women and girls of Madison County were alarmed, but if the stalker – whomever he was – struck, they were preparing for battle. The Karate classes at Mr. Moto's were overflowing with new female members, and the mace sprayers flew off the shelf at the Ace Hardware Store.

After sundown, the town stood still. Pappas' Restaurant and Barney's Burger Barn both closed early due to lack of traffic. That Friday's football game with neighboring Upton County was still scheduled, but kickoff time had been moved up to one o'clock in the afternoon, and there would be extra security from the Georgia State Highway Patrol.

Chief Callahan persuaded Uncle Buddy to stick around in case the dogs were needed to sniff out any new lead that might appear. The old man agreed to stay, but only after returning home to gather emergency rations – several jugs of corn whiskey – to sustain him while in Wrightsburg.

Margo Johnson became despondent when Cha-Cha's mother had a change of heart and drove down from Atlanta to pick up her daughter and take her back home. She reasoned that it was better to fight the devil she knew, Cha-Cha's stepfather, than the demon in the bush, the Wrightsburg Stalker – as Beth's killer had become known. Margo had first lost her best friend, Ginny, and now she was losing the only other pal she had.

Finally, the Atlanta newspaper writers dug up the stories of Wrightsburg's other missing girls. The front-page headline under Ginny's picture read, "Second Girl in One Month, Missing in Madison County." On the inside pages, there were stories about Armanda Lockett, the black girl who went to a traveling carnival, back in 1978, never to return; Anna Jennings, who left home, in 1982, and never came back; and then Beth Campbell.

Things were a blur at the police station and the mayor was up to his eyeballs in inquiries from all over the country. Another futile meeting of the investigators was drawing to its miserable conclusion when an officer opened the door to the chief's office and stuck his head inside.

"Lou, the phone's for you," he said. "You want to take it in here?"

"Yeah."

Lou, praying that this was not an anonymous tip about another dead body, got up from the conference table, walked over to the chief's desk, and then placed the receiver to his ear. "Brazell, Homicide."

The coroner's voice came on the line. "Lou, the lab report on the Campbell girl came back this morning. Are you ready for this?"

"Yeah, shoot," Lou said, sitting at the chief's desk and picking up a pencil.

"The cause of death is asphyxiation by strangulation."

"But you said there were no marks on her throat," Lou shot back.

"There was soil in Beth's lungs and her body was riddled with Pavulon. That's a--"

Lou's eyes widened and his face contorted as he cut in. "I know what it is. It's a muscle-paralyzing drug." His voice trailed off, but then he managed to end the conversation. "Thanks, Doc."

Lou's face hardened as he slowly hung up the telephone and turned to Lola and Chief Callahan, still seated at the table.

"What?" Lola asked upon seeing the horrified look on her lover's face.

"Beth Campbell was buried alive!"

Lola gasped and Chief Callahan looked on in horror.

Lou and Lola went back to their cubicles and Chief Callahan began working the telephones. The mayor had begun funneling his queries to the chief, who had written a statement that he routinely read to the out of town press. Russ Callahan had just fielded a call from Johnsonville, Tennessee, when there was a soft knock on the office door. "Yeah, come on," he said after hanging up the telephone.

When he looked up from his desk, Tyson Chandler, Jr. stood in his doorway.

"Oh, Mr. Chandler, how're you doing?"

"Fine, Chief, and you?"

"Just fine," the chief said. "Come on in. Have a seat."

"That's alright," Ty Jr. said, moving closer to the desk, "I'll only be a moment. I saw the article in the morning's paper."

"Oh, about the missing girls being linked together?" the chief acknowledged. "You know, we've been thinking along those same lines. We just haven't gone public with it. What about the article?"

"I think you need to add another name to that list," Ty Jr. said, and then placed a picture of Maryella Chandler on the chief's desk.

"Maryella?" the chief said, in shock, and then rose from his seat. "But I thought she was--"

"Living in Europe and married to a nobleman," Ty Jr. completed the chief's sentence. "That was my father's story, God rest his soul."

"Yes, that's what we all thought."

"Chief, on second thought, I think I'd better take that seat."

Chief Callahan ushered him to the conference table, and it took the better part of an hour for Ty Jr. to lay out the story of his sister's disappearance.

Down the hall, Lola was catching up on a back log of paperwork. On her desk – along with a long list of calls that had to be returned to people who had phoned in about Ginny and the reward – lay a thick packet from the Farmer's Bank. Lola had returned several calls, including one from a psychic in Atlanta, which proved to be interesting but not very informative.

The woman gave many details of the missing girls and Beth's grisly body, all of which could've easily been harvested from the pages of the Atlanta newspaper. Lola was about to give up and go to lunch, but she decided to take a look at the bank packet before doing so.

Not having the automated facilities of the Atlanta bank that had taken only a few days to deliver Hadley Frazier's records to the FBI, it had taken the Farmer's Bank two weeks to compile the recent transactions on Beth Campbell's account. Purely as a formality, Lola sifted through the pile of photocopies of checks and deposit slips. She was down to the last few pages when it popped out at her.

"Lou," she cried out. "Come take a look at this."

Lou was joking with another officer at the coffee center.

"In a minute," he said, waving a hand dismissively.

"Now," Lola demanded, rising from her seat and walking toward him.

"What is it?" he asked, now dismissing the joking officer and turning to her.

Then he saw it. Lola was holding up a check for him to see. It was a Bradley & Post company check for two thousand dollars – made out to Elizabeth Campbell and signed by Constance Bradley.

"Je-sus!" Lou said. "Who would 'a thought it."

"Not me."

"This doesn't make him a suspect, but Mr. Constance Bradley is gonna have a load of explaining to do," Lou said. "Let's go pay him a visit."

Ginny had no idea how long she had been in this dark place. Her life had become a jumbled mixture of dreams and reality, some of which could be remembered with vivid clarity, but other parts she had very little recollection of. Some of the imaginings were horrid nightmares while others could be as pleasant as a Sunday-school picnic. There were dreams of the forays into Simpson's Woods, where she would stumble upon Beth and the other girls.

One of Ginny's more vivid memories was of becoming horrified when the missing girls encircled her as if preparing to set upon her. They gnashed their teeth and stared at her – with blazing red eyes – until the blonde haired girl came to her rescue.

But she could also remember soaring with *the girl,* high over the expansive Golden Gate Bridge of San Francisco, the bright lights of Peachtree Street in Atlanta, and the monumental Sears Tower in Chicago.

In this state of betweeness, Ginny would sometimes feel herself beginning to awaken, but then there would be a prick on her arm and the dreams would start all over again. But now, Ginny realized that she had been drugged and that the chemical being constantly injected into her body, like Dr. Turner's medicine, was beginning to lose its effect. However, she still could neither fully distinguish dream from reality nor remember how she came to be in this dark hole, which smelled of mold and mildew and was as cold and damp as a riverbed.

But wasn't she on the verge of losing her mind? Well, that's it. She'd finally done it … lost her mind, and this is what it felt like. *Don't be silly,* she thought. *It's just a dream.*

But if it were a dream, Ginny Westbrook was ready to wake up. There were times when she tried to move her arms and legs, but couldn't. Her body was paralyzed. But now, sensing the movement of her fingers, she knew that she was *definitely* awake. As the feeling slowly drifted back into her extremities, Ginny sensed that she was lying on a bed, facedown. *That's it! I'm home,* she thought. But when she rolled over to get out of bed, her body slammed down, hard, on the concrete floor. "Aw, my head" she cried out.

Ginny was not at home, but had been sleeping on a cot, tucked into the corner of a shadowy dank basement. Her eyes blinked as she looked up into the streaks of light that filtered through a small window. Then it came to her. Ginny remembered how she had gotten there and who had brought her. "BUT WHY?" she wailed, opening her arms in entreaty.

Then Ginny tried to assess her situation. No bones were broken and she could now move her body, somewhat, so she got up from the floor and sat on the side of the tiny cot. She was too afraid to be hungry, but she was thirsty, had a terrible headache, and had to pee, badly. Then in the light from the window, Ginny saw a large bucket.

When she rose from the bed and moved toward the unsightly utensil, Ginny tripped and went sprawling to the floor. In astonishment, Ginny Westbrook looked down at the shackle that was attached to her right ankle. Like an animal, she was chained to the wall.

"Oh, God," she cried out. "Please ... help me."

Then Ginny thought about how *the girl* had come to rescue her from Sonny and his gang. "Okay, mystery lady," she said, aloud, "you've been following me around. Go ahead, do something. Do your thing! I need to have a long talk with the police."

Ginny closed her eyes and waited as if expecting something mystical to happen, but nothing did. "Come on, Girl," she cried hysterically. "I saw you bring those bees down on Sonny. Get me out of here!"

When there were no more tears left to cry, Ginny strengthened her resolve to get out of this horrible mess. She was now becoming accustomed to the darkness and her eyes desperately scanned the room for a way out. On one side of the basement, she could see the stairway that led up to the rest of the house, and on the other side, there was a door, which might be a storeroom.

Her heartbeat quickened when she saw a large ring of keys hanging from a nail beside the door. Ginny looked down at keyhole on the archaic shackle around her ankle. *One of those has to fit*, she thought.

After abandoning all sense of decency and relieving herself in the bucket, Ginny crawled toward the door until the chain that restrained her allowed no further movement.

Then she saw it!

On the floor behind several bags, there was a shovel, and it was much closer to her than the key ring. If she could get her hands on that shovel, then just maybe...

After flattening her body out on the cold concrete floor, it had taken every fiber of Ginny's being to reach the handle of the shovel. But finally, she had it in her hands. She smiled and rested just a bit before attempting the next task. Getting the shovel in hand was one thing, however, maneuvering it into position to slip the handle through the key ring was another matter, indeed.

Ginny could already feel the warm blood trickling into her shoe from the huge gash on her ankle that the shackle made deeper each time she stretched to reach for the shovel. Undaunted, however, she pressed on. Grasping the shovel blade with both hands, Ginny extended the handle as far as she could. It was no use. Even at her fullest extension, the shovel handle was at least a foot away from the key ring. "Oh, no," she cried in despair, falling to her knees and dropping the shovel. Ginny burst into tears.

Chapter 20

The return trip home from Chattanooga was always the worst part of the journey for Charlie Westbrook. The truck was empty and there were no more stops to make, therefore, the long stretch of Interstate-75 gave him too much time to think. There was too much time ... to take too much blame for the things he'd done. Whenever he had this much time to himself, Charlie would try to pinpoint that single moment in time when if he had done things differently there might've been a much different outcome.

Jay Dee was sleeping now. For him, there had been too much of Uncle Buddy's corn whiskey and too many cases of fruit and vegetables to unload. The hum of the truck engine and the hypnotic effect of the oncoming white lines, racing to meet him, sent Charlie zooming back down the highway of yesteryear.

September, 1972.

Not only had the news of the interracial romance between the rich man's daughter and the star athlete reached the Chandler household, but the

Westbrook's as well. Charlie was furious as he, Miriam, and his brother, Billy, sat around the breakfast table.

"You know what you're doing is wrong," Charlie screamed at his brother.

"Wrong! How can this be wrong? Isn't that what the Civil Rights Movement was about? Being yourself and being with anyone you choose."

"Please! Will you two stop fighting," Miriam said. "I hate it when you do this!"

"But that girl is gonna cause you nothing but trouble!" Charlie said.

"If there's trouble, we'll just have to deal with it!"

"Listen, Billy, I don't want to argue, but there's nobody but you and me, now. And you know Mom and Pop wanted you to go to college. Going into the Army is just downright foolish!"

Charlie and Billy Westbrook's parents had died young, both were only in their fifties. Their mother died from lack of proper medical treatment for a congenital heart condition. The saying was that she died of a bad heart and their father died – a few years later – simply of a broken heart. Whatever the case, this sad turn of events left Charlie as the primary breadwinner of the Westbrook family and as Billy's legal guardian.

"Billy, your brother is right," Miriam said pleadingly. "You have a scholarship. How can you think of not going to college?"

Billy jumped up from the table, now with tears in his eyes. "Because I don't have a choice," he said sadly. "Maryella's pregnant."

Miriam gasped and Charlie shook his head. "I knew it! I knew it!"

Billy walked over to his brother. "Charlie, you know I would never do anything to hurt you. And I knew what Mom and Pop wanted for me," he said remorsefully, reaching out to his brother. "I didn't mean for this to happen. It just did. And I love her, Charlie."

Charlie looked at his brother scornfully, and then brushed his arm away before stomping out of the house without a word.

Fort Benning, Georgia, December, 1972

"Do you, Maryella, take William ... to be your lawfully wedded husband, to love and to cherish, for as long as you both shall live?" the Base Chaplain solemnly asked Maryella Chandler.

"I do," she answered with a smile.

"And do you, William, take Maryella ... to be your lawfully wedded wife, to love and too cherish, for as long as you both shall live?" the stately looking officer asked Pfc. Billy Westbrook.

"I do," he answered, and then also smiled.

"Then, with the power vested in me by God and the United States Army, I now pronounce you man and wife. You may kiss the bride."

Maryella's bridesmaid, Billy's best man, and Miriam Westbrook, all of whom sat on the front row of the base chapel, clapped as the newlyweds kissed.

Although a Chandler was getting married today, this was *not* a "Chandler wedding." Other than Linda Wilcox, Maryella's best friend, and Buster Satterwhite, Billy's running buddy, the only other witness to the nuptials had been Miriam, who had come in defiance of her husband Charlie's strict instruction not to do so.

"I don't know if I'll have a husband when I get home," she later told Billy.

Last summer when Luanne Haney, Maryella's first cousin, got married at the mansion, things were much different. Luanne's was a true Chandler wedding. Over a thousand guests attended the catered affair, which was so gigantic that fifty extra workers were hired just to serve food and drink.

The private ceremony was held inside the mansion, but after Ty Sr. had given the bride away and Reverend Clark had made things legal, Royal Stevenson, the groom, kissed the bride before they all moved outside to the grandest reception that Madison County had ever seen.

Two circus tents were erected on the grounds to accommodate the reception crowd. There was a twenty-six piece orchestra in each tent, playing waltzes, show tunes, and love songs as the hordes ate and drank up everything in sight, and then danced the night away.

Instead of the traditional Chandler gown – made of pure white silk, smuggled in under the blockade of Savannah during the Civil War, and worn by every Chandler bride since – Maryella wore a simple white maternity dress. Instead of the tails and top hat that Royal Stevenson wore, Billy stood handsomely tall in his dress-blue military uniform.

Ty Sr. had promised a wedding twice as big for Maryella and Ransom Meriwether, a boy her family handpicked for her, but that she could *not* stand – his father was running for governor. However, none of that mattered now. Maryella was Mrs. Billy Westbrook and she was married to the man she loved.

After the wedding party left the base chapel, they all had a sumptuous nuptial dinner at the Enlisted Men's Club before piling into the car for the drive to the Trailway Bus Station. Linda would stay for a week to help Maryella fix up the modest apartment that she had rented over in Columbus, only ten miles away. Buster and Miriam would take the bus back to Wrightsburg.

While Billy and Buster unloaded the suitcases from the trunk of the car, Maryella had a chance to talk to Miriam as they stood waiting.

"I hope we didn't get you into trouble, Mrs. Westbrook ... but thank you so much for coming."

"Aw," Miriam said with a hand of dismissal, "don't worry about me. And don't you worry about those two old stubborn fools back home, either. They'll come around, both of 'em."

"I hope so," Maryella said. "I feel so alone without my father, and Billy says the same about his brother."

"You just take care of yourself and that baby," Miriam said, smiling as she hugged her new sister-in-law.

The two women held each other for a long time.

"Oh, that smells nice. What kind of perfume are you wearing?" Miriam asked.

"That's not perfume. I can't wear it. The stuff makes me break out in hives. It's just a touch of lilac toilet water."

"Well, remember … I'll always be just a telephone call away," Miriam said.

Miriam had just finished work on her practical nursing certificate, and upon her return home, she would begin working at Wrightsburg General. She scribbled her work number on the back of a card and pressed it into Maryella's hand. "Call me, if you need me."

Billy and Buster shook hands before his friend boarded the bus, and then Billy hugged Miriam.

"Talk to 'im," he said. "Try to make 'im understand."

"I will," Miriam said, hugging him tightly. She turned and waved before walking up the steps of the bus. Little did Miriam know it, but this would be the last time that she would see her brother-in-law alive.

Although news of the interracial romance had circulated widely and was readily available to the Chandler household, it had taken all of two weeks for the news to reach Ty Sr.'s ears. Not even those among them with the stoutest heart wanted to be the bearer of – what they all knew would be – crushing news to the old man. Then one day, he overheard two of his workers talking about the scandalous affair.

To this day, no one can remember such a raucous being raised. Upon hearing the reprehensible news, Ty Sr. cursed everybody he could think of, including the Supreme Court for handing down the school desegregation decision. However, sensing that nothing could be done to the boy, legally, he turned his wrath inwardly upon his daughter.

From that day on, Tyson Chandler, Sr. neither acknowledged her presence nor ever spoke another word to Maryella. He even sent his demand that she immediately leave the house and surrender the keys to her new Thunderbird convertible, by his son, Logan.

Homecoming queens routinely fell for star athletes. It was the American way, as was the case with Billy and Maryella. It just happened that he was poor and black and she was rich and white, which was what caused the problems. As soon as he had learned of Maryella's pregnancy, Billy Westbrook had stunned the Big Blue Wave loyalist. He quit the football team in the middle of a pretty good season, dropped out of school, and then joined the Army.

Within two weeks, he had reported to Fort Benning, Georgia, for Basic Training, and was nearing completion of the eight-week stint when Maryella called him with the news of being kicked out of the house. They had expected reprimands, but certainly nothing this harsh. However, they hastily made plans for Maryella to join him.

The next day, Maryella boarded a bus for Columbus, Georgia. Including her savings and the money Ty Jr. and Miss Ida forced upon her, she $2500, a tidy sum for the time. When she arrived in the Southwest Georgia city, Maryella bought a second-hand Chevy for $800 and rented a modest one-bedroom furnished apartment in a good part of town. Things were going well.

As she prepared for Billy's graduation from the training program, Maryella was well treated when she was on base. She had to go there once a week for counseling with the Base Chaplin, who later performed the wedding ceremony. He provided her great comfort since she was not allowed to see Billy at all. He could only call her on Sunday, and they could hardly talk for more than five minutes.

The wedding was over and their future well planned. Now that Billy had finished basic training, he would have to report to Fort Hood, Texas, for advanced infantry training. Maryella now had access to a military doctor and the base commissary, where food could be bought for almost half price. And she would soon begin receiving a hundred and fifty dollar monthly spousal allotment.

They had decided that she would remain in Columbus until the baby was born. Then, heaven forbid, if Billy had to go to Vietnam, she would stay there until he returned from his tour of duty. However, if Billy were to be deployed to Germany, they would all go together. There, the family would have on-base housing and there were schools where Maryella could get her high school diploma.

Later, Billy would go to night school and do the same. Then when his Army days were finished, there would be college for the both of them. Things would work out just fine. They both were sure of it.

Things took a turn for the worse, however, when Billy pulled the Chevy into the parking space in front of their apartment. The manager, a big slovenly-looking man, stood waiting as they got out of the car.

"Lady, over here. We need to talk," the red-faced man called out to Maryella.

She walked over to him while Billy and her friend, Linda, went into the apartment.

"Here, take this," he said, handing her an envelope.

"What's this?" Maryella asked.

She flabbergasted upon opening the envelope and pulling out a check that was made out for $600, the precise amount of the deposit on the apartment and the first month's rent.

"We don't 'llow no jungle bunnies here," he said contemptuously. "You've got twenty-four hours to get out!"

Maryella had seen the man give them a peculiar look when she, Billy, and Linda returned home the night before. However, she thought nothing of it. She and Billy always drew stares whenever they were together.

The three of them spent the night at the local Holiday Inn, where the mixed group also drew stares from the desk clerk and sneers from some of the other guest. The next day, Linda Wilcox hastily beat a path back to Wrightsburg. Maryella loved her best friend, dearly. She had stuck by her through thick and thin. Although in principle, she did not agree with what Maryella was doing, not once did Linda say, "I told you so."

Later that day the newlyweds scoured the city, apartment hunting, but with no luck. They soon faced a harsh reality about racial attitudes. Changing their search strategy, the couple was accepted at the first all-black apartment complex where they applied.

Upon moving in, they put their cares behind them and spent the next two weeks that Billy had left on leave in marital bliss, enjoying a honeymoon of sorts. Each day they rose early and eagerly shopped for a few pieces of furniture, a used bedroom set, a kitchen table and chairs, a stereo record player, and a stack of the latest 45-rpm records.

Although their money was getting low, they threw caution to the wind and enjoyed a lavish dinner each night, even once going to a club to hear a band that played soul music. They drank champagne, danced, laughed, and loved the night away. Living in the black community was a better fit for the interracial couple. There were some inquisitive eyes, but not nearly as many as on the other side of town.

It was the first day in May and things were going badly for the Westbrook's of Columbus, Georgia. The eighteen weeks of advanced training had come and gone with the swiftness they had anticipated, but at its end, there was bad news. Instead of diminishing, as President Nixon had predicted, the war was escalating. As were most of the new recruits, Billy had been unceremoniously shipped to Vietnam.

To add insult to injury, Maryella's pregnancy was progressing horribly. In fact, had it not been for her quick thinking next-door neighbor, Edwina, quickly driving her to the base hospital, Maryella might possibly have miscarried.

After that night, she suffered pangs of guilt. For a fleeting moment while she was propped up in the back seat of the Chevy as Edwina ran half the traffic lights in Columbus, Maryella had thought, *maybe this will be for the best.* How could she think of such a thing? How could the loss of her baby ever be for the best? She cursed herself then and ever since.

Maryella soon found out how the black students must have felt when they were bussed across town to the all-white Madison High School, two years before. Though aware of how blacks were treated by whites, she was totally unprepared for the contempt in which some of her black neighbors held her, especially the women, and particularly when her handsome black husband was home on leave.

Edwina had laughingly said, "Them women don't like y'all white girls takin' the black men, especially good lookin' like your man is. I could dig on a lil' piece 'a that sweet potato, myself. Girl … he is fine. Just kiddin', just kiddin'," she said, quickly recanting the comment made in jest, now cracking up laughing.

Maryella joined her friend. It felt so good to laugh for a change.

"Don't you let them niggers git to you," Edwina said, now sounding serious. "Do they put any food on yo' table?"

"No," Maryella said, still laughing.

"Well, there."

Edwina, the only friend Maryella had cultivated during her six-month stay in Columbus, always had a way of equating everything to dollars and cents. She was a heavy-set woman in her early thirties with a wide bottom and a very pretty face. Wina, as they called her, had three children, all out of wedlock, which qualified her for a monthly welfare check and Section-

8 housing, a federal program that allowed low-income mothers to move out of the housing projects into mainstream apartment complexes.

Not all good complexes, such as the one in which they lived, accepted Section-8 dwellers. Although Maryella and Billy paid full price, there simply were not enough units to go around. This, Edwina explained, accounted for most of the animosity some of the neighbors had for Maryella. They felt that she was infringing upon their turf, first by claiming a handsome soul brother and now a precious apartment.

That morning, the two women were sitting at the breakfast table, finishing off the last of the ham and eggs that Maryella had made for Edwina and the kids. The girl, Loretta, was sitting in the corner, playing beautician with her doll's hair. But the boys, Clarence and Othello, were running around the apartment like holy terrors.

"Clarence, you sit your butt down," Edwina yelled at the boy who kept doing exactly as he had been, prying at Maryella's cabinet door with a butter knife. "And you, too, Othello. Don't y'all let me have to get up from here!"

"Let 'em play, Wina," Maryella said. "They're just children."

Then the telephone rang. Maryella got up from the table, walked over to the wall-phone, and picked up the receiver.

"Hello," she said.

When Edwina looked up from her ham and egg sandwich, she screamed. "Ella, what's the matter?"

The telephone dangled by its cord and Maryella's face turned pasty white. She just stood there – in a state of shock.

Miriam Westbrook walked smartly down the hallway of Wrightsburg General Hospital. She was dressed in a highly starched white uniform with a matching white cap tilted proudly to the side of her head. Mabel, the receptionist, called out to her as she passed. "Miriam, where have you been? Everybody's been looking for you."

"I've been on break. Why? What is it?"

"The telephone," Mabel said, holding up the receiver. "It's for you. They say it's an emergency!"

Nearing panic, Miriam thought about her husband who was constantly on the road. "Oh, God," she said, "don't let it be Charlie."

She quickly took the receiver in hand and placed it to her ear. "Hello?"

After listening for a moment, Miriam uttered three words. "Oh, my, God."

Miriam could not force her mind to contemplate which was worse, the fact that it had happened or the realization that she would have to tell her husband that his baby brother was dead.

The record states that, "On April 28, 1973, during a fire fight in the Mai-Cong Delta, Cpl. Billy Westbrook was killed in action. Due to his courageous efforts, however, his company commander and six others were spared their lives as Cpl. Westbrook returned enemy fire, even after being cutoff from his unit. Pursuant to his heroic action, the United States Army awards Cpl. Westbrook the Silver Star for Valor and a Purple Heart – posthumously.

On the day that General Harvey Reynolds, from Fort McPherson in Atlanta, came to the Wrightsburg courthouse to present the medals to Charlie, the steps were crowded with local dignitaries. Conspicuously absent, however, were the Chandlers. The general gave a stirring speech of Billy's bravery before handing Charlie two leather cases containing the medals. To this day, both are proudly displayed on the Westbrook's mantelpiece for all to see.

To some extent, the war medals helped to salve the wounds made a few days earlier when Charlie was told that he had no control over his brother's funeral arrangements. He was peeved to no end, but being the next of kin, it was Maryella's gut-wrenching decision to make. She had to decide whether to have the funeral in Columbus – where Billy would be mourned only by herself and a few others, mostly military personnel, and even then, only out of a sense of duty – or have the body shipped to Wrightsburg, where all of his friends and family were.

After many telephone calls and much soul searching, Maryella and Miriam planned a funeral in Wrightsburg that Maryella knew she would not attend. She could not go home because of poor health, caused by the bad pregnancy, and because of the disdain her father and most of the white townspeople had for her.

But all in all, they gave Cpl. Billy Westbrook one of the finest funerals that Wrightsburg, Georgia, had ever known. On that rainy day, seven soldiers were on hand to fire three shots each into the air, completing the twenty-one-gun salute, which was always reserved for heroes and high-ranking officers. At the end, thinking Miriam was Billy's mother, the officer presented her with the flag, which had draped the coffin.

It had been a battle, but Miriam was able to keep the flag for Maryella. Charlie, however, would never ever think of surrendering the Silver Star or Purple Heart. Miriam thought that it was a fair compromise as she boarded the bus for Columbus.

When Miriam arrived, Maryella was already bed-ridden. She had an abnormally high fever and her body was swollen almost beyond recognition. Her face was puffy as cotton candy and her legs and feet were more than twice their normal size. The apartment was a mess, since there was only Edwina to look after things, and she already had her hands full with her children. Miriam immediately called the hospital and got a leave of absence from her job. There was no way she could leave her sister-in-law alone in this deteriorating condition.

Miriam immediately identified herself as a nurse to Maryella's doctor, and it took the two of them the better part of a week to bring down the swelling and high temperatures. She wanted so desperately to call Maryella's family. In Miriam's brief experience as a nurse, she had seen many patients in Maryella's condition who did not survive. Nevertheless, she beat back the urge to call the Chandlers and, over Charlie's protests that she return home immediately, the two of them moved on – one day at a time.

Then it happened. Miriam was asleep on the sofa in the living room when she heard Maryella's agonizing scream. Reacting to a pre-arranged plan, Miriam banged on the wall until Edwina answered. It took only minutes for Wina to shuffle her kids down the street to a neighbor and rush back to the apartment. Miriam, with a screaming Maryella hanging on one shoulder and a suitcase in the other hand, was standing in the doorway when Edwina arrived.

"Get the car. The keys are on the table," Miriam called out.

"Alright," Edwina said nervously. She snatched up the keys, and then moved as quickly as her short stubby legs would allow. Within minutes, Edwina had driven across the grass and pulled the Chevy up to the apartment door. She held the back door open and helped Miriam get Maryella inside the car.

"Breathe, breathe," Miriam shouted to Maryella, trying her best to comfort her.

"I'm trying," Maryella shouted back between cries of pain.

Edwina hurried around to the driver's side, and then rammed the accelerator to the floor. The tires dug ruts into the lawn as the Chevy bucked, and then skittered into the street. As Edwina commenced another midnight scurry through the streets of Columbus, Maryella's pain subsided enough for her to speak.

"Did you think about what I said?" she gasped.

"No," Miriam replied, sternly, "and don't you think about it, either."

"You have to do it, Mrs. Westbrook. I've already seen to it."

"I can't," Miriam protested. "Charlie would kill me."

"I don't know what I'm going to do, or where I'll be going when all of this is over. But I do know one thing. I can't take care of a baby," Maryella went on. "I don't know how."

"Well, neither do I," Miriam shot back.

When they reached the hospital, two orderlies were waiting at the emergency room entrance. Maryella was already in labor and it was going badly. After a quick gurney ride to the delivery room, a team of doctors and nurses immediately went into action. Maryella was crying like a baby and screaming with each contraction.

"Push, push," the doctor yelled to Maryella, who was now screaming louder than ever.

"I can't! You get this thing out of me, right now. Do you hear me?" she yelled between groans and screams.

"My God!" the doctor said, visibly shaken when he saw the baby's head as it broke through the opening of the vagina.

"What is it?" a nurse asked frantically.

"Give me scissors, quick! The head's wrapped in the placenta!"

In his haste to cut the translucent membrane from around the baby's face, the doctor, accidentally snipped Maryella's flesh. She screamed horribly, and then passed out.

As Maryella had been, her baby daughter was also "born under the veil."

The next morning, a nurse entered Maryella's hospital room carrying the baby. "It's a girl," she said smiling. "Do you want to hold her?"

Maryella painfully looked toward the nurse, but then turned away. "No, no, I just can't." However, when the nurse turned to leave, Maryella had a change of heart. "Yes, yes, please, just for a moment."

The nurse gently placed the crying baby into her mother's arms. Then the sandy haired baby girl stopped crying and looked up into her mother's eyes. And for the most fleeting moment, they both smiled. But then Maryella called out to the nurse, "Here, take her."

When Miriam and Edwina arrived, they both stopped by the viewing window of the maternity ward. One look at the little pink bundle of joy, and Miriam could no longer say no.

After Edwina, who had lifted Maryella's spirits as she joked about her driving skills, had left them, the nurse entered with a clipboard full of papers, and a pen.

"Are you sure you want to do this?" the nurse asked Maryella.

With tears in her eyes, she answered, "Yes."

Maryella and Miriam took turns signing the papers, and then the nurse signed. When the nurse had left the room, Maryella turned to Miriam. "Oh, Mrs. Westbrook, there is one thing."

"Oh?" Miriam said.

"Somehow, in the naming of girls in my family, one of my grandmothers got overlooked. Could you name her Virginia?"

It was around midnight, and Charlie Westbrook was waiting at the gate, when the bus from Columbus pulled into the station. He stood grim-faced, with both arms folded tightly across his chest, as the passengers got off the bus. He couldn't wait to give Miriam a piece of his mind. Several passengers were ahead of her, but then suddenly, Miriam, with baby in arms, stood on the bottom step of the bus. The sight of the two of them took Charlie aback.

"No you didn't," he exclaimed as Miriam walked toward him. "I know you didn't bring that baby home! I ought to make you turn around and take it right back where you got it from!"

Miriam, who had already been smitten by the tiny tyke, just smiled as she reached Charlie. "It's not an 'it'," she said roughly, but then smiled. "She's a girl."

Miriam pulled the blanket away from Baby Ginny's face. "Come see."

When Charlie looked down at the baby girl, she gave him a dimpled smile, and then cooed. It was love at first sight – for both of them.

Charlie quickly hustled both of them into the car, slung Miriam's suitcase into the trunk, and then set out for home. They could *not* let anyone see the baby, who was clearly white. It wouldn't take much for the Chandlers to put two and two together, and Charlie couldn't afford to clash with the powerful clan. After much debate that night, they arose before dawn the next morning and had driven fifty miles south before stopping along the road and making two telephone calls.

Miriam called the hospital, telling her supervisor that she was having difficulty with a pregnancy and would not be coming back to work, but would be living with her people in Florida until the birth of her baby. That way the women could look after her, and Charlie wouldn't be hampered in his work by that chore. Charlie called his office, alluding to a sudden need to take his pregnant wife to Florida and giving that same reason.

It was not an easy year for the couple, but it seemed the only thing to do. For medical reasons, Charlie and Miriam were not able to have children of their own, therefore, this seemed to be a Godsend. Charlie made frequent trips to Florida, and at the end of the year, Miriam and the baby returned. With pride, Baby Ginny was presented to the black society of Wrightsburg, Georgia. A few of the light-skinned kin people came along and stayed for a few days. *That way,* Charlie thought, *people could see that there were other light-skinned members of the Westbrook family.* It worked.

Miriam went back to work and soon things were back to normal for the Westbrooks and their new daughter. They had both agreed, however, that Charlie would sit down with Ginny and have a talk about her real parents. Knowing how cruel children could be, and there were already some rumors around, he promised to do this before Ginny entered school.

Charlie would always have a big belly laugh when he heard the rumor that the baby's real father had been a doctor at the hospital. *Sometimes, people could be so cruel and yet so stupid,* he thought. However, this actually helped the cause. During that time, no black person would dare question the validity of a black woman having a white man's baby.

Maryella Chandler was certainly not suspect. Her father said that she had run off to London, England, where she married the son of a nobleman whom she had met while attending a dog show.

When Ginny went off to the first grade, without the two of them having that talk, Miriam admonished Charlie. He contended that she was too young to understand things of that nature, therefore, he put it off until junior high. However, it was only after Charlie neglected his duty even after Ginny entered high school that Miriam decided to step in and do it herself. But things were going so well, and she didn't want to disrespect her husband. *Lord knows the white man does enough of that already,* she had thought.

One of the first things that Miriam did when they returned from Florida was to call Maryella's apartment. The telephone had been disconnected. When she called the rental office, Miriam was told that Maryella had left six months earlier, headed for Atlanta.

Miriam was ashamed that she breathed a sigh of relief instead having a feeling of concern for her sister-in-law. What if she had reached her and Maryella had changed her mind about the adoption? Miriam knew that she had done the right thing but, sometimes, she just didn't feel right about it.

Ginny was theirs to keep, and in Charlie Westbrook's mind, she was his natural daughter. Sometimes, if you live a lie long enough, it becomes entangled in the truth. Anyway, the Westbrooks never heard from Maryella Chandler again.

Chapter 21

"Peter, Peter, Pumpkineater," exclaimed a jubilant voice over the telephone wire.

"Had a wife, but couldn't keep her," another voice responded in similar tone. "Raggedy Man, how's it going up there?"

"What's happening down there, with those girls?" Rags asked. "I saw it on the national news."

"Oh, yeah, reporters are all over the place."

Before hanging up, the two lifelong friends talked for almost an hour about the goings-on in Wrightsburg and of much lighter fare.

Rags lived in Milwaukee, where he sang with the City's Symphony on weekends and sold houses and condominiums during the week. His dream of fame and fortune as a singer had not been realized, nevertheless, he was doing quite well, thank you.

It was always good to hear from an old friend who still called him Peter instead of the girl-sounding name that he was sure his mother had given him, out of spite. At precisely eleven o' clock in the morning, as he had done for the past five years, Francis Murray – whose nickname had been Peter since Kindergarten – walked out of his office and closed the door. He turned to his secretary, Miss Marable and said, "I'm going to lunch. I'll be back in about an hour."

As Principal Murray walked out of the school building, he thought about the next line of the nursery rhyme that had been the source of his nickname. "But then he put her in the dell," he said aloud, laughing sardonically. "And there he kept her … very well."

Although Francis (Peter) Murray had completed his pre-law studies, fate had thrown him a curveball. His father, Corliss, a mechanic at Chandler Enterprises, did, in fact, have to work late an awful lot, but not on the canning machines of the processing plant, for which he was paid. Most of Corliss Murray's late night work was with one of the nightshift women.

During the summer after Peter's graduation from Emory University, Corliss and the woman left town together, never to be heard of again. Corliss also drained all the money from the law school savings account, so that was the end of Peter's law career.

The entire school community had been genuinely surprised that it had been Mojo, Connie Bradley, a boy of no more than average ability who went on to become an accomplished lawyer instead of near-genius Francis Murray.

But stranger things have happened.

Peter's mother, Arlene, never quite got over it, actually going into a diabetic coma on two occasions. It was always believed that she missed taking her insulin shots on purpose. After she barely survived the second coma, Peter – Francis, that is – personally took over the administration of the lifesaving injections along with the preparation of the low carbohydrate meals that they both needed. He, too, had been diagnosed as diabetic and placed on insulin when he was just a child.

The state school board gave him a provisional certificate and Francis Murray took a job at his old high school as a social studies teacher. During the summers, he hired a live-in nurse to take care of his mother while he studied for a Masters' degree in education over at the University of Georgia. Francis became an excellent teacher and climbed the career ladder in record time, moving from teacher to assistant principal to full-fledged principal in only ten years.

On the personal front, the kindly principal fought a daily battle between good and evil. But today, there was little doubt as to the winner. His old friend, Rags, had called him out.

Peter – the evil persona – hated not only the feminine name of Francis, but also his alter ego's glaring weaknesses. Peter referred to Francis as a pansy and treated him terribly whenever he was the dominant one. Peter loved to create a mess while he was in charge, and then leave Francis to wiggle his way out of it.

A classic example of his tomfoolery was when Peter took over while attending a teacher's convention, enticing a female teacher into going to bed with him. He still laughed himself silly whenever he thought about how Francis looked when he woke up the next morning with the naked woman. He'd almost had a heart attack. Francis just didn't like girls … anymore.

Today, Peter Murray would do things differently than Francis, and would take a long lunch. Not being much of a driver, whenever he was in charge, Peter would walk home. It was a beautiful day and he didn't live far away. Besides, everybody knew that a leisurely stroll was always good for your health.

Peter followed the long curving driveway in front of the school to Amsterdam Avenue, and then began walking in the direction of his house. The air was brisk and clean. This allowed him to clear his head and gave him time to think. He wanted to think about everything. This was part of the pleasure that came with being the Prince of Demons, the Angel of Death.

As Peter moved onto the sidewalk that led home, he thought about them all, from the stupid police, who were virtually chasing their tails, to the even stupider girls, whom he had serviced – as he called it – when he freed them from their sinful ways.

"Heh, heh," Peter chuckled as he thought about his old elementary school nemesis. *That Russ Callahan has never been the sharpest pencil in the desk drawer, but he is just as dumb now as he was when I used to whip his butt in the county spelling bee.*

"Except for the time they cheated," the bad persona angrily said aloud, and then kicked a can that was lying on the sidewalk. Peter's eyes turned red as he glared venomously ahead.

Russ Callahan and his Keystone Cops are so dumb, they couldn't spit in a river if they were all standing in the middle of the bridge, he thought, and then bowled over laughing. Peter was rolling now – in sidesplitting laughter – waving his hands in the air, and then slapping his thigh.

Lately, Principal Murray was having great difficulty in keeping his darker side in check. Sometimes after a bad night, Peter, the bad persona, would literally take charge the next morning and, like today, it would be well after lunch before he could be suppressed. Francis had heard his teachers speak – in hushed tones – about his wild mood swings, and he also knew that his days as an educator were numbered.

After all of this was over, he would think about an early retirement, go to Florida and buy a condominium and maybe even a boat. He could afford it. After all, his only vice was buying flower seeds.

After doing the deed to Beth Campbell, Peter had also been pleasantly surprised when he'd found almost a thousand dollars in Beth's handbag.

"Well, she won't be needing this," he had said. "Not where she's headed."

Peter launched into another outburst of laughter upon thinking about how he had spent the dead girl's money. He had bought cigarettes, booze, and a tailored suit, which Francis never let him wear. *One of these days, though*, he thought, still laughing his fool head off.

"What's so funny to the principal?" a woman said to her husband as they drove past Mr. Murray, who was now laughing hysterically.

"I always thought he was a nut," the man said, looking back at the laughing principal.

Francis (Peter) Murray was now in another dimension, talking and laughing loudly to himself as he walked down the sidewalk. He was oblivious to any and all.

"Sometimes my job can be so hard," he said, "but other times it can be ... so ... doggoned ... easy. Take Beth, for instance..."

Beth Campbell and Coach Dixon walked out of his Spring Valley apartment and got into his car. As the Coach's convertible passed through the security gate, Principal Murray's car pulled from the curb and followed them. From a distance, he watched Beth's charade of leaving the coach's car and walking toward the library, but then changing her mind and rushing to meet her other lover.

He was also looking on as Joe Meriwether pulled Beth out of Barney's Burger Barn and when she, reluctantly, got into his car. As the two of them argued vehemently, the quarreling lovers were totally oblivious to the car following behind, still at a discrete distance. Suddenly Joe pulled to the side of the road, Beth got out of the car, and then he pulled off.

Peter Murray was about to pull his dark sedan to the curb in front of Beth, but he had seen the headlights behind him and quickly drove on. Circling the block, Mr. Murray returned to see Beth, still walking down the street. He quickly pulled to the curb, leaned across the front seat, and called out through the passenger side window. "Beth Campbell, what in the world are you doing out this time of night by yourself?"

Beth, still seething with anger, came up to the car and stuck her head into the window "It was Joe, Mr. Murray," she said. "We had an argument."

"You get into this car right now, and let me take you home. I'll attend to Mr. Joe Meriwether, tomorrow."

"Thank you Mr. Murray," Beth said, smiling now as she got into the car. "I'm so glad you came along. It's really dark out tonight and kind of scary."

"So doggone easy," Peter said aloud. He smiled, and then whistled a few bars of *Mary Had a Little Lamb* as he neared his house. They all had been easily coaxed into his car. After all, what high school student would be afraid to get into the car with their principal? Or as was in the case of Armanda Lockett, back in '78, her favorite teacher.

But then there was the smart one, Miss Westbrook, who actually turned out to be just as dumb as all the rest. Again, he luxuriated in his accomplishments, savoring the moments.

Ginny looked up from her novel as the car pulled to the curb alongside her. Mr. Murray, with a look of anguish on his face, leaned across from the driver's side. "Ginny, Ginny, come quickly! It's Dewey! There's been an accident, and he's calling for you!"

Stunned, Ginny looked at him with fear in her eyes.

"What? Dewey, hurt? Where?"

Ginny quickly got into the car, and then Mr. Murray guided it onto the street as he continued. "He had a seizure while in detention. He fell and struck his head."

"Oh, God!" Ginny said.

She looked horrified as he went on. "Did you know about his seizures?"

"No, he never mentioned them."

As he neared his house, Mr. Murray turned to her. "Ginny, I have to make one quick stop to check on my mother. Do you mind?"

"No, of course not."

"Good, I'll only be a minute," he said, pulling the car into the garage, and then bolting for the house.

Ginny fidgeted as she waited. Five minutes passed, and then ten. She gasped in exasperation as she looked at her watch. Finally, she got out of the car and walked up to the kitchen door. She hesitated, but then knocked.

"Mr. Murray," she said softly.

There was no answer. Ginny turned the doorknob, and then slowly pushed the door open. "Mr. Murray," she said, a little louder.

There was still no answer. Ginny slowly walked through the doorway. As she entered the kitchen, an arm slipped around her neck as a hand pressed a white cloth to her nose. She groaned and struggled valiantly, but then – like a rag-doll – slumped to the floor. Mr. Murray's eyes glistened and his teeth bared as he picked Ginny up into his arms and walked toward the basement door. "You little trollop! You're all alike!"

Now fully in his evil persona, Peter Murray's eyes glazed over as he carried Ginny down the steps to the basement, and then dropped her – like a sack of potatoes – on the cot beside the wall. He went to a storeroom, unlocked the door, and then walked inside. Shortly, he returned with a set of handcuffs, a roll of duct tape, and a Polaroid Camera.

233

Peter Murray whistled *Old McDonald Had a Farm* as he posed the unconscious girl for the grisly picture. He sat her up on the cot, placed a strip of duct tape across her mouth, snapped the handcuffs around both wrists, and then prepared Ginny for the crowning touch. With his bare hands, he ripped the leg of the slacks she wore, and then locked a rusty iron shackle around her right ankle before pulling both legs up on the cot so that the horrid looking manacle could be seen in the picture.

"Now that looks good," he said cheerily. "You must always have a little something for the book."

Peter Murray laughed, sardonically, as the light on the camera flashed. Afterwards, he released her from the handcuffs. Ginny grunted when he stripped the tape away from her mouth.

"Let's get you comfy now. You'll be here a while," the maniacal man said, puling out a syringe from a medical kit and filling it with a clear liquid. "This might sting a bit," Peter said as he plunged the needle deep into her arm.

"You know, I don't know who said it, but he was certainly right," Peter Murray said, smiling as he walked alongside his back fence. He reached up to a rose vine that had climbed to the top of the trellis. He took a long smell of the lush red rose before snapping it from the vine and placing it into his lapel. "You really do have to stop and smell the roses."

Peter opened the side gate and stepped into his lavish flower garden. *But there is still work to be done,* he thought. *There's a bird in the hand to be dealt with, and one still out in the bush.*

The two-story frame house, on the corner of Amsterdam Avenue and 2nd Street, was built by Corliss and Arlene Murray. The corner lot afforded a large portion of the two-acre plot of land to the garden that Arlene had started, but Francis Murray had greatly embellished. While Peter loved flowers, too, he politely left the gardening to Francis – sissy work, he called it.

A magnificent array of vegetation spanned the front and back of the building, but the centerpiece was the main garden that covered the entire left side of the house. In the middle of the garden, there stood a gazebo, which was always painted sparkling white. There was a circular cement pathway around it that led to the house, and also a tall white slated fence, which served as a trellis for the Rambling Roses and other climbing vines that ringed the entire property.

Summer in the South could be particularly hard on plant roots, but Francis Murray had seemingly overcome that obstacle. Regardless of the season, flowers in his garden always seemed to be in bloom. When asked of his secret formula, all that he would ever venture was that it was a slow-release variety of fertilizer. Some of his flowers were almost twice the normal size, and they all had a vivid radiance that defied description.

As he entered the garden, Peter walked past the red, yellow, and white azaleas and the bright yellow daffodils, which were nearest the fence, and then came row after row of red hyacinths, pink hydrangeas, and white chrysanthemums.

Nearing the center of the garden, he stopped to smell the large Easter lilies, which had no right being so big or even blooming this time of year. Then he moved to the white gardenias, which were never known to have grown in this part of the country before. And no visit to the wonder garden could be complete without a visit to the coup de grace, the gazebo. It was surrounded by a bed of white orchids, flowers that simply would *not* grow in this area, except inside a greenhouse.

Then suddenly – as if changing gears in an automobile – the smiling Francis returned and things became pleasant again. The good persona was back. You could always tell because Francis loved to laugh and joke, but Peter was usually all business and, lately, mostly foul of mood. But still from, time-to-time, Peter also loved to whistle a familiar nursery rhyme while he worked. And today would be a busy day. They always were when there was company in the house.

Francis decided that he would have to make his mother something special for lunch. Arlene was always a little jealous whenever company came – with her being bedridden and all.

"I have been neglecting her. Today, I'll make her tea and crumpets," Francis said aloud. Now that he had stifled Peter for a time, he was all the way back in charge. Then he laughed. "Of course, I like 'em, too."

Ginny's shoe was now filled with blood. The lunges that she made toward the keys had exacted a dear price. Each forward trust made the cut around her ankle deeper and wider. After several attempts, she still was unable to reach the keys. With each stretch, however, her body was becoming suppler, and she now needed only a few more inches to reach, what for her would be the pot of gold at the end of the rainbow.

Then she heard the kitchen door slam shut. The monster was back. Ginny panicked. Shock ran through her as she planned her next move. *I have nothing to lose now*, she reasoned. *He'll kill me, for sure, for trying to escape.*

With all of her sinew and an extra surge of adrenaline, Ginny picked up the shovel blade with one hand. It was terribly heavy, but if she could extend it as far as she could and hold it for just a second…

It had been an enjoyable lunch, and Francis had stayed in control throughout the meal. Arlene Murray always enjoyed tea and crumpets. Today the tea was her favorite, Chamomile with just a bit of lemon and honey, and the crumpets were just as she liked them, lightly browned and crisp. They were also made with a sugar substitute, in deference to both of their medical conditions.

After giving his mother and himself their insulin injections, Francis looked down at the other two vials in the medicine kit. *Uh, uh, I almost forgot*, he thought. *We have houseguest.* Then purposely, he allowed Peter to come back. It was time for dirty work and Francis wanted *no* part of it.

Peter whistled *A Farmer in the Dell* as he walked down the steps to the basement. When he reached the bottom, he flipped a switch and dim light filled the space. Peter gasped in horror when he saw the empty cot. Ginny was gone!

"What the --?"

"Wham!" a shovel blade crashed hard against his head. Peter slumped to the floor as Ginny dropped the shovel and skittered up the stairs. It had taken a miracle, but when she had only strength left for one final lunge, the shovel handle had barely slipped under the key ring. Ginny couldn't wait to get out of that house and down to the police station.

She could only imagine what her family and friends were going through, not knowing where she was. Then she had a sense of foreboding. For the first time, Ginny now realized that it was not some unknown stranger, but her high school principal who had killed Beth and possibly the other two girls. But why?

Ginny rushed through the kitchen to the garage door. She twisted the handle, and then pulled up. The door did not move.

"What?" she exclaimed loudly. "Come on!"

Then she saw the large padlock that secured the long metal release bar and kept the door from sliding up.

Do not panic, she thought, *Front door!*

Ginny ran back through the kitchen into the living room in search of a way out. She turned the knob on the front door, and then pulled, hard. It didn't budge. Then she looked down at the locks. There were two of them. Ginny disengaged the thumb lock, but froze when she stared down at the second.

"Darn, need a key!"

The second security device was a double-key lock, the same kind that Charlie had installed at her house. Ginny knew in a flash that this particular lock was designed, not to keep others out, but to keep someone inside the house.

Windows, she thought, and then dashed to the front window. "Oh, no," she cried, looking down at the padlocks. Ginny was now in frenzy as she ran from window-to-window, shaking the locks on each of them.

Then she saw the pole lamp. When Ginny picked up the lamp and thrust its base through a nearby window, her heart sunk. There was a tinkling of broken glass but also a clang of metal-on-metal. The lamp base had struck burglar bars. "Oh, no," she cried sadly.

Ginny was at wits end, but then she heard the faint sound of a television set. It was coming from upstairs. She thought for a moment, and then rushed back into the kitchen. She took a large knife from the rack, and then returned to the living room.

With knife drawn back, Ginny crept, slowly, up the stairwell. Stopping at the top of the stairs, she noticed a light coming from a door, which was slightly ajar. Ginny slowly moved closer to the door. "Hello," she said softly. "Is anybody home? Hello."

Ginny, slowly, pushed at the door with her foot.

"Arrrrrrrrrrrrr!" went the sound of the rusty hinge as the door slowly opened.

"Eeeeeeeeiiih!" went the sound of a girl frightened out of her wits.

The knife fell to the floor as Ginny raised both hands to her face and continued screaming at the top of her lungs, staring, in horror, at the emaciated mummified body of Arlene Murray. The body had been placed in the sitting position on her bed, which was still filled daily with lime. A food tray still sat across her lap with a full cup of tea and two freshly made crumpets on a saucer.

Although a hefty woman in life, Arlene Murray's skeletal remains had shrunken almost to the size of a little girl. Her eye sockets were empty, and her dark splotched skin had dried and tightened around her mouth, baring her teeth – in a bizarre misshapen smile of death.

Arlene's hair had grown long and willowy, and had turned pure white. Her fingernails also had grown so long that they curled into tiny balls. She was dressed nicely in a flowered robe, and a fresh bouquet of flowers was in a vase beside her bed.

Ginny forced herself to look away from the sickening sight and composed herself. And then she saw it. There was a telephone on the nightstand beside the bed. She slowly edged toward the nightstand, being ever so careful not to touch the bed. The dial tone hummed as Ginny picked up the receiver. Delighted that the telephone was still working, she quickly dialed the operator, and the telephone rang on the other end until a voice came on the line. "This is the operator. How may I help you?"

Ginny exuberantly spoke into the receiver. "Hello, this is --"

Suddenly the telephone fell to the bed and Ginny staggered backward, slowly sagging to the floor with a hypodermic syringe protruding from her neck.

"Hello, this is the operator," said the voice on the other end of the telephone line. "Is everything alright?"

"Yes," Mr. Murray said after picking up the telephone, "everything is just fine. My daughter is just a bit too playful today. I'm sorry. I'll see that it doesn't happen again."

Chapter 22

When Principal Murray returned to work, Peter was still in charge, which was unusual since he was the kind who usually liked to take a nice long siesta after a midday meal. And while there was no doubt as to which the darker side belonged, Francis also had his little devilish quirks. Sometimes he had been known to throw a tantrum or two and would almost always goad Peter into an argument when they went home for lunch.

It would usually start out as a disagreement over what they would eat, and then evolve into what they would fix for their mother before the usual finale: whom did their mother love the most? Since Peter first showed up – the night of the Chandler affair as it was called – Arlene had taken deference to the new side of a son, whom earlier she deemed to be too weak.

Today, however, it had not been Francis who had upset Peter. It was that Westbrook girl. *She'll pay for this*, Peter thought as he walked into the outer office.

"What happened to you?" his secretary asked, looking at the large lump on the back of his head and the grimace on his face.

"I hit my head on a low hanging shelf in my garage."

"Oh, well, you just have to learn to be more careful."

Peter Murray hastily walked past her into his office, and then slammed the door shut. She had seen him this way in the afternoon, but not often. However, the few times when he *had* come back in such bad humor, things had really gotten sticky.

Woe be unto anyone who enters that office this afternoon, the secretary thought, shaking her head, *be they student, teacher, or parent.*

She's right, Peter said to himself as he sunk into the big leather chair behind his desk, *he would have to be careful. Bad things always happened when he wasn't. But the hellion from Satan would pay, tonight, at the stroke of midnight – the bewitching hour*

The principal stayed in bad-persona the rest of the day. Francis was unable to squeeze in but for a few minutes and, as his secretary had predicted, Peter Murray was holding court. Three students were suspended for what, under Francis, would have been no more than detention. A faculty member received an official letter of reprimand for reporting late to class, and if Francis had not slipped into persona for just a few minutes, Peter would have told a parent where she could go and what she could do once she had gotten there. It was times like these when Francis knew that his working days were numbered. Peter was out of control.

When Lou and Lola entered Chief Callahan's office, they both had hangdog looks on their faces.

"Let me guess," the chief said, "your talk with Constance Bradley netted zero."

"Less than that," Lou said dejectedly.

"Well, come on, give," the chief said, giving his two detectives a hand signal to join him at the conference table.

"The two thousand dollars was just another contribution to the Beth Campbell Transportation Fund," Lola said despondently.

It was sad commentary, but in the end – as they say, the acorn does not fall far from the tree. The fact of the matter was that Beth Campbell, like her mother before her, was little more than a common whore. But unlike her mother, Lizzy, Beth had very expensive tastes.

Although the chief gathered that it would be a waste of time, he sat back and listened as they summed it all up. The visit to Constance Bradley's law office proved to be more of an embarrassment to the State Senator than anything else. At first, he denied knowing anything about Beth other than what he had read in the newspaper. After Lou presented him with the copy of the cancelled check, however, it only took a little prodding for Constance to sheepishly admit that he, too, was another link in the young cheerleader's "chain of fools."

Like Coach Dixon, he, too, had run into Beth at the Moulin Rouge – while attending a bachelor party for one of his staffers. As soon as the two of them discovered that they had Madison County in common, they had an off and on relationship up until she was murdered.

Neither Lou nor Lola could remember having worked on a case that had so many dead-end streets. After listening to their sad tale, the chief took a long sigh before he spoke.

"Well, folks, I guess we've done everything we can. The mayor's right. We *are* grabbing at straws. And now," he said, rising from the table and walking toward his desk, "we've just run out of straws."

Chief Callahan picked up the telephone and began dialing numbers. "It's time for me to make that call."

"Call? What call?" Lola asked.

"The one I should have made long ago. I'm bringing in the GBI."

"Go away, Francis," Peter said, banging his own head against the kitchen wall. "You have no balls! So why don't you just stay out of this? In fact, why don't you just get lost, forever?"

Then suddenly his body relaxed. He walked over to the table and took a seat. Francis was back. "Peter," he said calmly, "this foolishness has got to stop. You're running me away from my job. And I love my job! Do you hear me!"

This only agitated Peter more. "Teaching school is a job for sissies. I want to buy a boat," he said with a certain flair, "and sail the seven seas."

This infuriated Francis. "It's just like you to want to do something stupid like that," he said harshly. "And I could kill you for what you did to my mother!"

It was getting dark and the two personalities had been battling over their single body all that afternoon. It had been just such an extended argument that had led to the demise of Arlene Murray.

"It was an accident," Peter shot back. "And you were just as much to blame as I was."

Almost two years earlier, back when Francis' persona was almost as strong as Peter's, one Friday night, the two of them were locked in mortal combat. They argued all day and, physically, fought the entire weekend. Then realizing that if Francis died, so would he, Peter had allowed him to take his insulin shots, but would *not* allow Francis to climb the stairs to his mother's room at all – during the entire weekend.

It was the next Monday morning before they discovered her body. She had died in a Diabetic coma. When Francis tried to call for help, Peter would have none of it. He convinced Francis that there would be too many unanswerable questions put to him by the authorities. Questions such as, how did you get *your* insulin shots but she didn't get hers, and why didn't you call the doctor earlier?"

"You're right," Francis had finally said. Then Peter went to the basement to get a bag of lime to take the smell away from his mother's dead body. A skill she had taught Francis the night of the Chandler murder.

Suddenly Francis rose from the table and walked toward the basement, but Peter put the brakes on, stopping at the door and turning toward the table as if to speak to someone sitting there. "And where do you think you're going?" Peter snarled.

Francis turned back toward the door and spoke serenely. "I'm going to the basement," he said calmly. "I'm going down there and release that girl so she can go home to her parents."

Turning back toward the empty table, Peter bellowed at Francis. "Are you stupid? If you release her, the first thing she'll do is go to see Lou Brazell and his little nigger whore. And then what? Do you think they'll let you go back to your precious school and your darling little children? I don't think so," he said, singing the last few words.

His body relaxed, and then Francis Murray returned to his seat at the table. "You're right, Peter. You were right about mother. You're always right."

"That's a good boy," Peter said softly, stroking his own cheek as if it belonged to another person. "Let's make a deal."

"What's the deal?" Francis asked.

"This will be the last one."

"What about the other one?"

"I'll let her go," Peter lied. "I like it when we work together."

It was a cold night and the moon shone so brightly that it gave the illusion of daylight. The clock at Courthouse Square struck for the twelfth time just as the first dog hit the street. Down on Cherry Lane, the little Chihuahua sprang through the trap door and waddled down the driveway. Across the street, a hand opened the door and the barking Rottwieler also bounded down the walkway into the street.

The two dogs barked loudly as they followed the apparition of Maryella Chandler as it glided through the streets of Wrightsburg. Maryella looked back at the growling dogs, and then suddenly the barking ceased. The ominous trio moved on to the center of town.

The sign across the office window read, "K-9 ACADEMY." At the rear of the building, there were two large pens, both enclosed by tall fences. Four Dobermans bounded around anxiously in one pen while two German Shepherds nervously pranced in the other. Suddenly the dogs began to bark loudly.

Inside the building, one of the dog trainers sat in the break room, drinking coffee and watching television. He looked up as the heavy barking continued. Then the security guard walked into the room. "Did you feed those animals?" he asked the trainer.

"Yeah, I don't know what's got 'em so riled up!"

"Well, feed 'em again," he said. "Shut 'em up! They're drivin' me crazy!"

The dog trainer, carrying a bag of feed, walked outside and opened the gate of the Doberman's pen. As soon as he walked inside, a Doberman pounced upon his chest, knocking him to the ground. The dogs barked loudly as they ran from the kennel into the street. One Doberman stopped long enough to use his pointed nose to open the gate restraining the German shepherds, and then they, too, skittered into the street. As soon as the K-9 dogs joined Maryella and the other two, all barking ceased. As Maryella Chandler and her canine convoy moved through Wrightsburg, picking up strays along the way, the little Chihuahua struggled to keep up with the much larger animals, but somehow it did.

Francis Murray, like many others back in the '70s, had used marijuana freely during his college days. He had even participated in a campus rally to legalize the potent plant. Also like many of those who came out of that tumultuous time, he had grown out of the habit and was now a teetotaler.

Peter, who had only come into existence during that horrid affair with the Chandler girl, never touched the Cannabis weed. But he smoked Pall Mall cigarettes as if his mouth were a fireplace and his nose a chimney. Peter also loved hard liquor, bourbon, and plenty of it. When he drank heavily and chained smoked, Francis, who hated both liquor and cigarettes, stayed away completely.

After their battle that evening, Peter had drunk Jack Daniels and smoked Pall Malls all that night. He needed no interference from Francis. And he had no idea how he was going to do it but ... someway ... somehow .... after all of this was over, Peter was going to get rid of his alter ego, for once and for all. Maybe one of those head shrinks could help him turn the trick. It was almost time to leave, however, and there were still preparations yet to be made.

With practiced precision, Peter followed the procedure that – over the years – he had perfected. When he left his bedroom and walked down the stairs to the basement, he was dressed in black from head to toe. He wore a black scull cap, a black Navy pea-jacket, black pants, and a pair of black sneakers. His face was painted black with camouflage grease. When Peter slowly emerged from the basement, carrying Ginny Westbrook in his arms, he ritualistically walked to the garage, where the dark sedan awaited with opened trunk.

When he, callously, dropped her body into the trunk, Ginny's eyes blinked open.

"Well, you're awake," he said, looking down into her eyes. "I knew you would be. I went easy on the sleeping potion today. Ha! What would be the point if you slept through the whole show? But I put a little surprise in tonight. I'm sure you'll like it." He laughed loudly, peering down at the helpless girl.

"No," Ginny's mind sent the command, but neither her vocal cords nor lips responded. There was no sound as her body lay deathly still. Ginny was wide-awake, but the only muscles she could move were those that controlled her eyelids. Then she remembered Dr. Turner's words, "... a chemical is released that paralyzes the body ... paralyzes the body ... paralyzes --" In a flash, Ginny Westbrook realized that she was about to die. She began to pray silently, *Oh, God, please help me.*

Peter slipped into the front seat of the car and pushed a button on the electronic garage opener. The heavy door slowly rose. When he turned the key in the ignition, the engine came to life, and then he drove the black sedan off into the night.

With the speed of the wind, the ghost of Maryella Chandler moved through Wrightsburg, collecting the city's canines. Like birds of a feather, except in wild packs, dogs of different breeds did *not* usually run together. However, on this night they did. Dogs of all kinds – large, small, and those in between – ran swiftly and silently. Maryella Chandler was doing in death, what she had done so many times while living – working with different breeds of dogs at the same time. She was their leader and they her followers. There was but one more stop to make.

Maryella swung by Jay Dee's house to pick up Uncle Buddy's dogs. Jay Dee and Uncle Buddy, who had drunk moonshine well into the night, were in the living room sleeping it off. Like a synchronized high-jumping team, the Bloodhounds and Pointers easily cleared the backyard fence to join the cohort of canines.

Two police officers sat in a cruiser parked near a street corner. One of them looked on in disbelief as the dogs headed for Simpson's Woods. He turned to his partner. "Did you see that?"

The other officer, shaking his head in incredulity, said, "I saw it, but I sure as hell don't believe it. We'd better get a hold of Animal Control."

Then the officer, seeing only the dogs, picked up the microphone from the control-panel of the cruiser. "Headquarters," he blared into it, "this is car nineteen. You'd better get Animal Control over to Simpson's Woods in a hurry! We've got a pack of dogs running loose!"

It was just after midnight, and there were over twenty dogs that followed Maryella's ghost as she made the turn into Simpson's Woods. Shortly, not far behind the rest, the Chihuahua skittered into the forest. As soon as they entered Witches' Hollow, the lead dogs, the Dobermans, began to emit a low growl.

Just then came the first clap of thunder, so hard and loud that it shook the earth. Then a bright yellow flash of lightening struck, traversing from the heavens to the ground near the front gate and back up again. Just as suddenly black clouds gathered, passing over the moon and sending the night into pitch-darkness. Then the first drops of rain fell.

Since the tractors and backhoes had already cleared most of the forest during the earlier searches, the digging went easier tonight than ever before. Ginny lay, helplessly, on the ground, staring up into the blackness as Peter eagerly dug her grave. She screamed and screamed, but no sound emitted. *I'm dreaming,* she thought. *This is just a dream.*

Although the thunder rolled, lightening struck, and the rain now fell in sheets, Peter whistled *Mary Had a Little Lamb* as he shoveled the last of the soft dirt from the hole, making a large pile alongside it. Wiping the water from his face with the sleeves of his jacket, the maniac spoke. "Well, my little curly locks," he said, looking down into her horror-filled eyes, "It'll be over in a little while, and you'll be going home to the angels."

Further back along the trail, Maryella's ghost quickened its pace as it glided along the path. Now the dogs growled ferociously, baring their teeth and running more swiftly to keep her pace.

Unceremoniously, Peter rolled Ginny into the shallow grave. Landing face up, she screamed just as the first clump of wet dirt hit her face.

"Eiieeeek!" she cried out in pure horror.

The drug was beginning to wear off now. Ginny's voice had returned, but she still could not move. Now she realized that it was cold and began to shiver.

Shovelful after shovelful of dirt rained down on the helpless girl, but the paranoid-schizophrenic lunatic of a high school principal continued to throw the suffocating muck into the hole – stopping only to laugh sardonically and revel in the fear and agony of his prey.

Ginny's heart dropped as another shovelful of dirt hit her face. *Oh, my God*, she said silently, *I'm going to die!*

Back along the trail, Maryella and the bizarre assortment of dogs picked up even more speed – the larger animals leaving the little Chihuahua in their wake. The dogs were barking louder now and growling even more ferociously.

Peter threw another shovelful of dirt into the hole. Suddenly he stopped and turned toward the sound of the barking dogs. Then, off in the distance and through the driving rain, he could see the apparition of Maryella Chandler, leading the dogs straight toward him. Frozen in his tracks, he screamed hysterically, "Maryella! No! Stay away!"

Then he could see the pack of dogs, their teeth bared for action, and Maryella's face, now distorted into a menacing grin.

"Go back where you came from!" he said. "You're dead! I killed you!"

From the hole in the ground, Ginny caught just a glimpse of Maryella as she passed over.

"Whump!" there was a loud thud as Maryella struck Peter's chest, and then passed straight through him. For one fleeting millisecond, parallel universes converged and ghostly ectoplasm collided with human cells. He was looking down in astonishment at his chest when the first dog, one of the Dobermans, leaped into the air. Peter quickly recovered from the shock of seeing the ghost from his past just in time to swing the shovel, hard, striking the dog on its side.

The Doberman squealed as it fell to the ground. But then, another one pounced on the arm with the shovel, sending it flying off into the night, just as a third Doberman clamped onto his other arm. Peter turned and ran a few steps, but two Rottwielers caught each of his legs, sending the entire pack sprawling over a ledge and down into a ravine.

Ginny could see each dog as it vaulted over her would be grave until the last big dog was gone. Then there stood the little Chihuahua, whining and staring down at her, as if standing guard.

Violent screams and vicious growls could be heard throughout the forest. Now the Bloodhounds, Pointers, and the rest of the dogs got into the act, all seeking a piece of the psychopathic principal.

Then, all was quiet. The rain stopped just as suddenly as it had begun, and all of the clouds drifted away toward the sea – to refill for the next rainy day.

Chapter 23

At the K-9 Academy, the sound of barking dogs distracted the trainer from his television show. He got up and looked out the window, and then turned to the security guard who was now sleeping on the sofa.

"John, wake up! It's the dogs, they're back!"

This scene was played out all over Wrightsburg, Georgia, as Maryella's warrior dogs sauntered home after a night's work. Down on Cherry Lane, the man patted the head of his Rottwieler. "Duke, you're back." Then he shook his finger at the dog, scolding him, "You've been a bad dog."

Across the street, the little Chihuahua sprung through the trap door and into the arms of the little old woman. "Thank the lord," she said. "Mama's little baby is back home."

Jay Dee and Uncle Buddy were still dead to the world when the Pointers and Bloodhounds cleared the backyard fence and settled into their kennels as if it had all just been a jog in the park.

Yellow crime scene tape cordoned off the area in Witches' Hollow and spotlights shone down around Ginny's would-be grave. By now the woods were filled with police officers and detectives. Milton Hicks, the coroner, and Brian Pollard, the crime scene investigator, were also on duty.

Two emergency attendants lifted the stretcher bearing Ginny, with a breathing apparatus over her nose, into the ambulance. Sirens wailed as they left Simpson's Woods headed for the hospital. A patrol car had already been dispatched to pick up the jubilant parents, Charlie and Miriam, so they could meet their daughter at the hospital.

As Milton worked on the badly dismembered body, Brian, as usual, was down on his hands and knees – flashlight in hand – combing the bottom of the ravine for clues. The two men from Animal Control filled Lou Brazell and Lola Morgan in on how they had stumbled upon the girl in the grave while chasing down stray dogs.

Following the sound of a barking dog, one of the men actually stumbled into the hole on top of the girl. He was nearly scared out of his wits.

"I heard this little pup, yapping his head off," the man had said with a chuckle. "The little tyke saved her life. But when I climbed out of the hole, it was gone."

After giving up the chase for the dogs, who had taken the long way home, the men from Animal Control called the police.

When the coroner and his two attendants finally had the body loaded on the stretcher, Lou walked over and pulled back the cover. "Yikes! He's a mess. Could you tell who he was?"

"Nah." The dogs tore him to pieces," Milton said. "No face left."

"I got it," Brian said, approaching the group while shining a flashlight on a tiny piece of a driver's license. "I found pieces of his wallet. His last name is Murray. I can't make out the first name."

"The only Murray I know is the principal," Milton said, "over at the high school."

"Principal Murray?" Lola asked in surprise. "No, it couldn't be him. Let me see."

"No! Go back! You don't want to see this," Lou said, waving Lola away as she approached the stretcher.

"Get him out of here," the coroner said to the attendants, and then turned to Lou. "If it is him, somebody's going to have to notify his mother. She's bed-ridden, you know?"

"Yeah, I heard." Lou said.

When Lou knocked on the front door of the Murray house, it was almost daybreak. Lola stood behind him and watched. There was no response. Lola stooped and looked down at the window that Ginny had broken during her escape attempt. "Lou, look at this. Something's happened here."

"Yeah, we've got to get inside," he said after seeing the broken glass scattered about the porch.

"Gotcha." she said, and then pulled out her two-way radio. "This is Detective Morgan. We need back-up at the Murray house over on Amsterdam. Bring a battering ram."

The double-locked door splintered as two officers sent the battering ram crashing through it. Then Lou, Lola, and the two uniformed officers, all with guns drawn, carefully entered the house.

"Alright, people," Lou said. "Until we know different, this is a crime scene, so let's treat it like one."

As they walked into the living room, Lou turned to the officers. "One of you guys check the garage and the other take the basement."

After the officers left, Lou turned to Lola. "I'll take the lower level. But you'd better check on the old lady upstairs. We've probably already scared her to death with the noise."

"You're right," Lola said. "I'll take it easy."

The sound of a television set blared as Lola walked up the stairs. Lou was walking out of the kitchen just as Lola screamed. "Lou, come quick!"

Lou ran up the stairwell and entered the bedroom. He found Lola standing mesmerized by the sight of the mummified body, which was still propped up on the lime entrenched bed. Lou's jaw dropped and he shook his head.

"Je-sus!" he exclaimed.

Lola struggled to keep from vomiting. Just as Lou pulled her out of the macabre mausoleum, one of the officers called out from downstairs. "Lou, you'd better get down here! In the basement!"

Lola was repulsed by the rank smell of mildew and urine as she followed Lou down the steps into the basement that Francis (Peter) Murray had converted into a dungeon of death. They both stared, in horror, at the cot by the wall with its filthy mattress and foul smelling blanket, the grimy bucket that still smelled of urine, and the manacle and chain the fiendish principal had used to bind his prey – his own students.

Lou turned to one of the officers. "Get on the horn. Get the chief and Brian Pollard down here ASAP," he said. "Oh, and get the coroner, too. There's a body upstairs."

It was almost noon. The coroner had released Arlene Murray's pitiful body to the county morgue, and the investigative team had searched the house from stem to stern, but found nothing else. There was plenty of evidence that linked Principal Murray to Beth Campbell's murder and Ginny's abduction, but since there was no murderer left to prosecute, Emory Sheppard and Chief Callahan had come and gone.

Brian related that, sometime ago, when he had gone to the hardware store, the manager *did* verify that the white stuff found at Beth's gravesite was lime, the kind used for fertilizer. But thinking it unimportant, he didn't mention it to Lou. The lime evidence and the manacles tied Beth's abduction, false imprisonment, and murder directly to the Principal. And they couldn't wait to talk to Ginny, sure that she would have *some* tale to tell.

But for now the investigation was over, and most of the officers had left. Lou, Lola, and the coroner were standing in the kitchen, about to do the same.

"But why would he do a thing like this?" the coroner asked with a look of concern on his face.

"Who knows?" Lola said.

They were about to walk out the door when Brian called out from the basement. "Lou, wait. I've found something."

The crime scene investigator raced up from the basement and placed an old battered scrapbook on the table. "Take a look at this. You won't believe it."

Brian's meticulous search had revealed a secret compartment behind a wall of the storeroom. There, he found handcuffs, duct tape, a Polaroid camera, and the old scrapbook.

Lola opened the old book to the first page. There was a badly faded color picture of a pretty blonde girl with a handwritten inscription across the bottom that read, "To Peter, with love." Under that inscription, there was another but in a different handwriting, which read, "Mary, Mary."

The coroner's eyes narrowed as he studied the picture. "Why, that's Maryella Chandler, Tyson Chandler's daughter."

"Her brother was right," Lola said.

"About what?" Milton said.

"About her being missing, too."

Lola turned the page, and then gasped before placing her hand over her mouth. She had to take a seat. The three men hovered around her and peered down at the page. This page was different. At the top of the page, there was a yearbook photograph of a beautiful black girl and, at the bottom, a gruesome Polaroid picture of the same girl – bound and gagged with her eyes closed.

"Why, that's the Lockett girl," the coroner said in aghast.

"Oh, my God," Lou said. "There *were* others!"

In disbelief, Lola turned page after page. Each new page revealed another girl with the same before and after scenario, Anna Jennings, Beth Campbell, and finally Ginny Westbrook.

When she turned to the last page in the book, a wave of dizziness washed over Lola, almost causing her to keel over. But as she stared down at the content of the page, anger replaced fear.

"It was him, Lou," she shouted. "That bastard was stalking me! He was going to kill me, too!"

They were all flabbergasted at the disturbing sight of the picture on the final page. The *before* picture, at the top of the page, was a newspaper article that featured a picture of Lola Morgan. The caption underneath read, "Homegrown Detective Returns to Wrightsburg." The article had been published when she joined the force. There was no picture at the bottom, but Lola knew that she was to have been the killer's next victim.

"Why?" asked a perplexed Brian Pollard.

They all just shook their heads, but when Lola saw that her picture had been added to this gruesome gallery, she looked up at Lou. Neither spoke, but both understood. For the interracial couple, the motive for Murray's madness was no longer a mystery. Lola's mind quickly flashed back to the other girls. Since he had not been in Wrightsburg long, Lou would not have known that both, Armanda Lockett and Anna Jennings were dating across racial lines, but they both could relate to Beth Campbell and the black football coach.

Lola turned back to the picture of Armanda Lockett. She was a beautiful dark brown girl, with an immaculately kept Afro hairstyle. Upon closer observation, like the picture of Maryella, there was a small inscription at the bottom of the photograph. It read, "Lucy Lockett."

"Was her name Lucy?" Lola asked the coroner.

"Not that I know of," he said. "They might've called her that."

Then Lou examined each page even closer. "Seems to be some kind of pet name he calls his victims."

Lola pondered as she turned, and then re-turned the pages. "Nursery rhymes, she said excitedly. "They're nursery rhymes."

"What?" the coroner said quizzically.

"Think," Lola said, pointing a finger to her temple and recalling a verse from the rhyme. "Lucy Lockett lost her pocket."

"Yeah," Lou said. His eyes widened as he looked at the inscription under Ginny's picture. "Curly Locks, will you be mine?"

Lola's eyes flashed wildly and she began to smile as she read the inscription under the first picture. "Mary, Mary, quite contrary. How does your garden grow? With Silver Bells and Cockleshells--"

"**And pretty maids all in a row!**" Lou cut in. "Ha! The flower garden!"

A backhoe stood nearby in the freshly dug soil of what was left of Mr. Murray's magnificent flower garden. The TV reporter stared into the camera as she spoke. "I know you've heard that a dog is a man's best friend. But here in Madison County, several dogs proved to be a girl's best friend. It seems as if a group of dogs just happen to be in Simpson's Woods when..."

What caused that pack of dogs to come together and happen upon Simpson's Wood's was a mystery that remains yet to be unraveled, even to this very day.

After the last of the three bodies had been dug up and carried away, Lou and Brian knelt in the rich dark soil near one of the graves. Brian picked up a handful of dirt as he shook his head. "I blew it, Lou. I should've known."

The two men rose to their feet as Lola joined them.

"How could you?" Lou asked.

"You know, I told you there was something strange about Beth's body," he said.

"Yeah," Lola said, "did you figure it out?"

"Yes, after the fact," he said. "There were two kinds of soil. Beth was buried here first, but then re-buried in Simpson's Woods."

"Don't feel bad, Youngblood," Lou said. "We wouldn't have thought to look here in a million years. For Christ's sake, he was a frigging principal."

"How did you know that the body was in Simpson's Woods?" Brian asked.

"An anonymous call," Lola said.

"Yeah, now I see," Brian said. "He wanted the body to be found so we would take Dixon down."

"That's right," Lou said. "If Coach Dixon had been convicted, he would've been home free. Free to kill – again and again. But why would he go after the Westbrook girl so soon? He could have taken her any time."

"Well, it seems that she was doing something that we weren't," Lola said.

"What?" Brian asked.

"Linking the cases," Lou said. "She was doing a lot of nosing around about the other missing girls for a story in the school paper."

"It doesn't matter," Lou said, putting his arm around Brian's shoulder. "You got 'im in the end."

"Me?" Brian said quizzically.

"If it hadn't been for your diligent search of that old storeroom, we would never have found the other bodies."

"Yeah, that's right," Brian said, smiling. "Yeah … yeah!"

Lou held up his hand for a hand-slap, which Brian was happy to give. Then Lola did the same. They were finally giving the young investigator his due. He had earned it. They all had.

Epilogue

Charlie and Miriam sat on either side of the hospital bed. They had not left Ginny's side since reaching Wrightsburg General after getting Chief Callahan's call of glad tidings. Miriam held her hand as Ginny slowly opened her eyes. "Oh, Ginny, I'm so sorry," she said.

Ginny struggled to sit up as Charlie took her other hand. "Mom, I'm alright," she said. "Just a bit drowsy. I slept, it seems like, for ages. And guess what?"

"What, baby?" Charlie asked.

"No nightmares. Only beautiful, magnificent, dreams."

"Oh, Ginny, that's so wonderful," Miriam said, lovingly massaging her daughter's hand.

Just then nurse Grimes, a heavy-set black woman, entered the room. "How's my little patient?" she asked cheerily."

"Just fine," Ginny said, now with a smile about as wide as the State of Texas on her face.

Lois Grimes – one of Miriam's best friends – had pampered Ginny for the past two days. Not wanting her to panic at the inability to move her limbs, the doctors had kept Ginny heavily sedated until the effects of the Pavulon had worn off.

The nurse took Ginny's blood pressure and pulse, and then looked up at her. "Looks like you're about ready to leave us."

"Good," Ginny said. "I sure am ready."

Nurse Grimes smiled as she left the room.

Charlie moved closer to his daughter and said uneasily, "Ginny, ah, er, we haven't been perfectly honest with you. There's somethin' I've been meanin' to tell you."

Ginny stroked his hand. "About my other mother?" she said, looking dreamily into her father's eyes. "It's all right, Dad. I know."

Miriam's eyes grew to about the size of saucers. "How do you know?"

"Trust me, I know," she said, now beaming. "And it's just fine. Not many girls have two moms who love them as much as mine love me."

Miriam was flabbergasted and Charlie looked befuddled.

Just then, Dewey Colton appeared through the doorway, carrying a large bouquet of bright yellow roses. Ginny grinned as Dewey walked straight past Miriam and Charlie into her waiting arms. They kissed passionately.

"Oh, Ginny, I love you," he said.

"And I love you, too," she said.

Charlie cleared his throat and looked over at his wife. Getting the message, Miriam rose from her seat. "We're going to leave you two," she said. "Seems like you have an awful lot of catching up to do."

Dewey turned to Charlie, who had also risen from his chair. "Oh, I forgot my manners," he said, extending his hand to him "Hello, Mr. and Mrs. Westbrook."

"Hello, Dewey," Charlie said, shaking his outstretched hand. "We're gonna have to do a better job of taking care of our little girl."

"Yes, sir, all of us," Dewey said.

After Charlie and Miriam had left, Ginny turned deadly serious as she looked at Dewey. "Did you finish my new article?"

Two weeks earlier, Mr. Robinson had finally relented and allowed Ginny to write another in-depth article on *all* of the missing girls.

"I sure did!" he said, "but with a few changes. I hope you don't mind."

"No," Ginny said exuberantly as Dewey unfurled a newspaper with a headline that read, "School Reporter Helps Police Solve Missing Girl Case."

"Oh, Dewey, thanks," she said as the two of them hugged. "I love you so much."

Nurse Grimes, now with a puzzled look on her face, stuck her head into the doorway. "Ginny, you have another visitor. It's some white man. He says he's your uncle."

Ginny looked up into the smiling face of Tyson Chandler Jr. as he stood tall and handsome in the doorway. He was holding – what had to be – three dozen red roses in one hand, and the biggest box of chocolate candy Ginny had ever seen in the other.

Charlie and Miriam walked silently toward their car in the parking lot. When they reached the Taurus, Miriam stopped and spoke warily. "Charlie, do you remember the night Ginny had that really bad dream?"

"Yeah. What?"

"There was that familiar smell in her room. A perfume."

"So?"

"It was lilac toilet water. The same kind that Maryella wore."

"Listen, Miriam, I know what you're gettin' at, but don't you say that to *anyone* else. There's no such thing as ghosts. Everything that happened has a perfectly logical explanation."

"Well, you explain to me how she found out about the adoption," Miriam said sarcastically, placing one hand on her hip in mock expectation of an answer that she knew would never come.

Charlie hesitated, and then just stood there, scratching his head. "Well, maybe she, ah, er," he stammered. "Will you get in the car? I gotta go to work."

For Francis Murray, it was a sad ending to a sorry situation. Although Maryella Chandler's murder might have been considered accidental – that is – until Peter, the evil alter ego, stepped in and took charge – much later, some would try to figure out what might have been the spark that lit his powder keg and caused Francis to commit a string of such heinous crimes.

It would be a sure bet, however, that no one in his or her right mind could phantom that good old church-going, bible-thumping Arlene Murray had been the cause of it all. It had all begun when the evil side of her son emerged to deal with the mongrelizing Chandler girl – as Arlene called her. She liked him a lot. Then not long after that, her husband, Corliss, ran off with a mulatto woman, called Delia. In her twisted little mind, interracial liaisons had made the Murray family pay too high a penalty. Something had to be done. Retribution had to be exacted. But from whom?

When it became widely known that the black girl, Armanda Lockett, was running around with Constance Bradley, she became the logical candidate. It had been Arlene Murray who badgered her son, Francis, the girl's homeroom teacher, into allowing Peter back into the family. During his time over in Athens, a shrink had help rid Francis of the unwanted entity.

Francis had just made principal when Anna Jennings became the talk of the town by dating a black boy who was the star of the basketball team. Again, Arlene cajoled him into allowing Peter to return, even going so far as to replace the contents of the capsules, which were prescribed by his psychiatrist, with baking soda in order to lower Francis' resistance to the persona intrusion.

Then in the twinkling of an eye, Peter was back – bigger and bolder than ever. Soon Anna, too, dropped off the face of the earth. Little did Arlene know that her decision to pressure Francis into keeping Peter around to do her bidding would lead to her own demise. Soon Peter had gained so much strength of will that – as they say – the genie could *not* be put back into the bottle.

The day after the "Midnight Mauling by Mongrel Mutts," as he called it, Mitch Bradley had scooped the Atlanta papers, and for the first time in five years, the *Herald* actually published a weekday edition. There had been a full-page spread that laid out the entire story of the serial killings, including a large picture of a smiling Ginny Westbrook in her hospital bed, which he sold separately to both the *Atlanta Journal* and *Macon Telegraph*. There was also an excellent piece on Chief Callahan and the Wrightsburg Police Department, alluding to the mayor's comments, which extolled the virtues of the same investigative team that he had once called a waste of both time and money.

The investigators would go on to fight crime in Madison County for many years to come, with Brian Pollard eventually rising to the rank of detective and hiring his own CSI. Lou would divorce his wife and marry Lola. Later, they would have a house full of beige-colored kids running around the place.

Since Constance Bradley had not been accused of any wrongdoing, Chief Callahan thought that it would serve no purpose to mention his affair with Beth Campbell. Constance brilliantly, as usual, defended Coach Dixon, talking Judge Iverson into dropping the flight to avoid prosecution charge. "There was nothing to prosecute," Constance argued and the judge agreed.

The assistant principal, George Willis, who had been promoted to full principal in light of recent events, even offered the beleaguered coach his old job. Coach Dixon said thanks, but no thanks. He was glad that he no longer had to dodge the law, but said he'd had enough of the South. He would later marry, settle down, and become a scout for the Green Bay Packers.

And to this day Hadley Frazier has never stood trial. When Chief Callahan last heard, the former stockbroker had jumped bail and left the country, presumable to a place where there were many women but no extradition treaty with the United States.

It was a beautiful fall day in Wrightsburg, Georgia. Ty Jr. and the other Chandler men, Walter and Logan, had eschewed the usual, large and regal, Chandler funeral in favor of a graveside service.

At the about same time, a similar event would be held for Armanda Lockett. The remains of the other murder victim, Anna Jennings, had been cremated and shipped somewhere up north, where the rest of her family had moved.

"It was what Maryella would have wanted," Ty Jr. had said, referring to the modest burial arrangements, and the others agreed.

Still, mourners came in droves, lining both sides of the driveway as the funeral procession passed through the gates of Richland Memorial Cemetery. Ginny, Charlie, and Miriam rode in the lead limousine with the Chandler men, who had instantly taken to their newly found niece as if she were their very own daughter.

Ty Jr. was sincere in his fondness of Ginny, having formed a bond with the budding reporter as she interviewed him for the newspaper article – while having no idea of their kinship. Or was it his sister's aura about Ginny that had drawn the two of them so close, so quickly. Deep down inside, he felt that Maryella had been there that day, helping to forge a bond between the two of them that could never be broken.

On the other hand, Ty Jr. had his doubts about the sincerity of his two brothers, thinking that it was more or less their feelings of guilt about not having been that close to their sister, along with the fact that if they had done more to side with him when Maryella was driven away from home, things might have been different. Logan certainly had come to rue the day that he was sent by the old man to do his dirty work – to confiscate Maryella's keys to both car and house. Whatever the case, the two of them saw this as a chance for redemption and were determined to make it up by way of royal treatment of Ginny.

Reverend Clark, who had been a busy man as of late, had just begun to recite the eulogy as the bronze coffin, bearing the remains of Maryella Chandler, sat on straps atop the open grave. "Man that is borne of a woman hath but a short time..."

Ginny turned to look just as the apparitions of Maryella Chandler and Armanda Lockett, both wearing pure white, whisked through the cemetery gates. Ginny chuckled as Maryella approached them.

Miriam nudged her. "Ginny, pay attention," she said.

"And I commit thee ashes to ashes and dust to dust," the minister continued.

Armanda's translucent figure continued across the cemetery toward her funeral, where a small group of black mourners – except for Sarah Steele and her family – were gathered. Members of the Steele family stood on either side of Emma Lockett, who sat emotionless in her wheelchair as Sarah reached down to hold her hand. The old woman looked up just as the specter of Armanda Lockett smiled down upon her. Emma Lockett inadvertently squeezed Sarah's hand as she returned a smile, which she had not seen in years.

"What is it, Aunt Emma?" Sarah asked, looking down at the beaming woman while thinking, *What in the world could be funny at a funeral?*

At Maryella Chandler's gravesite, the guest of honor smiled as she turned and waved goodbye to Ginny. Ginny giggled as she waved back. Miriam looked at Ginny and shook her head. "Ginny, don't. Please," she said.

As the casket sunk slowly into the grave, the last vestiges of the ghost of Maryella Chandler quickly decomposed and disappeared into it.

It was Thanksgiving Day at the Chandler mansion, and today's turnout was the largest that anyone could ever remember. All of the Chandler kin drove in from the surrounding counties, and the Westbrook's entire Florida clan came to town for the grand occasion.

After a scrumptious meal, Ginny and Ty Jr. left the others to their own devices, talking for hours while bringing each other up-to-date on their hopes and dreams for the future. That summer, they all agreed, Ginny would serve as an apprentice in her uncle's office before heading off to the University of Georgia in the fall. There, as she had planned long ago, she would major in journalism and minor in drama.

Upon hearing of her horrendous treatment on the school bus, and over Charlie's strong protests, Ty Jr. bought Ginny a brand new tomato red convertible Chevy Camaro. He had wanted to buy her a Corvette, but the sports car had only two seats. Ginny prevailed upon him to make it a Camaro, so that there would be plenty of room for her friends, Margo and Cha-Cha, whose mother had allowed her to return to Wrightsburg.

Each morning, the three girls would let the top down, regardless of weather, and drive to school, seat dancing to hip-hop music all the way. Ginny was beginning to like hip-hop, in fact, so did Sarah Steele, who now sat with the girls every day during lunch. The four girls would go on to become life-long friends.

Ginny soon regained her thirst for living. She had never been so happy in her whole life. Then one day when she got home from school, there was a large envelope for her in the mail. The handwriting was barely legible. She hurriedly tore it open, already knowing its origin.

Inside was a heart-shaped card with the simple words, "Thanks, Emma Lockett."

It was over.

THE END